A HERO FOR
WONDLA

SIMON & SCHUSTER

presents

A Hero for WondLa

by

TONY DiTERLIZZI

with illustrations by the author

SIMON & SCHUSTER

First published in Great Britain by Simon & Schuster UK Ltd, 2012
A CBS COMPANY
Originally published in the USA in 2012 by Simon & Schuster Books for Young Readers, an imprint of Simon & Schuster Children's Division, New York
This paperback edition published in 2013

Book design by Tony DiTerlizzi and Lizzy Bromley.

1 3 5 7 9 10 8 6 4 2

Simon & Schuster UK Ltd
1st Floor, 222 Gray's Inn Road
London WC1X 8HB
www.simonandschuster.co.uk

Simon & Schuster Australia, Sydney

Simon & Schuster India, New Delhi

A CIP catalogue record for this book is available from the British Library

PB ISBN 978-0-85707-302-0
EBook ISBN 978-1-4711-0496-1

Printed and bound by CPI Group (UK) Ltd, Croydon, CR0 4YY

Within

the pages of this book you will find a hidden feature: a three-dimensional interactive game in which you pilot the *Bijou* through various terrains, just as Hailey does in *A Hero for WondLa*. This is brought to life through the wonders of WONDLA-VISION (also known as Augmented Reality).

The illustrations on pages 19, 79, and 280 are the keys to unlock this hidden feature. Just visit

WONDLA.COM

for directions. You'll need a computer with Internet access and a webcam to get started.

Contents

PART I

PART II

PART III

"THE UNIVERSE
is not required to be
IN PERFECT HARMONY
with human ambition."
—Carl Sagan

A HERO FOR
WONDLA

PART I

CHAPTER 1: LEAVE

Eva Nine watched a turnfin flap its triple pair of wings to join its flock. The alien birds squawked in an otherworldly harmony as they soared through the eroded sun-bleached remains of buildings that had once stood as New York City.

Over the eastern horizon the morning sun was shining down on mountainous white clouds sailing slowly over the ancient ruins. Eva made her way through the twisting labyrinth of crumbled brick walls and rusted steel beams, stopping in

front of a lone column blanketed in gigantic leafy lichen. She pulled her empty drinking container out of her satchel and removed the cap. Eva yanked a large corrugated leaf from the column with her hands and began to roll it up. She wrung the leaf tighter and tighter until water began to trickle from its stem.

Really? That's it? Eva thought as the dribble of water ran to the bottom of her drinking container. *This is going to take forever. I wish I'd kept my hydration tablets.* She sighed and tore off another leaf.

Traveling down the bygone avenues of a withered world, Eva paused at the gaping shadowy entrance of a tunnel that led down into the earth toward the remains of a forgotten library. Her mind flickered to the memory of the giant water bear, Otto, digging that tunnel like an enormous puppy. Eva closed her eyes. Though her loyal companion was with his herd far from here, Eva knew he was relaxed and content. She had a connection with Otto. She could understand what he was thinking when it appeared no one else could. Eva could not explain how it was that she could do this. She just *felt* it.

She opened her eyes and took in the endless barren horizon beyond the ruins. Eva whispered,

"I'm happy for you, Otto. I am going to join my herd too." With a smile she continued on toward her camp.

Under the shade of a deteriorating steel archway, a lanky blue alien sat on backward-bending legs. The Cærulean, Rovender Kitt, appeared to be organizing the scattered contents of a saddlebag that hung from a parked gull-winged glider.

"You were right, Rovee," Eva said, joining her friend. She shook her mostly full drinking container. "I was able to get quite a bit of water. But with only one good hand my fingers got sore from all that squeezing."

Rovender glanced up at Eva, then continued on with his task. "Your wounds will heal soon enough." He spoke in a soft, gravelly voice. "And do not worry about your hand. You will become stronger and it will become easier." He unbuckled a second saddlebag and began rooting through it. "We shall have to hunt down some breakfast soon, though."

"Food, huh? I don't suppose you'd be interested in these at all?" Eva pulled out a voxfruit from her satchel and smiled.

Rovender stopped, a look of genuine surprise on his whiskered face. "Oeeah! Voxfruit! Out here? Well done, Eva Nine. Well done." He held up a thick-fingered hand, and Eva tossed him a piece of fruit.

"Yup," replied Eva. "I found them growing in some sort of underground transit station. I grabbed all I could carry." She opened her satchel. It was stuffed full with the exotic fruit.

"That is a good discovery. Now come." Rovender patted the ground next to where he sat. "See what I have found."

Eva knelt down next to Rovender and poured water into his empty bottle. Then, after taking a swig from her own container, she shuddered as she glanced over the booty. Like the glider, these items had once belonged to the Dorcean huntsman, Besteel. Now the huntsman's belongings had been sorted into little piles that were spread out over Rovender's sleeping mat.

"I told you I think it's weird going through all his stuff," Eva said, returning her drinking container to her satchel. "I don't want anything from that monster." Besteel's raptorial visage was still fresh in Eva's memory. She still half-expected the huntsman to jump out of the shadows and capture her once again.

Rovender took a sip of water and nodded in agreement. He picked up a small wooden contraption with many knobs. "Yes, yes, Eva, but you never know what we may need. Like this." He handed the gizmo to Eva.

"Uh, I give up," she said, looking at the item without the slightest interest. "What is it?"

"It is a Variable Bird Caller. You turn the knobs to attract all sorts of birds." Rovender turned one of the large knobs, and the familiar squawk of a turnfin was produced.

"Okay . . . but why would I call more turnfins? There are enough here already, don't you think?" She gave the bird caller back to Rovender.

"Perhaps," Rovender said sagely as he pocketed the item. "But then again, its use may come in handy."

Eva wondered if there were turnfins everywhere in Orbona. "Fine. But what else of Besteel's do we *really* need?"

Rovender moved his hand over the piles of odd accoutrements and opened a pouch—out of which rolled a handful of vocal transcoders. "How about these?" Rovender plucked up one of the spherical devices. "See if our new arrival would be receptive to using one. I am sure he would feel more comfortable if he could understand what I am saying." He rolled the transcoder over to Eva.

"Okay, you're right—as usual." Eva rose and held up a voxfruit. "I'll see if he's up for trying some of the local food too."

Through the scattered rubble of a desert plain Eva arrived at a sandy plot where a round airship rested on heavy landing gear.

In the late morning sun she could see that the ship had once been painted in a brilliant black and gold check, but years of neglect had taken their toll. As though the ship were an enormous insect shedding its skin, a corroded metal carapace was visible beneath the flaked-off patches of ancient enamel. Along the many rows of small hover-thrusters lining the ship's body, dried grime and exhaust ran down to the patinated chrome underbelly.

Next to one of the headlights, just below the cockpit window, a name was painted in decorative lettering: *Bijou*. Underneath the lettering were rows of decals, each in the cutout shape of a human. As Eva counted the decals, wondering what they represented, the entry ramp hissed open from the belly of the ship. Eva caught a glimpse of her reflection in the lens of a headlight before she entered. The girl looking back at her was a dirty disheveled mess.

Wriggling about, Eva pulled and tugged her rumpled tunic in an attempt to straighten it. To further smooth it she ran her bandaged hand down the front—but all she accomplished was to smear the dust that had invaded every wrinkle of her clothing. Shifting her focus from her outfit, Eva unwrapped one of the long braids that held her hair up off of her neck. Now loose, the wad of dirty-blond hair drooped down over her shoulders. Eva combed through the mop with her thin fingers trying to style it, but the effort was fruitless. Already her neck was sweating under the thick tresses. "Ugh!" Eva said with a frustrated sigh. "Whatever." She pulled her hair back up and wrapped it tight with a braid.

Nearing the open entry ramp that led into the ship, Eva heard the pulse of electronic music thumping from within. She stood at the foot of the ramp and called up, "Good morning, Hailey. Are you hungry? Hellooooo in there!"

The music did not pause, nor was there a response. Eva called out again. Finally she tiptoed up the ramp and peered around the cramped cargo hold of the ship. Inside, the distinct scent of motor oil greeted her. This was a scent that Eva knew from her old home, her Sanctuary, and so it was somehow reassuring to her. It was the scent of machines. Machines made for people. Machines, just like this ship, that would whisk her away to a city full of people. It felt as if, after all of the searching and running, her dream—*her WondLa*—had come true.

That little crumbling picture of the girl and the robot and the adult had given Eva hope that there were others like her—humans, just waiting to be found. But the lands she searched through were not like the Earth she had learned about. These lands were full of monstrous sand-snipers, bird-eating trees, and evil alien queens. Just when she had given up all hope of the existence of other humans, a ship had fallen from the sky. A ship piloted by a boy named Hailey . . .

Last night Hailey had told Eva and Rovender that he'd come to take them to the human city. He'd come to take Eva home.

Explaining that the ship would need to recharge overnight, the young pilot had offered up sleeping accommodations in the ship's cabin. But, despite Eva's pleas that they stay on board the ship, Rovender had preferred sleeping outdoors. Eva said she had so many questions she wanted answered, but really she was curious and excited to spend time with the first human she'd ever met in all twelve years of her life.

Hailey had had to admit that he was tired from travel and needed rest. Of course Rovender had concurred. Eva's questions would have to wait. Back at camp she'd tried to fall asleep despite the electricity that coursed through her.

Lying next to the crackling fire, Eva had wondered how exciting the life of gallant Hailey must be as he searched for helpless humans to rescue from the wilds of Orbona. But thoughts of being rescued were soon interrupted by memories of Muthr.

Muthr.

For all of Eva's life her only caretaker had been Multi-Utility Task Help Robot zero-six, or Muthr for short. As Eva had grown older, her yearning to explore the surface of the planet had often led to arguments with the robot. Regardless, Muthr had taken good care of her . . .

. . . even when Besteel had ransacked their underground home.

. . . even when their trusted technology had been ineffective against the dangerous new world they faced.

. . . and especially when she saved Eva's life,

although it had meant sacrificing her own.

Muthr had loved her. Eva still grieved over the robot's passing.

"Hey there," Hailey called out over the music, rousing Eva from her thoughts. A tanned teenage face peered down from an access hatch in the ceiling of the cargo hold at the bow of the airship. Even upside down the pilot's shaggy brown and blue-dyed hair was stuck to his face by a thin layer of perspiration. "Hi." He waved. "Hold on a sec. Music volume: minimum," he said. The ship responded.

Eva made her way past the disorganized stacks of crates in the hold and stood at the bottom of the access ladder. "Good morning." She pulled out one of her prized voxfruit. "I've brought you breakfast," she said, pleased with herself.

Hailey grabbed the side rails of the ladder and slid down to the floor. He took the fruit from Eva with black greasy hands. "Thanks," he said, turning it over and examining it. "What is it?"

"It's voxfruit." Eva took the fruit and ripped open the translucent rind. "You eat the berries inside." She handed the peeled voxfruit back to Hailey. He wiped his dirty hands on his stained flight suit and then gingerly grabbed a handful of the green berries from within.

"Hmm. Oh, yeah," he said through a mouth full of food. "These aren't bad."

"I also brought you this." Eva produced the vocal transcoder. "Or do you have one of these already?"

"That depends," said Hailey, eyeing the device. "What is it?"

"Well, I wasn't sure how many languages you know, but I could tell last night that you couldn't understand Cærulean. . . . You know, Rovee's language." Eva put the transcoder near her mouth. "So this little thingy will allow you to understand *all* the different languages of the aliens. You just press this button, speak into it, and inhale the micro transmitters that it releases. It will do the rest." She dropped the device into his palm.

Hailey examined the transcoder, a look of awe on his smudged face. He caught Eva's eye and straightened up. "Well, thanks. Thanks a lot, Ella."

"Eva," she corrected him, and brushed her bangs out of her eyes. "Eva Nine."

Hailey regarded her for a moment. "Well, Eva Nine, we won't be ready to leave until tonight. I suggest you get some REM and gather any belongings you may have. . . . Oh, and don't forget your Omnipod." He began to climb back up the ladder.

"My Omnipod? Do I really need it?" Eva picked at her nails.

"Yup," said Hailey as he continued climbing. "It holds all of your Sanctuary records. It's the only way you can be admitted as a citizen of New Attica."

Eva followed Hailey up the ladder. She felt like she was climbing, ascending, toward some answers from her mysterious rescuer. "*New Attica?* Is that the name of the human city? Is it far? What planet is it on? How long will the flight take? What will we do when we get there?"

"Boy, you sure do talk a lot for a reboot. I guess it's 'cause you don't know much about stuff," Hailey said with a laugh as he entered the main deck of the ship.

Somehow the tone of those words stung Eva. "*Reboot?* What's a reboot?"

"You are," Hailey replied in a matter-of-fact tone as he sat down in a floating hovchair in the galley.

Eva joined him at the small table and studied Hailey as he devoured another piece of fruit. He was somewhat slovenly when he ate, just like Rovender. *Muthr would disapprove of his upbringing,* Eva thought.

He continued through a mouth full of food, "You're Sanctuary-born, right?"

Eva answered with a nod of the head, then tried to appear uninterested. She looked away from Hailey and glanced around the galley. An array of dispensers lined the low walls, each with their synthetic contents labeled: nutriment pellets, Susti-Bars, Pow-R-drink packets, and flavored hydration tablets.

Hailey finished the fruit and wiped his mouth with his sleeve. "So, then, you're a reboot."

Eva was quiet. The way he said "reboot" bothered her, but she would not let it affect her.

"And I am a *retriever*," Hailey continued proudly. "With this ship I track down newly emerged humans and take them to the great city of New Attica, 'Where a bright and beautiful new future awaits.' It's a ways out west, but the flight won't take too long."

"How did you track me? With my Omnipod?" Eva asked. She felt ignorant, like Hailey knew everything and she knew nothing.

"No." Hailey got up and approached her. "There's a tracking chip inside of you."

"Inside . . . me?" Eva replied. "I don't think so. Muthr never told me about a—"

"No, it's true," said Hailey. Very gently he ran his finger up the nape of Eva's neck. "The chip is . . .

right . . . here." He stopped at the little raised mole on the back of her neck.

"Heart rate BPM acceleration detected, Eva Nine," the shoulder patch on Eva's tunic announced. "Please—" Eva swatted the patch, abruptly shutting it off. Pretending she didn't hear it, she stepped away from Hailey and entered the cockpit. "Wow," she said. "This is where you pilot your ship?"

Behind a large domed windshield a single chair sat at an arcing dashboard. Gathered clusters of thin multicolored wires hung out from underneath the dash like the roots of an overturned tree. On the floor of the cockpit Hailey's Omnipod displayed a floating hologram of the *Bijou*, labeled as an HRP Compact Transcarrier.

"Yeah, this is where I operate the ship." Hailey leaned against the doorway. "And I can tell you, there is no feeling like it."

Eva spun a tracking ball set in the dash. "Is it easy to fly?"

"No," answered Hailey, gently brushing Eva's hand away from the dash. "It may look simple, but it takes a long time to master. The controls are very delicate."

Eva picked up the Omnipod and examined the hologram. The wiring diagram of the ship pulsed like an electronic nervous system. "Is everything okay with the *Bijou*?" she asked.

Hailey took the Omnipod from her. "Yes, of course. I am just doing some . . . refining." He guided Eva back to the access ladder leading down to the cargo hold. "So, if you and your blue friend want to relax here in the ship, I'll give you an update later today on our departure time. Just don't forget your Omnipod."

Eva turned back. "About that . . . You see, my Omnipod . . . It is, um . . . gone."

Hailey raised an eyebrow. "Gone?"

"Well . . . yeah." Eva felt oddly nervous explaining this to him. It was like she hadn't followed some set of unspoken rules. There was nothing about losing your Omnipod on her survival tests. Though, now that she thought about it, the device did seem integral to all the exercises. She wished Muthr were here to explain things. "You see, Rovee—that's the blue guy—and me and my Muthr were being followed—hunted, actually—by this big hairy monster, Besteel."

Hailey crossed his arms. A slight grin drew across his stubbly face. "Go on."

"Well . . ." Eva didn't want to talk about this. It was too soon. Too real. She wanted to change the subject. She wanted to leave.

"Hello?" Rovender's voice echoed up from the hold down below. "Eva Nine?"

"I'm . . . I'm here," she called down to him. "I'll be down in a second." Eva looked back at Hailey. His shaggy bangs concealed one of his deep umber eyes. She felt nervous and giddy. "I don't have my Omnipod anymore," she said. "I used it to kill Besteel."

"Kill him?" the pilot said with a smile. "What, did you throw it at his head?"

Eva's eyes narrowed. "No. I used it to lure up a sand-sniper, which ate him." There was venom in her voice.

"Okay, reboot. Whatever you say." Hailey dismissed Eva and opened up a supply cabinet in the main deck.

"It's the truth! My Omnipod is lost out in the desert somewhere!" said Eva.

"Well, you better go ask that sand-sniper to give it back to you, because you'll need it to get into the city."

Rovender called up from the bottom of the ladder, "Eva, is everything all right?"

"I said I'm fine!" yelled Eva. "What about Rovee? He doesn't have an Omnipod. He's never had an Omnipod."

"Humans need their Omnipods to register in the city." Hailey continued rifling through the supply cabinet. "I don't make the rules. I just bring you in."

"Thanks a lot," grumbled Eva, and she began to climb down.

"Hey." Hailey stopped her. "Hold on." He handed her a tarnished old Omnipod. "It's an older model that I hacked, and it barely works, but it might help you find yours."

Eva snatched the Omnipod from him and continued down the ladder.

By the time she crossed the cargo hold, the loud music had resumed. Eva stormed down the ramp and out from under the *Bijou*, with Rovender following close behind.

"Is there something wrong?" Rovender asked.

"I just want to get out of here."

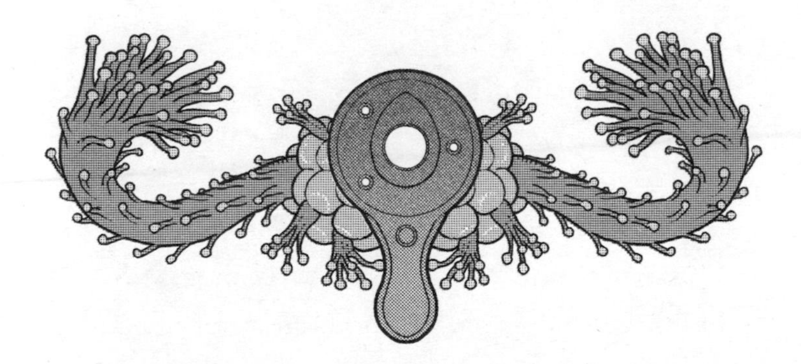

CHAPTER 2: MOTHER

On the walk back to the campsite, Rovender listened while Eva explained her dilemma.

"So the pilot, Hailey, tells you that you must retrieve your Omnipod in order for you to gain entrance to the human village, New Attica?" he asked.

"Yeah, pretty much." Eva pouted and kicked rocks out of her way.

"And what is your impression of this other human?" said Rovender as they walked under the broken arch at the entrance of their camp.

Eva gave pause, mostly because she wasn't sure what her impression was just yet. "He's okay, I guess. . . . I don't know," she said, twisting a bead on one of her braids. "I mean, he's here to rescue us and take us to the city, right? But he's also telling me I have to go find my Omnipod buried out there in a sniper-infested desert. Why can't we just leave without it?" She exhaled hotly.

Rovender stopped and lifted Eva's chin. With indigo eyes he studied her. "Eva, I recognize your confusion. It is not always easy to understand another's spirit, especially if you do not know where to look."

"He looks like a nice guy," Eva said. "Well, except that he is a bit dirty."

"No, no, no. That is not what I mean," Rovender said. "When we first met, I certainly did not know what to make of you. And likely you felt the same about me, correct?"

"You yelled at me and snatched away my Omnipod."

Rovender grinned. "I admit, I thought the device to be some form of weapon."

"And you kept telling me how you needed to go and how I was on my own," said Eva. Her voice became more thoughtful with recollection. "But then you stayed. You helped me. You helped Muthr. I couldn't have survived out here if it weren't for you."

"So, Eva Nine, you must sometimes disregard what one is *saying* and focus instead on what they are *doing*. Watch and observe. That is when one reveals his true self. Do you understand?"

Eva nodded.

"This Hailey knows the rules of your people. He tells you that he is trying to make it easy for you to become one with the human village." Rovender continued walking.

"So I just do what he says, then?" Eva asked.

"If your desire is to gain access to this New Attica, then we must trust him until his actions prove otherwise," Rovender said.

Yes. Maybe he's just eager to leave too, Eva thought, her mind somewhat at ease. *He was awfully busy fixing his ship.* She sat on the wing of Besteel's parked glider and began twirling one of her thin braids around her finger. "But how are we going to find my Omnipod? You saw what happened out there."

"I understand. All of this makes you upset," said Rovender.

"I just don't want to go back to that . . . place." Eva said. Thoughts of Muthr and Besteel's attack bombarded her all at once. "It's too much. I can't." The braid was wound so tight that her fingertip was red.

Rovender brushed away Eva's bangs. "Have you

told Hailey what happened to your Omnipod?"

Eva lied. "No. I didn't want to trouble him. He seemed busy working on his ship." She wished that Hailey had not said the things he'd said. She wanted him to not think of her as some helpless "reboot." She wanted to slap her Omnipod into his hand and prove to him how strong, smart, and resourceful she was. But that wasn't going to happen. Her Omnipod was down in the gut of some monstrous sand-sniper.

"You wait here, okay?" Rovender grabbed his walking stick and donned his wide-brimmed hat.

"No, Rovee." Eva let go of her braid. "Don't go. It's too dangerous. You saw the size of that sand-sniper. It's not worth it."

"It is worth it to you, so it is worth it to me," Rovender said, grabbing his bottle of water. "We have until sundown, correct? I will go take a look around and see what clues may be found."

"And if you come across a sniper?"

"I shall be protected." Rovender pulled out from the glider's saddlebag a holster holding a large sonic pistol. He tucked the weapon snug into his belt. "Now you wait here and get some rest."

Eva handed Rovender his saggy rucksack. "No way are you going out there alone. I'm coming with you."

"Very well. At least this way I can keep an eye on you."

Eva strapped her satchel on, her mind turning over what Rovender had said earlier. "Rovee?"

"Yes, Eva Nine?"

"Why did you decide to help me? I mean, how did you know the difference between what I was saying and what I was doing?" asked Eva.

Rovender knelt down in front of her. "Despite what we see and hear, there is a voice that will always be truthful to you," he replied. Rovender spread an open palm over Eva's heart. "If you listen from here, you will never be misled."

The glaring noonday sun baked the sand-worn remains of the ancient city. Rovender and Eva found themselves on the outskirts of the ruins facing endless dunes that stretched out in every direction. The hot breath of gusty wind whipped at Eva, covering her feet in loose granules of ashen sand. Not even the climatefiber in her utilitunic could keep her body cool.

"There is no way on Orbona that we are going to find this thing," Eva said, rubbing the sand from her eyes.

"Be patient." Rovender placed his hat on Eva's

head and climbed up onto a large piece of eroded rubble. He peered through his spyglass. "Perhaps luck may pay us a visit."

Eva stared out into the wasteland. It was like a sea of sand. And, just like the great lake near Lacus, the surface undulated and rolled with the blowing wind.

"Hmmm." Rovender continued to scan the horizon. "I was hoping for some kind of tracks from Otto's herd or a sinkhole from the sniper. But all is gone. Buried."

Eva wiped the sweat from her forehead and sipped her water. She sat on the rubble where Rovender was perched and suddenly recognized its shape and form. He was standing on the rusted carriage of a half-buried hovercraft. It was similar to the old golden hovercraft Eva had piloted over these wastelands. A thought came to her. "Rovee, look for the Goldfish."

"Yes, yes, yes," Rovender sang as he scanned the horizon. "Your hover-machine. That is a good idea, Eva Nine. A very good idea. . . . Aha!" He pointed out into the distance. "I see it! The Goldfish is this way."

The two trudged along in the blistering heat at the edge of the ruins, careful to avoid the open sandy dunes where snipers preyed just below the surface. As Rovender and Eva moved closer to the wreck of the Goldfish, Eva felt weird, like she was rewinding a program—a program she wasn't ready to revisit just yet.

"Oeeah! What have we here?" Rovender knelt down to examine something.

"Is it my Omnipod?" Eva rushed up to him.

"I do not think so."

Lying before them was a gooey sand-speckled blob about the size of Eva. Strange flies and unusual insects buzzed around it as they lapped up the milky goo that oozed from the cracks of the blob's dried skin. Rovender jabbed the viscous mass with his walking stick. The end of his stick caught on something inside the blob, and he tugged on it. From the mass came a coiled wire, which Rovender seized with his hand and began to pull out.

"What is that?" Eva winced. Now that Rovender was digging around in the goo, a nauseating stench drifted up amidst the swarm of flies.

"I believe it is a clue," he replied as he yanked on the coiled wire. Finally, from deep within, he pulled out a familiar artifact.

"That's Besteel's boomrod!" Eva said in shock.

"Indeed it is." Rovender dropped the huntsman's

weapon back into the mass. "It is as I suspected. Sand-snipers cannot digest metal or other similar materials. Do you remember the one near your old home that spit out my bottle?"

"I do." Eva flinched. "So, is my Omnipod in that?"

"Perhaps." Rovender wiped his hands on his tattered jacket. "But we'll have to dig through this spittle to know for sure."

The disgusting stink wafted back up, whirling around Eva.

"I'm not digging in that." She wagged her finger at the blob. "I'll puke."

"But, Eva Nine, your device may lie in there," Rovender countered.

Eva brightened and pulled out from her satchel the old Omnipod that Hailey had given her. "Hold on. Perhaps Hailey's old one can tell us for sure if it's in there."

"A good idea," Rovender said, and dribbled water over his hands to cleanse them.

Eva activated the old Omnipod, and the lights flickered for several long moments before it finally came on.

"Greetings, Van Turner," the Omnipod said through a static-filled hiss. Eva and Rovender exchanged glances. The device continued, "How may I be of service?"

"Can you locate the whereabouts of another Omnipod?" Eva asked.

"Initiating Techscan," the device replied. A flickering radar map projected over its central eye. "There is a faint signal approximately ninety meters to the northeast," it reported. "It carries a trace signal similar to an Omnipod. However, it is too far away to tell for sure at your current coordinates. Please rescan when you are in closer proximity."

"What about in this glop right here?" Eva pointed the Omnipod's eye at the mass that held Besteel's boomrod.

The Omnipod was silent for some time. At last it said, "There is Tech here that I cannot identify. It does not carry the signal of an Omnipod." Eva put the old device away and looked at Rovender.

"Let us continue," he said, and set out over the dunes in the direction the old Omnipod had instructed.

As the debris of the ruins became sparser, Eva spotted something glimmering in the sun. The duo ventured toward a golden fin rising out of the sand like a hologram of a swimming shark.

It was the rudder of the Goldfish.

"We can go no farther until we find out if there are any snipers present," said Rovender. He began thumping the ground around the wreck with his walking stick. "This vibration will attract them if any are present, but you may also want to use that Omnipod as well."

Eva crumpled down to the blazing ground next to the golden fin and clutched handfuls of hot sand. In one night the entire hovercraft had been almost completely buried in sand, save for the lone tail rudder. However, the events—Muthr's intercepting Besteel's lethal shot—were still fresh in Eva's memory.

Rovender knelt down next to Eva and put his arm around her. "Are you all right?"

"Yeah." She wiped her eyes with her sleeve. "I just want to get out of here." She took out the old Omnipod and commanded, "Initiate LifeScan, please."

The hissy voice of the old Omnipod replied, "LifeScan is inoperative at this moment. Aspects of the program's database appear corrupted. Please hold while I attempt program analysis and repair."

"Great! That's just great!" Frustrated, Eva threw the old Omnipod back into her satchel. "Doesn't anything work?"

"Patience, Eva Nine," Rovender said, leaning on his stick.

"I'm tired of being patient! I'm tired of waiting!" Now furious, she stomped around the wreckage as the sweltering heat hammered down. It felt as if the sandy ocean itself had been brought to a boil.

"Eva," Rovender called out to her.

She ignored him and continued yelling. "It's all everybody ever tells me. 'Wait for this!' 'Be patient for that!'"

"Eva!" Rovender called out again.

"WHAT!"

"Do. Not. Make. A. Move," Rovender whispered, and pointed behind her.

Eva turned to see an enormous sand-sniper towering overhead. The monster was an impossibly large, sand-colored crustacean armed with an arsenal of spiked claws and barbed graspers. At its head two bowl-shaped eyes moved independently of each other amidst an array of corded feelers and paddle-shaped antennae. The sniper was accompanied by its brood of clacking, snapping nymphs.

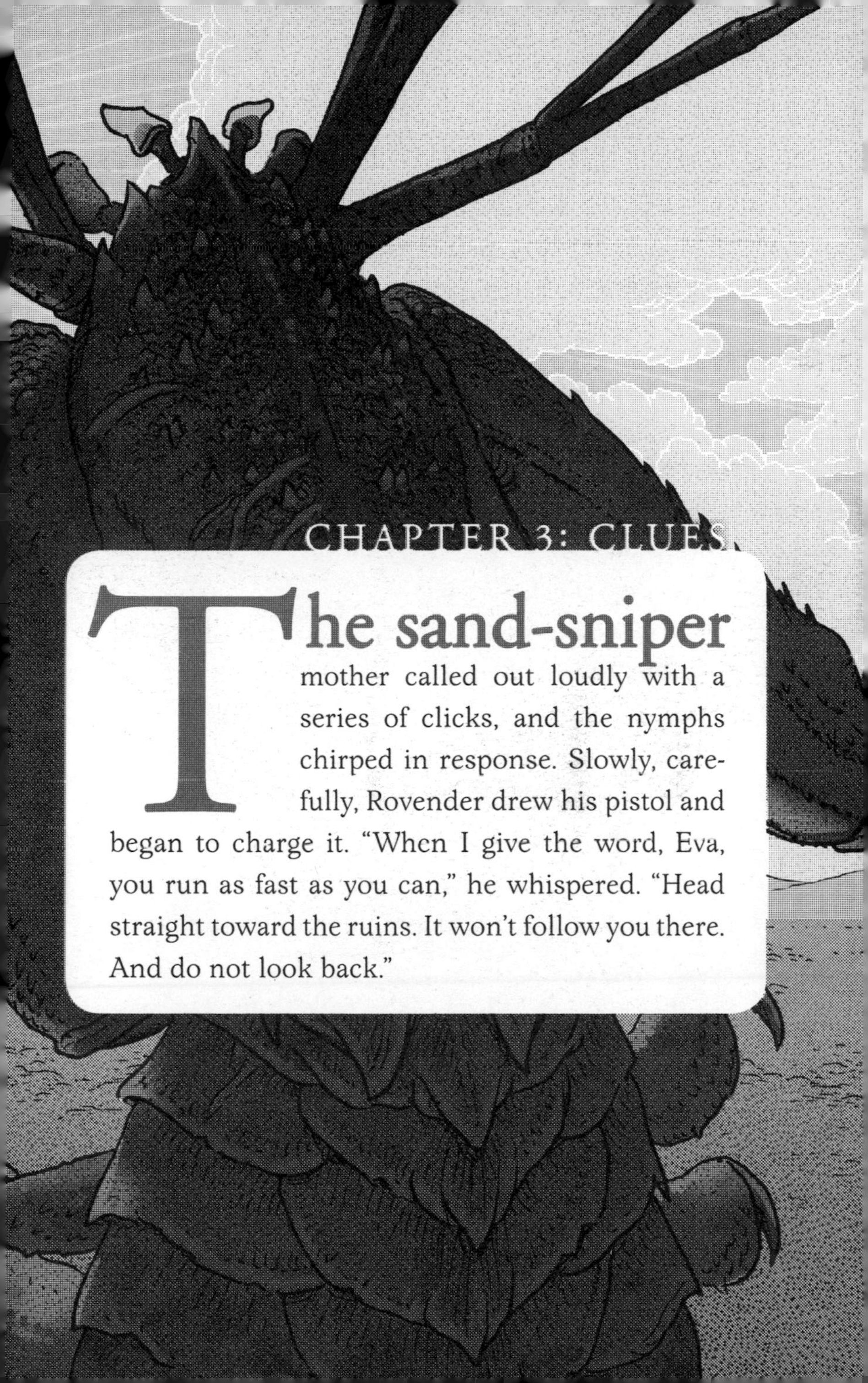

CHAPTER 3: CLUES

The sand-sniper mother called out loudly with a series of clicks, and the nymphs chirped in response. Slowly, carefully, Rovender drew his pistol and began to charge it. "When I give the word, Eva, you run as fast as you can," he whispered. "Head straight toward the ruins. It won't follow you there. And do not look back."

In a spray of sand another sniper shot up behind Rovender and pinned him down. The pistol fell from Rovender's grasp and was snatched up by one of the nymphs.

"Don't hurt him!" Eva called out to the mother sniper. Eva made a move toward Rovender, causing the sniper on top of him to rear up and flex its many graspers.

"It's a threat display, Eva." Rovender remained under the sniper, unmoving. "They're protecting the young. That's why they haven't killed us. You have to go now!"

"No. Let me help you." She took another step toward her friend.

Suddenly, Eva was whisked up several meters off the ground. Immediately she realized she was being held tightly by the graspers of another large sniper that had emerged directly behind her. As the blood rushed through her ears from her pounding heart, Eva fought all instinct to scream or struggle.

"Please don't kill me!" she called out. The pinpricks of the graspers that held her pierced her tunic and sank into her skin like dozens of long needles. The sniper could crush her as though she were a bug, but for some reason it had not. Eva concentrated on blocking out the pain inflicted by the pincers that held her. She needed to see what the snipers would do now that they had seized control of the confrontation.

The mother sniper's large eyes rotated independently, watching both Eva and Rovender at once. The monster's multiple graspers flexed in rhythm to the clacking sounds that emanated from deep within its spiky carapace.

Eva kept her gaze fixed on the mother. She calmed herself and thought out to the monster in the same way that she had communicated with Otto. *Please don't hurt us,* she thought. *We are just looking for something that belonged to me—my Omnipod. The clicking device I used to call you up from your home.*

Eva created a mental picture of the Omnipod in her mind. Just like an animated holographic program from her Sanctuary home, she replayed the events of the previous day. Besteel holding Rovender captive. Eva atop Otto with his herd close by. Eva throwing the Omnipod into the desert sand while it played the recorded call of a sand-sniper. The mother sniper rising up behind Besteel, skewering him.

One of the sniper's thick antennae quickly dropped down. It tapped Eva's head and rose back up. The sniper then called out loudly and opened up every pair of its mighty barbed claws.

Can you help me? Eva held her breath, waiting for some sort of thought response. She could feel a trickle of blood running down her arm. *Once we find it, we will leave you and your babies. I promise.*

One of the nymphs clicked and chirped loudly. The mother sniper turned one eye down toward it and chittered back.

In the nymph's mouthparts a milky ball, the size of Eva's head, formed. The nymph spit the ball out toward the sniper that held Eva, and it landed in the sand below. The mother sniper called out again. Slowly Eva was lowered, and the entire family sank back under the sandy dunes. Within moments the wind erased all indication of their presence.

Eva's legs gave out from underneath her, and she collapsed in the scorching sand. Rovender rushed over and helped her up. "Eva, are you all right?" he said. "We have to go before they return. We will tell Hailey."

"No!" Eva scrabbled toward the gooey ball that the juvenile sniper had spit at her. She thrust her hands into the warm mass and felt around inside. Though the substance was milky, Eva could see small bones and other indigestible matter suspended within. Finally she felt a familiar form that she recognized all too well. Eva pulled her Omnipod out and wiped it off on her tunic.

"Greetings, Eva Nine," the device said in its usual singsong voice. "How may I be of service?"

Eva stared at the Omnipod in disbelief. Rovender laughed out loud and put a hand on her shoulder. "Come, Eva," he said. "Let's get to safer ground."

Eva was quiet as she and Rovender trudged through the soft sand back to their campsite. While her tunic administered SpeedHeal ointment to her many bodily wounds, Eva's mind processed all that she had just witnessed.

At last she spoke. "Rovee, I think I can talk to the snipers, kind of in the same way that I can speak to Otto."

Rovender kept on walking, his face shadowed underneath his wide-brimmed hat. "Those snipers are vicious mindless fiends, Eva. You've seen what they can do."

"I have." Eva's broken fingers wriggled in her bandaged hand—a reminder of her encounter with the young sniper in the Royal Museum at Solas. "But I think somehow they can understand me. Almost like they can *feel* what I am feeling. . . . You know?"

"I believe what we just witnessed was a family satiated from their recent meal and a mother protecting her young. Nothing more," replied Rovender.

"But, Rovee, they could have just killed us. Instead I think they understood that we would do no harm—that we were just looking for something," Eva said.

Rovender was silent as the two continued on their trek.

"Remember what you said about people's actions?" Eva cleaned her Omnipod with the hem of her tunic. "Those snipers gave me the thing I desperately needed. It's sort of like—"

"The trees in the forest," Rovender finished her sentence. He nodded in agreement. "Perhaps you are right, Eva. Clearly your species is as ancient as this planet. Therefore, you may have a connectivity to its denizens."

Eva took all of this in. Both were quiet for the remainder of the hike back to camp.

"Hailey! Hailey!" Eva called up from the entry ramp of the *Bijou*. She sprinted across the cargo hold and scrambled up to the main deck.

"Ho there," Hailey said over the loud music. He

was now at the stern side of the main deck galley, opposite the cockpit entrance, in front of an open electrical panel. Grease and grime covered his hands, face, and undershirt. "Did you find your Omnipod?" He kept his attention on the tangle of wires he was combing through.

"I did," said Eva, satisfied. "It was in the stomach of a baby sand-sniper, but I was able to persuade it to give it back to me."

Hailey paused from his task, holding a sparking cluster of wires in one hand. A smirk grew on his face. "A sand-sniper, huh? And how were you able to do that?"

"I asked it." Eva stood tall and cocked her head to one side.

"You . . . asked it?" repeated Hailey, now with a broad grin. "Did you ask it for a new pair of sneak-boots while you were at it?"

He doesn't believe me, she thought. *I can't believe this. He doesn't believe me.* "I'm being serious! Do you know how scary these things are? Look at this bandage on my hand. I was wounded by a sand-sniper."

"O-kay. Yeah. Sure." Hailey chuckled and turned back to his work. "We'll be leaving just after sunset. So you can hang out here in the galley or go up to the cabin if you want to catch some REM before we take off. Don't forget to tell your blue buddy."

Eva glared at Hailey. She thought out to him the way she had with the sniper. *Turn around. Turn around and say you're sorry and that you're impressed that I found my Omnipod.*

But Hailey kept his back turned and began humming along with the song blaring from the ship's speakers.

Eva slapped his old Omnipod down onto the deck table. "Here's your junky old Omnipod back. Not that it helped much."

Hailey stopped the music and looked over at her. "Were you out in the sun for too long? What's wrong with you?"

Eva gulped. She hadn't expected him to ask, or even care, at this point. "You," she blurted out. "You're what's wrong!"

"What did I do?"

"You're not what . . . You're not like . . . Ugh!" Eva threw her hands up. "I've never even *seen* another human. I've dreamed all my life of finally meeting one, and he's . . . he's . . ."

"What?"

"Just forget it." She turned to leave.

Hailey grabbed her arm. "Look." His voice was

softer now. "I'm sorry you didn't get the warm welcome and all the attention you were expecting. But I need to finish some stuff on this ship so we can get you to New Attica as quickly and safely as possible. Okay?"

Eva relaxed and studied Hailey. She watched his Adam's apple move up and down in his throat as he swallowed audibly. *He's nervous,* she thought. *Is he telling the truth? Or is he hiding something?* She remembered Rovender's words about trusting Hailey until he proved otherwise. "Okay. I'll go tell Rovee to get our things," she said.

CHAPTER 4: DREAM

Eva sat on a bunk in the upper cabin deck of the *Bijou.* As she combed her wet hair, she felt cool air from the overhead vent cascade down over her. The crew's quarters had a small bathroom that had allowed her the chance to bathe. This had also given Eva a moment to inspect the multiple bloody pinpricks that ran up and down her sides where the sandsniper had seized her.

Dressed in a clean blue flight suit, Eva removed the bandage and splint from her right hand. The SpeedHeal ointment from her old tunic had mended her palm and fingers well, though a puffy pink scar traced where the caged sniper had struck her. *Would Hailey believe me now if he saw this?*

Down on her forearm the glyph—a circle within a circle—was still vibrant under the skin. The glyph had been imprinted there by the alien soothsayer, Arius. Its presence had saved Eva from being killed in the taxidermist's lab back in Solas, when Arius's brother, Zin, had recognized it. Eva was wondering if the glyph would disappear in time, when she noticed a ring of dots forming around the outer circle. *I never noticed those before.* Eva rubbed the image on her skin but felt nothing.

She leaned back against the wall of the cabin and remembered the chain of events that had brought her here. She thought of her WondLa and its joyous image of a family in a field of red flowers. She thought of what adventures awaited her and Rovender in New Attica.

She thought of Muthr.

Despite the fact that she had switched off the speakers piping Hailey's music into the cabin, Eva could still hear the electronic rhythm below as the pilot finished his work on the ship. She climbed up to the top bunk, knowing that Rovender would soon join her in the cabin. The lanky alien was down in the hold loading up Besteel's glider. Since flying machines were a rare commodity among the general populace of Orbona, Rovender thought it best to bring the glider along, though Eva wondered why he would need it once they arrived at their destination.

Outside a tiny porthole the red sun sank low in the sky, casting a wan beam into the cabin. Even through the thick glass Eva could hear the crying call of turnfins perched atop the airship. She peered out the window at the decayed buildings and imagined the city at the height of its splendor. Eva lay back on her bunk. *Will New Attica look like this?* She wondered why her Omnipod knew nothing of the city, as the cool air and the soft bed summoned Eva into a deep slumber.

A dream slowly materialized in Eva's mind. She was back in the waterfront village of Lacus. Amidst the distant call of birds, she walked along the rickety pathways that took her around the many tiers that made up the village. As Eva passed the rows of huts, it became apparent that the place was deserted. She looked out into the open bazaar that formed the center of the village, but it too appeared abandoned. Judging from the toppled carts and overturned baskets, the residents had left in haste.

Eva called for Muthr, her voice echoing out through the empty homes. The only reply was a sound like Hailey's airship rumbling across the darkened sky. From a dilapidated shanty emerged

Besteel clutching his boomrod. The huntsman was bloodied and battered, missing body parts and limbs. He knelt in front of Eva, laying his weapon down at her feet. Frightened, Eva ran off, searching for a hiding place. She found herself in the home of Arius.

Eva stumbled through the cluttered hoard of offerings and into the smoky den. The pale, plump alien floated near an open window illuminated only by the waning sun. Using her nine stumpy arms, Arius held up an ornate nesting doll. One at a time, Arius twisted a hollow doll open and removed a smaller doll from within.

"Is this your doll?" Eva asked. "I had a Beeboo doll when I was younger."

Arius lined the dolls up on the windowsill. It was clear from their descending size that one of the dolls was missing. Arius looked back at Eva through small slit eyes but said nothing.

"Are you asking me where that missing doll is?" Eva asked.

The soothsayer remained silent.

Eva felt frustration creep over her. "Arius, where is everyone? And why is it so dark out?"

An enormous mottled snake slithered down from the ceiling above. Its jaw was unhinged as it consumed a giant egg.

Eva backed away from the snake. "Arius, what is going on? You know, your brother, Zin, is looking for you." A chill breeze swept through the room, knocking one of the nesting dolls over. It rolled on the sill for a moment before dropping to the floor. Eva looked down, and the doll materialized in her hand.

Eva watched the last fiery rays of the sun slip out of the room as she walked to the sill and reunited the doll with the others. Arius held out a stumpy hand, and Eva took it. She felt her body go limp and was overcome by the sensation of weightlessness. Eva and Arius were now adrift in outer space, floating among the constellations. Without moving her large mouth the alien soothsayer began a chant that reverberated in Eva's head:

"The ancient hive returns again,
to claim a land no longer to claim.
A nymph, born of the earth, forged by
machine,
will lead a way through hate, through fear,
through war.
The heart will be thy ally, and the feast will
come to an end."

The words felt so familiar to Eva, like a long-lost childhood song summoned from her memory.

Then new words came. Words Eva did not know:

> *"Ancient beliefs, ancient leaders, and a*
> *shadow rule the roost.*
> *Illusion shepherds a flock just as a queen*
> *protects her hive.*
> *A gift has been given, a gift many wish for*
> *themselves—*
> *yet a gift none may own.*
> *And so one society flourishes as another*
> *one perishes.*
>
> *Soon there will be a reunion,*
> *but it will end falsely in death and then*
> *truly in rebirth.*
> *Foster your wit, your heart, and your soul,*
> *for the waters of life will quench your*
> *thirst,*
> *heal all wounds, and allow your spirit to*
> *soar."*

With the last incantation Eva found herself back in Arius's den. The sun finally set, smothering the room in darkness. As Eva searched about the gloom for the soothsayer, she soon discovered that she was alone. There was no Arius, no

Muthr, and no Rovender—only the hollow ache of loneliness.

Eva blinked as the dream evaporated into the recesses of her mind. Through the porthole she could see that it was now dusk. She sat up and looked around the cabin. Rovender's belongings were there, but he was not. Eva lay back on her bunk and thought of Arius and the dream. "What was with those dolls?" she wondered aloud. "And that creepy snake?"

Her thoughts were interrupted by the whine of the *Bijou*'s engines resonating through the cabin walls. Eva sat up as the sound rose higher and higher in pitch. The whine was soon muffled as the air pressure dropped in the cabin. Eva hopped down from her bunk and felt the floor under her sway back and forth. She rushed out of the cabin and down a ladder to the main deck.

Rovender was standing in the doorway of the cockpit watching Hailey pilot the airship for take-off. Through the expansive windshield the grand silhouette of the ancient ruins dropped away, and the *Bijou* rose straight up into the evening sky.

Good-bye, Muthr, Eva thought as she watched Muthr's final resting spot vanish below the clouds. *I'll never forget you.*

CHAPTER 5: FLIGHT

"We're off!" Hailey glanced over his shoulder at Eva and Rovender as he worked the controls. He seemed more relaxed now that they were airborne. "The return trip should take a little less than three hours, depending on the weather. I'll let you know when we're getting close."

Eva watched quietly as the ship broke through the cloud cover and soared up to the stratosphere. High above in the twilight the Rings of Orbona glimmered brightly. They arced like mighty ribbons over the horizon and under the waning moon. It was as if the *Bijou* were traveling through another world, another dimension entirely, to

arrive at its final destination. Eva felt light-headed and energized all at once. "Is there anything else we need to do?" she asked.

"Nope. Just sit back and enjoy the ride." Hailey kept his attention on the ship's instruments. A detailed hologram of the *Bijou*, along with numerous readouts regarding wind, weather, and other virtual controls, hovered over the dashboard.

"What about Rovee?" Eva looked over at her friend. "Is there anything he needs to do to register with New Attica?"

Rovender mumbled in agreement with Eva's question and took a sip from a bottle. His breath carried a pungent smell.

"I've got it under control. Don't worry, Emma," Hailey said.

"It's Eva. Are there a lot of other Orbonian aliens there?" Eva replied. "I hope we meet some Halcyonus. I really enjoy their company. Do you know any? They prepare the best seafood."

Hailey drew in a deep sigh. "Just go back to the galley and grab a SustiBar or relax up in the cabin. We are coming up on some turbulence, and I've got to concentrate."

Eva and Rovender backed out of the cockpit, and the door hissed shut. From within Eva could hear Hailey command the ship, "*Bijou*, music, please. Play me my ancient rock and roll collection infused with electronica and filtered into a fast-track beat. Thank you." Hailey's music began thumping in a steady driving rhythm throughout the ship.

Rovender hung his hat over the galley speaker, effectively muffling the sound. He took a seat in one of the hovchairs at the table. "Did you give him the transcoder?"

"I did," said Eva, looking back at the closed cockpit door, "but I don't know if he used it."

"He has not," Rovender said into the mouth of his bottle, and took a swig.

"That stuff." Eva gestured at the bottle. "You've drunk that before. What is it?"

"This? This is Nuccan usquebaugh, so called because it is made from the fermented milk of a nucca plant." Rovender tilted the glass flask, causing the contents to swish about. "Apparently Besteel enjoyed it as I do. I found it among his many things."

Eva crinkled her nose. "It smells . . . gross."

"It helps to ease my nerves, Eva Nine. You know how I feel about machines. Traveling in one, to a village I know nothing about, makes me wary. My methods are usually more . . . cautious."

Eva reached out and held his large hand. "This is a big change for you, too, huh? I guess I was so excited about leaving that I didn't think of how all of this would affect you."

"It is okay. Where you go, I go," Rovender said.

"Thanks for coming with me."

"For you it is important we go to this place. I must confess I am curious to see what sort of essence inhabits it." Rovender took another swig.

"Essence?"

"Yes." Rovender grabbed his rucksack and began rummaging through it. "The essence will be evident everywhere. In all that the citizens do: in their art, music, food, and their buildings. If the essence of a place nourishes your spirit, then it is a good place to be."

Eva sat back and absorbed his words. "Yeah, I can't wait to explore it with you and find our new home."

"Home?" Rovender pulled out a voxfruit and a strip of cured turnfin meat. "Eva Nine, a village of your kind does not necessarily make a home."

"Of course it does," said Eva. She seized one of the voxfruit berries. "It is where you fit in. Where you find happiness."

"Bluh!" Rovender washed a piece of meat down with his drink. "One can find happiness in a variety of places. It can be in a busy city of many, such as Solas; but it may also be alone, deep in a tranquil forest. It is not always among your kind."

"You mean *your* kind, don't you?" Eva said. She knew that Rovender had left his village after the death of his partner and child, never to return.

The Cærulean put down his food and bottle. Eva realized that his eyes were watery—but she wasn't sure if this was simply a reaction to the dank aroma of his drink, which lingered in the galley.

Looking down at his bottle, Rovender spoke softly, "If you are referring to those I left behind, Eva, then you are right. They were my kind in that we were of the same sort, but not of the same mind. I see their faces in my memory every day that I wander, but the place where they dwell is no longer home to me."

Eva felt awash with remorse. As she watched Rovender return to his meal, she wanted to take back the words she'd just said to him.

She thought back to when Rovender had confessed to being a widower running far away from his pain. *Am I running away too?* she wondered. *Am I running from the pain of losing Muthr?* A realization drifted into her mind, filling her with dread. "Rovee, if something goes wrong, will you leave me? Or will you stay with me as you promised?"

Rovender took a drink from his bottle and looked up at Eva. "I'll always be there for you, Eva. You have my word."

She smiled at him, but this only hid the notion that, though Rovender had given his word, somehow Eva felt there was something he wasn't saying. All this was too much to ponder at the moment. They would be arriving in New Attica before long.

She changed the subject. "So, I was checking in with my Omnipod today—which, by the way, seems to be working perfectly. Can you believe that? After where it has been?"

Rovender cracked a grin, lightening in mood. "That is something."

"It is," Eva said, "and my Omnipod reminded me that tomorrow is my birthday!"

"Your birth-day?" Rovender tilted his narrow head, looking confused.

"You know, the day I was born. The day I arrived."

"Ah, your hatching."

"Yes!" Eva giggled. "I guess with all that we've been through, I'd forgotten it was coming up. So we have to celebrate and do something fun. Maybe Hailey will join us."

Rovender continued eating. "Yes. Your hatching

is important when you are a little nymph. But as you grow older, it becomes lost amidst the other great events in your life journey."

"Well, arriving at New Attica is about the best event, the best birthday present, I can think of. Don't you think?"

"We shall see, Eva Nine. We shall see," said Rovender, and he finished his meal.

Back in the cabin, Eva Nine tossed and turned in her bunk. Excitement prevented her from sleeping, as did the fact that Rovender was snoring in the cot below. Eva peered over her bunk and realized that her friend had passed out on the floor instead of his cot. She hopped down and wrapped him in his worn woven blanket. Rovender mumbled something incoherent as he rolled over and buried his head under a pillow. Eva smiled in the dark and gave him a loving pat.

The ship turned ever so slightly, causing the cabin to tilt. Rovender's bottle rolled out from his grasp and under the lower bunk. Eva heard the half-full bottle clink against something before it rolled back out into the room as the ship stabilized its pitch. She grabbed the bottle and returned it to Rovender's rucksack, then investigated what it had bumped into. Using her Omnipod's light, Eva discovered a small carton tucked far under the bunk. She slid it out into the open and wiped off a thick layer of dust. A logo, similar to one she had seen in her Sanctuary, was stamped into the lid. It was an emblem with the letters *HRP* printed in the center.

Eva's eyes darted around the room. With the hidden carton now revealed, a guilty feeling crept over her. *Does Hailey care if I have a look in his box? Should I ask?* Eva looked around the cabin for cameras. Seeing none, she seized the carton and climbed back up to her bunk. Sliding the lid off the carton, she shone her light inside. The carton was full of old holographic programs.

The programs all looked alike: small transparent discs stored in perfect rows with aged foam lining. Eva carefully grabbed the first one by its edges, as she had been taught, and snapped it over the central eye of her Omnipod. So as not to disturb Rovender, she whispered, "Please initiate program."

Matching Eva's volume, the Omnipod responded, "Initiating."

"Welcome to the Historical Holography Project." A portly man with bushy gray eyebrows and a beard flickered above the Omnipod. "I am Leonardo Pryde, lead programmer on this monumental undertaking.

Here you can interact with some of history's most famous names, all brought to vivid life through the magic of holog—"

Eva pulled the program out and snapped in another one. It was titled *Manufacturing Your Own Synthetic Foods.* A farmer greeted Eva and began explaining how to instill the natural flavor of fruits and vegetables into easy-to-produce pills and pellets, enough to feed the masses. *Masses of what?* Eva thought as she plucked out the program. *Why eat that stuff when you can find real fruit to enjoy?* She inserted a new program and continued going through them one at a time, hoping to find any information on New Attica.

When the last program activated, a bespectacled man with a goatee materialized over Eva's Omnipod. He was similar in appearance to the man in the first hologram, but thinner with an aquiline profile. His voice had a welcoming folksy tenor to it, as if he were about to tell a story by the campfire. "Hello. I am Cadmus Pryde, and welcome to my future world vision for all mankind. It's called the Human Repopulation Project, or HRP, brought to you by the Dynastes Corporation."

DYNASTES
CORP

CHAPTER 6: HRP

"We have determined that the reality of cost-effective manufacturing of in vitro labs for planetary orbit, or deep space travel, has too many variables and therefore greatly diminishes any chance of success." Cadmus addressed a small audience from behind a lectern on a small stage. The Dynastes logo flashed about in an animated fashion behind him.

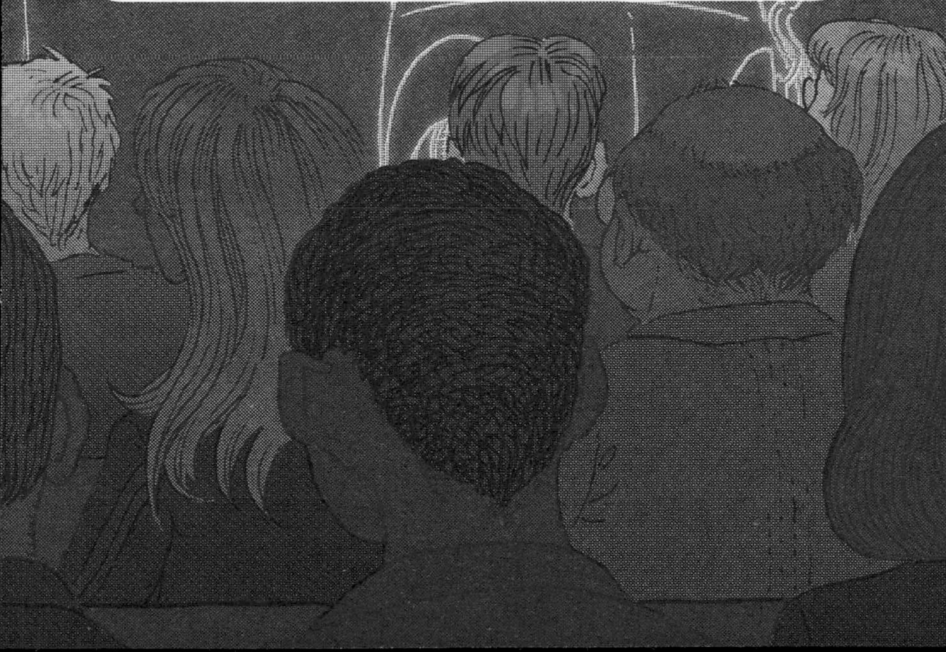

Eva set the program to 360-degree mode, and the hologram of Cadmus and the stage filled the ship's cabin at actual size as it projected from the Omni-pod. Rovender snored softly underneath the light show. *Finally,* Eva thought as she leaned forward and watched from her bunk. *Answers.*

Cadmus continued with his presentation. "You've all witnessed the tragedy that occurred with the colonies on the moon, so there is no chance of 'waiting this out' off-planet. Therefore, I am proposing the creation of a network of automated subterranean laboratories that would remain inert until surface conditions restabilize to viable levels."

Eva had a hard time understanding all that Cadmus said. In fact, he sounded a lot like Zin, the curator at the Royal Museum of Solas. Still, she paid close attention, hoping for more clues about her existence. Behind Cadmus detailed architectural renderings of a Sanctuary and its many rooms were projected. An audience member raised his hand. Cadmus pointed to him and said, "Yes?"

A distinguished man with short white hair stood. "Bradley Tofield, Virtual Syndicate Press. I want to make sure I understand the premise here, Mr. Pryde. You are proposing to build underground labs—"

"We are calling them Sanctuaries," Cadmus interjected.

"Sanctuaries," Bradley continued, "where you want to grow test-tube babies?"

"That is correct."

The audience's murmur carried on for several long uncomfortable moments. Cadmus shifted, obviously nervous, behind the lectern.

The reporter continued his questioning. "But if your theory of Terra Terminal Hibernation is correct, and we are all to perish, then who would raise these children?"

"An excellent question, Bradley." Cadmus touched the screen on the lectern, and a new set of images projected around him. "It is sort of a chicken-or-the-egg dilemma, but I believe I have found a solution. Our research in robotics has grown in leaps and bounds since the approval of the Organ Integration Act. We've been able to interface the latest cutting edge technology with cloned human brain tissue. More specifically, we've created robots that don't just mimic human emotion based on preset circumstances built into their programming. They can actually react emotionally and cope with a human in a real-time situation." Eva watched as technical drawings projected behind Cadmus rendered into the familiar shape of Muthr.

"Robots raising test-tube babies?" an unseen attendee spoke out.

Bradley added, "You can't honestly believe that a

robot could provide proper care for a child. They need parents."

"I agree," Cadmus replied. "However, the establishing generations will not have that luxury, because there will not be anyone left alive to care for them."

The audience grew restless with disapproval.

Cadmus tried to calm them, but no one was listening. Finally he gripped the sides of the lectern and spoke out loudly, hushing the attendees. "Listen. I understand your feelings and what you are thinking. No doubt these are radical ideas. However, our dire situation requires nothing less. You've seen it. The oceans have lost more than eighty percent of life. Our forests and fields no longer exist, and consequently the atmosphere is thinning, even with our CO_2 processing factories working overtime. As you know, we have tried to reestablish balance by cloning and releasing millions of every life-form that we've collected, but it is futile. All ecosystems are shutting down, and the Earth is entering a state of planetary hibernation. This is bigger than anything we can control."

Audience members got up and began leaving. Some of them booed Cadmus and threw cups and loose electra-papers at him. Cadmus called out to them, "If mankind wants to stake a claim on the future, we have to act now! There is so little time left!"

The historical program finished. Eva gently removed it and shut off her Omnipod. She leaned back on her bunk. *Rovender said that the Ojo family had the ability to wake dead planets.* As Eva had concluded back at the ruins, Earth must have perished, and Orbona had risen in its place. *So have the humans in New Attica lived here all this time?* Clearly Cadmus's plan was put into action at some point in the past. *Here I am,* Eva thought. *And a robot in an underground Sanctuary raised me, just as Cadmus predicted.* He'd been a true visionary.

Hailey's voice crackled out over the ship's intercom, startling Eva from her thoughts. "Hey. We are in our final approach, so if you two can get your things together and come on down, we'll be on the ground shortly."

From below, Rovender stirred and let out a loud yawn. "What is that? What did he say?"

"We are getting ready to land." Eva placed the program back in the carton and closed the lid. She hopped down and helped Rovender gather his belongings.

CHAPTER 7: REBOOT

The night sky was aglow from a distant circular city sparkling just below the horizon. As the *Bijou* zoomed beneath the clouds and approached its final destination, the lights of the city pulsed and twinkled like an enormous electric being.

"That's it. New Attica," said Hailey as he brought the ship low for its landing. The metropolis was surrounded on all sides by jagged dark mountains, which Hailey navigated through with apparent ease. As they entered an expansive valley, Eva realized that New Attica was situated at the bottom of

a gigantic quarry set deep in the earth. Above it hung a mirror image of the Rings of Orbona.

"Is it underwater?" Eva asked. "I see a reflection."

"Heh." Hailey chuckled and activated the landing gear. "No, it's not underwater. There is an atmospheric membrane stretched over the entire city. It helps regulate the temperature inside and protects against the elements." Hailey dimmed the *Bijou*'s headlights and navigated the ship around the perimeter toward a low flat canyon dominated by tall hydration spires.

Eva tore her gaze from the vision that now filled the entire cockpit windshield, and looked at Rovender. Though her heart was pounding with excitement, her friend seemed indifferent as he watched from the cockpit doorway. Eva walked over to Rovender. "Well, what do you think?"

Rovender stood with arms folded. "It is quite a sight. And it looks to be about the same size as Solas."

Eva leaned against him, thinking back to her experiences in that alien city. "I hope we fit in here. I hope these people accept us."

"Eva Nine." Rovender put his arm around the girl. "*You* should also accept *them*."

"We'll be landing in just a few moments," Hailey said. He brought the ship down into a gorge deep

in the canyon just outside the city limits. A loose congregation of campfires flickered from the canyon floor.

Eva and Rovender exchanged concerned glances. "We don't land in the city?" she asked.

"Nope. We put in here," replied Hailey as the ship touched down on the rocky flat ground. He taxied the *Bijou* toward an opening in the canyon wall. Outside, a band of shadowy figures could be seen running toward the ship. Even through the thick glass of the windshield, whooping and shouting could be heard mixed with the crack of gunfire.

The hairs on the back of Eva's neck stood on end, and she scooted even closer to Rovender. "Why here?" She tried to remain calm as she looked down at the dark shabby figures below dancing around the ship. "Are those . . . people? Where are you taking us?"

"Yes, they're people. Don't worry about them. They just get excited. Do you always ask so many questions? I told you I was taking you home, and I am. But we stay here for the night." The ship came to a halt in a run-down hanger deep within a widemouthed cave. Hailey shut off the engines, rose from his pilot's seat, and stretched. "What are you waiting for?" the pilot said. "Go get your stuff. We're here."

From the cargo hold of the ship, Eva could hear the murmur of many human voices echoing throughout the hangar. She leaned down and peered from the entry ramp of the ship to spy on Hailey. The pilot was addressing a small gaggle of people gathered at the entrance of the cavern.

The first thing Eva noticed was the dirt. All of the humans seemed to be covered in a layer of grime and dust—from their greasy hair to their grungy mismatched attire. Most carried weapons of some sort, even the few children that were present. Eva could not make out what Hailey was saying, but eventually the group broke up and the people filed off into the gloom outside. With the hangar now empty and quiet, Eva carefully stepped out of the *Bijou*.

The jagged cavern walls were lined with a store of crated supplies and provisions. Overhead lights buzzed loudly with electric current, fed by several large generators. Deeper within the cavern, next to the *Bijou*, lay the skeletal remains of another airship. Its ply-steel shell and other valuable components had long been scavenged. Hailey rounded the *Bijou* with a rolling ladder that he pushed snug up to its nose. Eva approached him, curious.

From a worn leather pouch the pilot pulled two decals shaped like humans. Carefully he adhered them to the hull of the ship in line with the others. He opened a small can of paint, hanging from the ladder, and painted one of the decals blue. Hailey hopped down from the ladder and examined his handiwork. "You've no idea how long I've wanted to do that. The blue one is for your friend."

There was a clanging sound from within the *Bijou*, and Rovender started down the ramp with the glider hovering low. "No, that's okay," Hailey said, running over to Rovender. He started pushing the glider back onboard. "You can leave it on the ship for now." He glanced around the hanger as if looking to see if anyone else were watching. "Let's just get inside."

Rovender looked over at Eva and shrugged his shoulders. It was clear he still could not understand what Hailey was saying. *I wonder why Hailey hasn't used the transcoder yet.* Eva thought. "He says to leave it on the ship for now, Rovee," she translated. Her lanky companion pushed the glider back up into the hold. He grabbed his belongings and joined Eva and Hailey underneath the bow of the *Bijou*.

"This way. Follow me," the pilot said, leading them to a recess in the back of the cavern.

"I don't like this," Eva whispered to Rovender. She held his hand tight as they trailed behind Hailey.

"Do not fret, Eva Nine. Let us see where he takes us and go from there," Rovender replied, lighting his lantern.

Chittering could be heard high above them coming from the shadows of the jagged ceiling.

"Knifejacks?" Eva asked.

"Perhaps," Rovender replied. "Try not to make any loud noises."

"It's just ahead," said Hailey as he rounded a thick stalagmite. "Here we are. Watch your step."

Eva and Rovender followed Hailey and arrived at a hovel nestled in the back of the cave.

Upon entering, Eva recognized the painted weathered pieces that formed the walls of Hailey's ramshackle home as the hull paneling from the wreck out in the hanger. Empty crates and hovchairs from the wrecked ship's galley made up a dining area, while a multitude of wires snaked over the floor, providing power to all aspects of the cluttered abode. Hailey dropped his bag of belongings onto one of the hovchairs and slid open a large rolling door. "You guys can use my room to REM in tonight. I'll take you to the city in the morning."

Eva looked at Rovender and stopped, not following Hailey into his room. "Why can't you take us now?" she asked.

"The city registrar is closed," the pilot replied.

"The registrar?" Eva asked. Cautious yet curious, she peered inside his room.

Like the rest of the home, his room's décor was made up of reconstituted parts of the wrecked airship. The majority of the space was dedicated to an enormous half-assembled engine held in place by stacks of worn tires. Intricate components and other bizarre parts littered the floor, creating winding footpaths to walk through. Empty upturned crates acted as provisional workstations, all of which were buried under an assortment of tools. Two cots sat alongside each other at the far end of the room.

"Yes," replied Hailey. He picked up a stack of loose electra-papers and dirty clothes heaped upon the two cots. "All reboots have to register and be admitted into the city's computer system to become a citizen. I'll deliver . . . er, take you to the offices myself. From there you'll be given a medical checkup and orientation."

"It sounds like a lot to do," said Eva.

"It goes quickly. So we'll leave first thing in the morning, okay?"

"Okay." Eva clutched her satchel strap.

Rovender picked up one of the tools and examined it. A hand-size heavy clip held a metallic rod tight in its pincers. Rovender sniffed the tool and set it back down. As he did, the rod brushed against the metal of the engine and ignited in a bright blue spark.

"Hey! Be careful!" Hailey rushed over. "I can't believe I left the arc welder on," he muttered, and shut off the generator that powered it.

"Sorry," said Eva. "He didn't know."

"It's okay," Hailey said. "Look, I have to go recharge the ship and take care of some other maintenance. There's Nutri-pills and bars in that crate over there, and the bathroom is here." He slid open one of the hull panels to reveal a simple bath, basin, and toilet. "Make yourself at home, but don't touch anything, all right?" He hurried out toward the hangar. "I'll be back in a bit."

Rovender leaned his walking stick against the wall and hung his hat from the top. He pulled his bottle from his rucksack and uncorked it. "Well?" he said, stretching out on a cot.

Eva stood in the room, still clinging to her satchel strap. The oily machine smell permeated everything here. It was much stronger than it had been on the ship. Somehow the scent wasn't as reassuring to Eva as it had been before. She let out a long sigh and sat on the cot opposite her friend. "Well, this is not what I was expecting."

"What were you expecting?" Rovender asked, unpacking his sleeping mat and blanket.

"A home. Not a garage full of junk."

"This is a home. This is *my* home," croaked a voice from the back of the room. Startled, Eva squealed and jumped off her cot.

"Who is there?" Rovender stood, aiming his lantern toward the voice.

A sound came from behind the engine. *Stomp-hiss. Stomp-hiss.*

"Oh, it's just me, little old me," the voice wheezed in a singsong manner. From behind the engine an elderly man limped out into the lamplight with the aid of a cane. *Stomp-hiss. Stomp-hiss.* His small frame was draped in a long tattered dirt-brown jacket, similar to Rovender's. A dingy flight cap sat atop his balding head. The grease on his cheeks contrasted with his stringy white hair and beard. He put a gnarled finger to his mouth and whispered, "Shhh. Don't tell the boy I'm here. He gets cranky." The old man smiled a yellow grin and hobbled toward Eva and Rovender. The *stomp-hiss* sound continued with every step he took.

"This one I can understand." Rovender's voice dropped to a confidential whisper. "He must carry a transcoder."

The man stopped in front of the duo and studied them both. "A reboot! A reboot traveling with a newcomer. And I thought I'd seen it all," he said to Eva, leaning on his cane. "We haven't had a Sanctuary-born here in a long time. A long time." A series of scars raked down the side of his withered face, causing his right eyelid to droop. With his good eye the old man winked. "Name's Van Turner. But you can call me Vanpa if you want," he said. He inspected Eva up and down. "You're young for a newbie. Did your Sanctuary go kaput?"

"It was raided," Eva answered, though she didn't quite know what to think of his questioning. "By an alien."

"This fella?" Van Turner pointed a crooked finger at Rovender.

"No!" Rovender paused while dimming his lantern. "It was a Dorcean—"

"Of course it wasn't you. I knew that. You blue ones

are nice," Van Turner said, patting Rovender on the shoulder. He sang, "The blue ones are nice, the gray ones are mean, and the pretty ones are something else in between." He gestured for Rovender to slide down. "Move over, slim. I need to take a load off."

Van Turner eased onto the cot next to Rovender. Eva could not take her eyes from the thick beard that grew from his face or the wrinkles that surrounded his eyes. It was as if Van were a different species altogether.

"Never seen a fellow as old as me, have you?"

Eva shook her head no.

"Don't worry. No one ages like this in the city."

He loosened his jacket and reached down to his left knee. Eva realized that his left leg was a makeshift assemblage of pistons and shafts, likely pilfered from the wrecked airship. Van Turner unstrapped the artificial leg, revealing a knotted fleshy stump underneath.

Van Turner caught Eva's stare. "Lost it to a sand devil years ago," he said, rubbing his stump.

"Does it pain you?" Rovender asked, offering his bottle.

"Not at all." Van Turner took a drink. "But you know, sometimes I swear I can still feel my foot, plain as day." He handed the bottle back.

"Who are you?" Eva asked.

The old man jabbed a thumb toward the hangar. "I am Hailey's grandpa. I've been taking care of him since he was a whiny whelp."

"Are you a returner too?" Eva asked.

"A *retriever*? No, ma'am," Van Turner said with a chuckle. He took the bottle from Rovender and paused, his eye sparkling in the low light. "I'm like you, little one. I was also conceived in a Sanctuary lab, almost two hundred years ago."

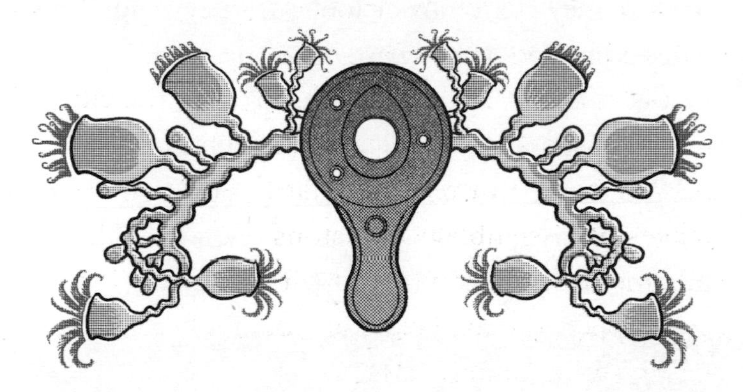

CHAPTER 8: TOILERS

"My given name was Evan Six, but I changed it when I registered with the city. After all, who wants a number for a name?" Van Turner took another swig. "You can do that too if you want, little one. Change your name, change your appearance, change your programming, change it all!" he said, and cackled.

"You came to New Attica two hundred years ago?" Eva relaxed a bit. She sat cross-legged on her cot and pulled off her sneakboots.

"Yup. I was a reboot like you, born and raised by ancient technology so that mankind can once again rule the world. Ha!" Van Turner handed the bottle back to Rovender. "I don't think they've seen one of us in the last hundred years. You may get quite a welcome."

"Are there not many in your village, New Attica?" Rovender asked.

"Oh, there are many," Van Turner replied. "Too many, if you ask me. But no reboots really. There are not many of us left."

"Well, I can't wait to meet more people, especially kids my age," Eva said wistfully.

"There were no others in your Sanctuary cluster? Had to settle with this guy, huh, newbie?" Van Turner nudged Rovender in a playful manner. Rovender nodded and took a sip of his drink.

"No," Eva replied. "I was the only one."

"Woo! You're both in for an eye-opening experience, then."

"If you went to New Attica, why are you now out here? Were you expelled?" Rovender asked before pulling a voxfruit out from his rucksack.

Van Turner shook his head. "I left."

With a longing in his eyes, he watched Rovender peel the fruit. Eva noticed this and handed him one of hers. The codger seized it with trembling hands and began clawing it open. "Oh, yes. Green berries." He closed his eyes as he put the fruit into his mouth. "I haven't had these in over a decade."

The three of them ate for some time without speaking. Eva looked over at Rovender, and he gave her a relieved smile. She exhaled a breath that she hadn't realized she had been holding. The old man seemed a little batty, yet somehow he made Eva feel more at ease than Hailey.

"Why did you leave, Vanpa?" she asked. Eva liked that Van Turner had offered his nickname right away.

"Too many rules, too many promises, too many things being done for you and yet for no one at all. I didn't want to exist in that cocoon forever. I wanted experiences. I wanted adventures. *I wanted to live.*" He pondered his meal. "It's like this green fruit here. Man was not designed to eat pills and powders and all the other chemicals they pump you full of. We were meant to live off the land in harmony with it. Not in some safety bubble."

Rovender gave a knowing look at Eva.

"But why here?" said Eva.

"Yes, this does seem a rugged existence," Rovender added.

"Oh, it is," Van Turner said, running his twisted tree-branch fingers over his leg stump. "But we have not always lived here. The others and I, we left New Attica many years ago to start our own colony near the green spot."

"The green spot?" Eva asked.

"Yes," Van Turner said. "It is Eden reborn. It is where the air is fresh, the waters run clear, and the trees creak with joy."

"You're talking about the Wandering Forest," Eva said. Rovender agreed.

"'Wandering'?" Van Turner said. "I like that name. It certainly wandered far away from this place, that's for sure," he said, and then cackled.

"So you left?" asked Rovender.

"Yes," Van Turner continued. "We took a couple of airships and left for greener pastures. But it wasn't as easy as we'd hoped for. Our Omnipods failed to identify anything. They proved practically useless. There were all sorts of newcomers poking around, like this blue fella here, some friendly—some not. And the Wandering Forest, as you call it, was dangerous in and of itself. We lost some good people."

Eva remembered how scary some of the trees and plants had been when she'd first ventured into the forest. Between the weeping bird-catchers and giant sundews, it was amazing she was still alive.

"So we moved camp to the outskirts of the forest, and that's when the sand devils got us. Picked us off one by one in the dark of night." Van Turner's hands balled into fists. His raspy voice cracked. "Those beasts took my leg, and they took . . . they took . . . my son . . . Hailey's daddy." The old man sniffled. Rovender offered his bottle, but Van Turner shooed it away. "I didn't want to have a new leg clone-grafted," he said. "When you get this old, you start to remember things in the wrong order, or forget them completely. I wanted reminders—mementos of my life. I never wanted to forget what had happened."

"And so you came back?" Rovender spoke softly.

"Yes, we returned. Defeated by the new laws of nature. We learned we are no longer rulers of the land. But what was worse is that Cadmus was furious that we'd broken away from his little utopia and left with his precious airships and technology."

"Cadmus Pryde?" Eva thought of the young man in the program. "He's still alive?"

"Yeah, the maker of us all still rules the roost. When we returned, he repossessed the working airships and most of our supplies, saying it was property of New Attica. He then forbade us ever to return to his city. And so, here we are on the outside looking in. Yet we survive. I don't know how, but all of us here manage."

"Where did everybody here come from?" Eva asked. She thought about the gathering of grungy people running out to the airship when they'd landed.

"They're like me—the disillusioned and disenfranchised. So they try to make a go of it out here. 'Toilers' are what they call us back in the city. I guess because we are willing to work for our rightful place out here in the real world. But those who live in the city are nothing but 'sheeple,' if you ask me. An overgrown flock of cloned sheep eating and sleeping whenever they are told. Safe with their shepherd."

"I'm confused," Eva said. "Why don't you all just leave on the *Bijou*?"

"Right," Rovender added. "Your flying machine will allow you to go anywhere. There are safer places to colonize."

Van Turner let out a drink-sodden sigh. "Well, that's been the plan. But for the past year the boy's been working on converting the *Bijou* into a fully manual air-breaker from scavenged parts. I think he's almost done. He's good with machines, just like his daddy was, but not so much with people."

"An 'air-breaker'?" Rovender took a drink.

"Yup, those retriever airships are completely automated. They'll sit dormant for decades waiting for a reboot signal. Even if there'd been no pilots around, that ship would have tracked you down and brought you here by itself—it's that smart. But since there have been no reboots in a long time, Cadmus has disbanded the retrievers. However, some pilots have figured out how to convert the airships to manual control. The boy is close to finishing. He just needs a few more components."

"So, Hailey isn't a retriever?" Eva asked. Her mind flickered to the rows of human-shaped decals on the nose of the ship.

Van Turner laughed. "No."

Eva shot a worried look to Rovender.

The old man continued, "I mean, the boy wants to be one, just like his daddy was. But Hailey was asleep on the ship when it took off."

"Asleep?" Eva asked. "Are you serious?"

Van Turner chuckled. "Yup. He must have been scared silly when the *Bijou* fired up and zoomed off after you." He picked up Rovender's bottle and gulped down the last swallow of the milky liquid. "There must still be some kinks to work out," he said, lost in a thought. "You don't want your only means of transport taking off in the middle of the night to pick up someone and fly 'em back to the city, right?"

The door slid open, and Hailey walked in, holding his Omnipod. "Vanpa, what are you doing?" he said in an exasperated tone. "I told you to leave our guests alone. They need REM."

"They're fine, boy. I'm just telling old stories." Van Turner winked at Eva and strapped on his artificial leg.

Hailey grabbed a pair of gray HRP blankets from a crate. "Well, don't believe a thing he says. He's a crazy old man." Hailey made a silly face, mocking his grandfather.

"Like you know everything at fifteen?" Van Turner said while Hailey draped a blanket over his shoulders.

"Come on. We'll sleep on the *Bijou* tonight." Hailey led his grandfather out of the room.

"We'd better. If that thing comes back on again to pick up another newbie, I want to be on it this time!" Van Turner laughed.

"Of course, Vanpa. I would *never* leave you

behind." Hailey rolled his eyes and ushered him along. "Come on."

"Good luck tomorrow. Don't let 'em rewire all your thinking," Van Turner said to Eva with a wave, and he left.

"Good night," Hailey said, and closed the door.

Fifteen, Eva thought. *He's barely older than me.*

Rovender lay back in his cot, resting his head on his rucksack. "I like the elder one," he said, eating the last of his voxfruit.

"I like him too," Eva replied. "Even Hailey seems more normal, more relaxed, around his grandpa."

"Agreed. And the pilot must have used the transcoder, because now I understand him," added Rovender.

Eva smiled. *Maybe Hailey isn't so bad after all,* she thought, and curled up under her blanket.

CHAPTER 9: NEW ATTICA

I can't believe he decided to go exploring this morning! Today of all days!" Eva said as she ripped open her last voxfruit. "Ugh! And after he gave his word he'd always be there for me."

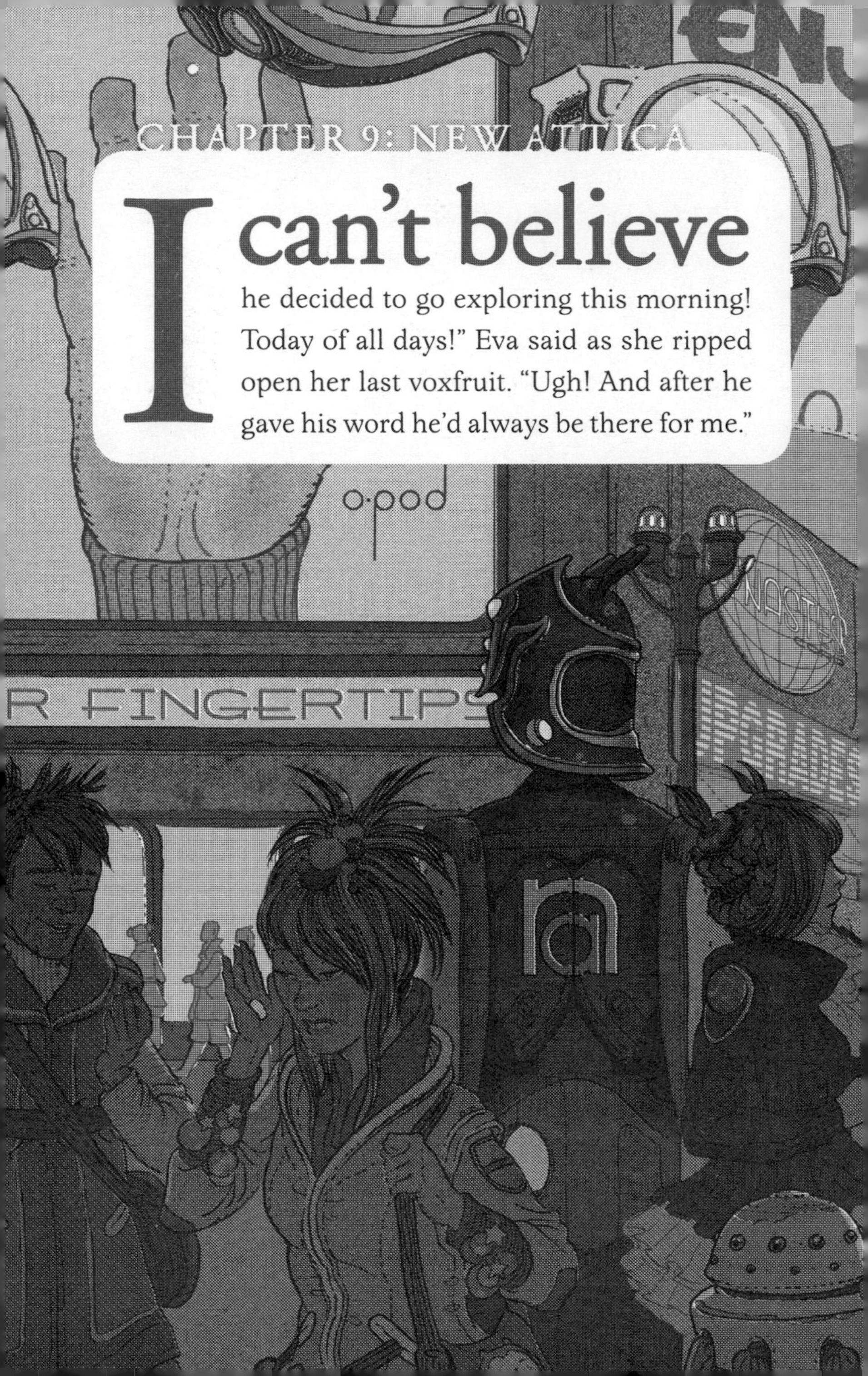

"Yeah." Hailey poured two cups of coffee. "He and Vanpa were both up at sunrise and wanted to take a look around. I think a few of Vanpa's friends even came with."

"Who knows when he'll get back? Ooo! How typical," Eva groused. "Rovee knew how badly I wanted to go to the city. *He did this on purpose*. It's another one of his stupid 'life lessons.'" She threw her voxfruit down into her satchel and sighed melodramatically. "What are we going to do?"

Hailey handed Eva a steaming mug. He dropped down into one of the hovchairs and sipped his oily black coffee. "Well," he said, thinking aloud, "we could go in and get you registered this morning, and then I could just send him over to meet you once they're back."

Eva took a gulp from her drink. The bitter hot coffee scorched her tongue. She set the mug down, careful to hide the sting of the burn on her face. "Yes," she said. "Let's go. Now."

"Welcome back to New Attica, Hailey Turner," a bodiless voice greeted the pilot while a green laser scanned his body. Eva and Hailey were standing at the bottom of an underground access ramp that led to the entrance of the city. Flanking the grand entryway were two stone pillars, one carved in the shape of a man and the other in the shape of a woman. Graffiti and other markings marred the ornate sculptures.

"Thank you." Hailey addressed the closed entry gate to the city. "I am here with a new citizen."

"Please remain still for initial body scan. This will take several moments," the gate instructed. The laser eye began to inspect Eva just as it had done with Hailey.

"Do you come to New Attica often?" Eva tried to stand still.

"I've been a few times. It's too crowded for me."

"Weren't you born here? Did you change your name, like Vanpa?" Eva asked.

"No," Hailey replied, uninterested. "This is the name my dad gave me."

"I might change my name to Dorothy," Eva said, watching Hailey for a response. "She was a girl in this old book I found. Have you ever seen a book before?"

"Please remain still until body scan is complete. Thank you," the gate said.

"Dorothy, huh?" Hailey leaned against a pillar and polished his Omnipod. "If that's the name you like."

"I'll have to find out what it means first," Eva said. "Do you know what 'Hailey' means?"

"Please remain still until body scan is complete. Thank you," the gate repeated.

"Yeah. 'Hailey' means, 'Sit still so we can get on with this,'" the pilot said with a smirk.

"Scan complete. Please insert Omnipod here," the gate said. A hatch slid open, revealing a small access port. Eva did as she was instructed.

"You are Earth in Vitro Alpha, ninth generation, from HRP Sanctuary five-seven-three. Is that correct?" the gate asked.

"Yes," Eva said, bouncing on her toes. Excitement buzzed through her like a wild electric charge.

"Access to city granted," the gate said. "Please take your Omnipod and proceed to the subferry dock for immediate departure. Welcome to New Attica." The heavy pocked ply-steel outer gates squeaked in resistance as they ground apart. Inside, a row of battered subferries sat docked at a steep angle facing down into a series of tunnels that led deep underground. The bobsled shaped, aged ships were waiting for their new arrivals with back hatches open.

"Please watch your step," the nearest subferry said in a friendly manner. "We shall be departing shortly."

"Let's go to the front. Those are the best seats," Hailey said, boarding the ferry.

Eva climbed in and scooted past two rows of seating. She joined Hailey in the front row and strapped herself into a worn seat. The hatch closed in the back, and Eva's eyes adjusted to the dim lighting.

"Thank you for your cooperation. Welcome aboard New Attica's subterranean ferry. If you are ready, we will be off in just a moment, with an approximate travel time of ninety seconds." The entry hatch sealed and locked shut. Eva tapped her seat's armrests in anticipation.

"Hold on," Hailey said. "This is quite a ride."

"Really?" Eva watched a series of lights activate along the length of the endless tunnel. In the background the ferry counted down. "Ten . . . nine . . . eight . . ."

Even without her life monitor to inform her, Eva could feel her heart rate speed up.

"Five . . . four . . . three . . ."

She gripped the armrests.

"Don't worry." Hailey smiled. "It's fun."

"Two . . . one."

Eva's stomach pushed against her throat as the subferry plummeted down. The lights outside became a glowing blur as the craft spun and whirled through the tunnel. Just when Eva thought the high-speed descent would never end, the ship slowed and leveled out, coming to a gentle stop at a platform.

"Thank you," announced the subferry. "Please take your belongings and make your way through the eastern corridor into the city limits. Welcome to New Attica."

"Quite a ride, huh?" Hailey asked.

Eva caught her breath and feigned a smile. "Fun."

Across the platform two layers of white doors unlocked and hissed open. Eva and Hailey entered a long white illuminated hallway and stepped onto a moving sidewalk. Electric billboards pulsed and flickered on as the two travelers were carried along. Low music warbled overhead from unseen speakers:

> *"Oh, great machines, great minds of man,*
> *you've come to rescue me.*
> *My tired world is now reborn,*
> *my air, my land, my sea."*

"This takes us through the atmospheric membrane and down to the ground level. It's gonna take a few minutes," Hailey said. "But it will put us at a busy sector of the city, where we should be able to get transportation to where we need to go."

"How many reboots have you brought in before?" Eva asked, though she knew the answer.

"Um, well, my dad was a retriever, and he brought in a lot of people," Hailey replied. "I want to do the same."

"Hello, and welcome to New Attica, where a bright and beautiful new future awaits." A hologram of an elderly man dressed in pure white flowing robes materialized before the duo and floated in front of them as they traveled down the sidewalk. His long white beard and wispy mustache barely moved when he spoke. "I am Cadmus Pryde, proud leader of this great city, and I've been waiting for you. No doubt you have many questions, and all of them will be addressed very soon. Please visit Attican Hall so that you may be admitted through the city's registrar. Don't worry. It's a quick, easy process. Afterward you'll be given orientation by one of our knowledgeable city guides. They know any- and everything about our utopian paradise. Thank you for visiting, Eva Nine. Till morrow's destiny." The hologram evaporated just as Eva and Hailey approached the end of the long hall.

"It's just a dumb recording," Hailey said. "It comes up every time you enter."

"He looks so different from how he looked in the programs I've seen," Eva said.

"Well, he's old. Really old," Hailey said, fidgeting with his Omnipod. "You might even see him today. He's pretty friendly, for an old guy."

"Please watch your step," an authoritative voice announced. Eva saw two helmeted ebony robots standing guard at the end of the hall. Their rigid form and shape reminded Eva of chessmen. Like Muthr they had multiple arms, though theirs were much thicker and shielded their bodies. On each glossy polished chest was printed TECH PROTECTS AND SERVES.

"Thank you, sir," Hailey said, mimicking the robot's voice and helping Eva off the moving sidewalk. A door hissed open that led to a small chamber, and both stepped in.

"Please raise your arms and remain still while we begin final identification confirmation and security check," a relaxed voice said. Eva and Hailey did as instructed, and a red laser scanned their bodies.

"Those were authoritons," Hailey said to Eva. "They keep the peace. Though I've never seen 'em do a thing."

"They look scary," replied Eva.

"I think they are mostly for show," Hailey said as the scan lines moved across his smug face.

"You know," Eva said, grinning, "today is my birthday. I'm thirteen. Maybe—"

Hailey shook his head and started laughing.

"Please remain still until final identification scan is complete. Thank you," the relaxed voice said.

Eva looked over at Hailey and giggled. "What?" she whispered. "What is it?"

"You are an old program with a lot to learn," Hailey whispered back. "They don't celebrate individual birthdays here. Only the Awakening."

"Oh, the Awakening. Okay." Once more Eva felt stupid.

"I'm sure it's just as much fun," he replied. "You'll see."

Eva tried to shake off her embarrassment. "Well, after I am registered and stuff, maybe you and Vanpa can join me and Rovee for dinner or dessert."

"Maybe," Hailey replied, looking away from Eva.

"Scan complete. Thank you, and have a pleasant day," the voice said. A final set of doors opened, and Eva walked into the city at last.

A mix of ambient music and melodious birdsong greeted Eva and Hailey as they entered New Attica. A cloudless azure sky was projected onto the atmospheric membrane high above, watching over the

modular cubic houses that ringed the high city wall. The stacking of the picture-windowed homes formed a stepped quarry. Around the various levels, floating spherical gondolas moved through the air, carrying passengers in all directions. Everywhere Eva looked, she saw people walking, playing, and conversing. There were dark-skinned individuals, orange-skinned, and violet-skinned too. No one bore any wrinkles or scars, like Van Turner, for no one was old. Tears pooled in Eva's eyes, and she whispered to herself, "I'm home."

A gondola glided down and landed in front of

Eva and Hailey. The empty vehicle was almost entirely transparent because of the large bubble-shaped canopy encasing its cabin. The words "New Attican Transit Share" glowed in bold letters on its side. In a calm voice it said, "Greetings. Are you Eva Nine and Hailey Turner?"

"Yes!" Eva said, bouncing up and down.

The door to the gondola slid open. "I have been summoned by the city to transport you to Attican Hall. Is this destination correct?"

"It is," said Hailey.

"Thank you," said the gondola. "Please watch your step as you enter."

Beaming at Hailey, Eva hopped in. Three cushioned seats in the center of the cabin welcomed the riders. Eva looked around the cabin and noted that the gondola lacked the controls that the Goldfish had. "How do you steer this?"

"You don't." Hailey flopped down and put his feet up on the low dashboard. "Just tell it where to go, and it takes you there. That's it."

"Wow." Eva slid over to the farthest seat and pressed her face against the window as the gondola gently lifted off.

An intricate map of the city projected onto the front windshield with a blinking red dot indicating the gondola's current position. "Arrival time to your final destination, Attican Hall, is approximately five minutes," the gondola announced.

"Oh! Is there a place to get food where we can stop first?" Eva asked.

"Uh—," Hailey started.

"Apologies, Eva Nine, but I must taxi you to Attican Hall for registration first," the gondola replied. "There are four eateries in the immediate vicinity that you may visit afterward."

"Sound good?" asked Hailey.

"Okay." Eva smiled.

"Very well, then." The gondola started a guided tour. "The thriving city of New Attica is approximately thirteen square kilometers. While the founders originally constructed it as a subterranean metropolis, the architects of the city later decided to . . ."

But Eva wasn't listening.

Instead she gazed down at the colorful geometric buildings below. The layout of the city was round, with all buildings ringing the central hub, as if they were in a gigantic basin. Like a wagon's wheel, the main roadway rounded the ground level, with spur roads leading toward the center of the city.

Soaring higher now, Eva could see that the spur

roads led through a lush green park that surrounded a large central pond, also circular in shape. At the center of the pond rose a colossal pyramid.

"That's it." Hailey nodded toward the city's centerpiece.

"We are approaching Attican Hall," the gondola said as it circled the pyramid. "Landing time is less than one minute."

Projected on each side of the pyramid's great height was an image of Cadmus Pryde. With eyes shut, as if dreaming, the aged man smiled through his snow-white beard. He then lifted his clenched hands high overhead and opened both up. One palm held a glowing microchip while the other cradled a human embryo. Projected between both hands was a rotating globe of the Earth. A parchment scroll circled the globe with the words "The Past Shall Prescribe the Future."

Mesmerized by this magnificent moving monument, Eva broke her gaze only when the top of the pyramid shone a brilliant light down at the gondola. Like in the holos of old lighthouses, the temple had a shining beam that rotated at its apex. Squinting her eyes as the bright beam moved past, Eva could make out a gigantic roving eye in the pyramid's peak.

The gondola alighted near the entrance to the

temple and opened its bubble-shaped doors. Eva stepped out among the city's bustling inhabitants.

People of various shade and hue brushed past, along with a variety of robots dedicated to maintaining the city. A gathering of sparrows chirped as they flew overhead and landed in a nearby tree. Above, a stream of gondolas moved in a steady flow around the pyramid. Brilliant three-dimensional holographic billboards flickered from atop many buildings. Overhead the citywide music lowered in volume, and a warm voice resonated over unseen loudspeakers. "Good morning, my fellow Atticans. The time is ten thirty. The weather today will be partly cloudy with a temperature of twenty-two degrees Celsius. We have scheduled a rain shower for tonight just around curfew at approximately twenty-twenty o'clock. We'll update with more news at the top of the hour. Till morrow's destiny."

Eva reached out and seized a passerby by the arm. A handsome man, older than Hailey, with pale green skin was speaking into his palm. "Hold on a nano, Steve. . . . Yes?"

Eva let go of his arm and watched an animated tattoo of flames flutter and flicker around his wrist. "Sorry," she said. "I just wanted to make sure you were real . . . that all of this was real."

"Real?" the green man said with a laugh. "You've overloaded on holos, haven't you? Do yourself a favor and take a break every once in a while. You'll find the real world is just as fun."

"Okay. Thanks," Eva said, confused at his response.

"Till morrow's destiny!" He patted Eva on the head and continued on his way.

"Hey, Eva," Hailey said, pointing to the open entrance of the hall. "We need to go. Come on."

"But I want to explore." Eva turned around. She heard an electronic chirp and noticed that she had stepped on a bright graphic logo cemented into the sidewalk. A hologram of a teenage girl rose up from the logo and greeted Eva. Her red hair was tied in a row of knotted twists, and dark makeup was drawn around her eyes and lips. "Wanna share your mood?" the hologram asked, and began expressing her mood by making various faces. First she pouted, then smiled, then sneered; and as she did so her frilly dress changed color to suit the emotion she was conveying. "Share your true colors for all the world to see. The latest Emote-Attire fashions are available at the Attican Galleria. It's rocket!" The hologram burst into a cloud of light motes and disappeared.

There was a tap on Eva's shoulder.

"Hey, you can burn through your quotacard later," Hailey said. "But first you gotta get registered, okay?"

A pale yellow Muthr rolled by with a pink baby swaddled across her torso.

A Muthr!

Eva watched the robot for a moment with longing. It met with a second Muthr, and both disappeared into the crowd.

"Eva, come on. Let's get this done," Hailey said.

"Okay." Eva followed Hailey through the multitude of pedestrians across a walkway that took them over the pond and into the pyramid. Great gilt-covered columns flanked the entrance, creating a majestic colonnade. Each column was decorated in etchings of ancient computer coding. It reminded Eva of holo-shows she'd watched on Egyptian temples covered in hieroglyphics. The duo entered the grand lobby, walking under a holographic projection of a manifesto.

"This place has a lot of offices, and I can never remember exactly where the registrar is," Hailey said, looking at a detailed floor plan on his Omnipod. "Let me grab an autoserver. I'll be right back."

"Okay." Eva moved to the side of the meandering sightseers and read the manifesto. Its words floated prominently in midair for all to see.

Man created Tech to aid man.
Tech carries many of man's burdens; it keeps his world safe.
Tech extends man's life. It eliminates sickness and perfects his offspring.
Tech creates man's home and city, accurate and steadfast.
Tech remembers man's collected knowledge.
Man trusts Tech as he trusts himself.
Man created Tech to remember the past.
Man created Tech to inform the future.
With Tech all dreams are attainable.

Eva pondered these words as she watched people wander past. *Out of the Sanctuary my Tech, my Omnipod, was hardly effective. Even Muthr struggled with the wild terrain.* Eva thought of Cadmus's presentation about creating the HRP and wondered how long ago that had occurred and how long this city had been here.

"The municipal offices are this way." Hailey returned with a waist-high cylindrical robot rolling on a single wheel.

"Welcome to Attican Hall," the autoserver said in a cheery tone. "Please follow me to the city registrar's office." The robot led Eva and Hailey to a glass elevator that took them high up in the pyramid. After exiting the elevator, the trio strolled down a winding corridor decorated with animated murals between the numerous office doors. Eva watched one of the murals, a landscape, transition from a lush rain forest to a lifeless desert before returning back to its original state. Across the corridor, adorning the public works office, an image of a turbulent ocean evaporated into a tiny creek, only to transform back.

"The registrar's office is the next doorway on the right." A rod arm extended from the autoserver's body, pointing down the hall. "Is there anything else I can do for you?"

"No, thanks," Hailey replied.

"Till morrow's destiny," the robot said, and zoomed off.

"What does that mean? 'Till morrow's destiny'?" Eva asked Hailey as they entered the small empty office.

"Hmph. It's how everyone says good-bye here," Hailey said. "'Until tomorrow's destiny reunites us once again.' It's a famous line from one of Cadmus's early speeches. It's sort of stupid, if you ask me."

"How come?"

"Of course these people will all see one another

tomorrow. Where else are they gonna go?" Hailey walked over to the round glossy desk located in the center of the sterile white office, and spoke. "Um, hello."

"Greetings, Hailey Turner," the desk responded. "Welcome back to the City Registrar. I've been notified of your arrival by the eastern gate."

"Uh, thanks." Hailey glanced at Eva through his unkempt bangs. "Well, I have a reboo—uh, new citizen to register with the . . . um . . . city. New Attica."

"The newly emerged imago, Eva Nine. Is that correct?"

"Yes," Eva answered.

"Great. We have been waiting for you, Eva Nine. Please place your Omnipod in the designated location." A soft glow indicated an Omnipod-shaped impression in the desktop. Eva placed her Omnipod onto the desk.

"Thank you, Eva Nine. Please take a seat while I transcribe your history," the desk responded. "Your wait time to meet with an HRP greeter is approximately ten minutes."

Eva sat in a hovchair and looked around at the row of vacant seats. As Van Turner had said, there seemed to be no other reboots entering the city this morning. Despite what Vanpa had said, Eva had hoped that there would be at least one other person present so that she would have someone to talk to. Someone who would relate to what she'd been through.

Hailey slouched down next to her and pulled out his Omnipod. Within the antiseptic walls of the room, the pilot's dingy flight jacket and greasy hair made him appear grimier than ever. It was apparent to Eva that he was out of his element, like the wild sand-sniper loose in the taxidermist's pristine lab back in Solas.

"Please enjoy this public announcement while you wait," the desk said. A hologram of Cadmus appeared. He congratulated the citizens for participating so earnestly in their Waste Not Want Not power-rationing program and promised a bright new future as a reward for their efforts. He concluded his announcement with a daily kernel of wisdom that reminded Eva of something Rovender would say.

Eva looked over at Hailey. The pilot was fiddling with his Omnipod and was not paying any attention to the announcement or to Eva. She thought aloud, "I wonder how Rovee and Vanpa are doing."

Hailey quickly tapped his foot on the gray tiled

floor. "I'm sure they're fine. Like I said, I'll send your friend over as soon as I get home."

"It's funny." Eva twirled one of her braids. "Did you see any aliens here?"

"Oh yeah, they're here," Hailey replied, still tapping. "They just don't always . . . come to Attican Hall. Specifically. I mean, why would they? Right?"

"Right." Eva tried to recall if she'd seen any alien types in her few moments in the city. There had been so many people moving about that it had been hard to take it all in, let alone focus on certain individuals in the crowd. However, now that she thought of it, there had been some hairless lavender-skinned citizens that had looked like they were from Solas.

A door in the back of the office slid open. An elderly man with a long white mustache and a beard entered, followed by his aide. Eva stood, recognizing the man immediately as he approached.

"Hello." His warm hand clasped Eva's. "I am Cadmus Pryde, and I am delighted to tell you that New Attica accepts you as one of its own. Welcome to your new home, Eva Nine."

CHAPTER 10: GEN

Cadmus Pryde looked over at Hailey. "Thank you for your services," he said. "My aide will see to it that your airship receives the necessary parts you've requested. Bring it to the western hangar by the end of the day, and we shall install them for you."

Hailey shook Cadmus's hand. "Thank you, sir."

Eva watched as Hailey gathered his things. "What? You're leaving?"

"His work is done," answered Cadmus.

"I've delivered you to New Attica as I promised," Hailey added.

"But . . . you're not staying?" Eva grabbed Hailey by the sleeve. "What about my birthday dinner?"

"Birthdays! How I adore the young imagoes," Cadmus said, and laughed. "I am sure we can arrange something for you, Eva."

Eva ignored Cadmus and kept her eyes on Hailey.

Without Rovender here, the pilot was the only person she knew in the entire city.

"Sorry," Hailey said. "Vanpa and I are loading up as soon as the *Bijou* is fixed."

"The *Bijou*?" Cadmus kept his attention on Hailey. "Is that the name you've given your airship?"

"Yeah."

Cadmus smiled. "How appropriate. To have your own airship is quite a little jewel indeed. I suppose, once the *Bijou* is repaired, you'll be looking for more functioning Sanctuaries for me?"

Hailey's eyes darted around the room. "Yeah. Sure. I know where there are lots more working Sanctuaries, and we'll bring you more reboots."

It then dawned on Eva what had transpired. "Wait. You just brought me in and traded me for parts, didn't you?"

"No," the pilot replied. "I provided a service in return for some much-needed components for my ship. That's it."

Eva's heart sank. "But . . ."

"Don't be so dramatic, Eva. You got what you wanted and I got what I needed. It's as simple as that."

"Eva, pay him no mind," Cadmus said. "You are with us now. You are home. And our young retriever was just leaving."

"What about Rovee?" Eva asked.

"You'll see him. He's already—" Hailey began.

"I am sure your traveling companion will be here soon enough," Cadmus interjected.

"I can't believe this," Eva hissed at Hailey. "I can't believe you!"

"Here, here." Cadmus put his arm around Eva. "It's not as bad as you think, Eva dear. Our boy Hailey was doing his job. The job his father once performed. Nothing more."

Eva Nine glowered at the pilot.

Hailey kept his gaze on the floor as the aide led him out. The door slid shut behind him, and he was gone.

"While the city computer finishes recording your life history, Eva, we'll bring you to the medlab for a quick checkup," Cadmus said, leading Eva through a back passage from the registrar's office. One of the many doors that lined the passage slid open to reveal a bright white lab, similar to the generator room back in Eva's Sanctuary.

A stream of holographic screens circled the medlab. Eva glanced at the screens in turn and realized that these were recordings of her at various ages. In one she was an infant learning to eat as Muthr mashed up a nutriment pellet in water. In another, she was a toddler stacking bricks and making a home for her Beeboo doll.

"These are your Omnipod's memories," Cadmus said. "It records everything so that we may get a perfect picture of your past. It helps us to understand each and every new citizen so that we may better serve them."

A medlab aide, dressed in a light blue ivory laboratory coat, handed Cadmus a semitransparent sheet of electra-paper. Even on tiptoes Eva could not read the paper's scrolling text from her vantage point, so she shifted her gaze to Cadmus. Like on Van Turner's face, a weave of wrinkles crisscrossed around Cadmus's sparkling eyes as they scanned the note. Eva touched her own cheek, wondering what it must be like to have wrinkles.

"You were conceived in Sanctuary five-seven-three, is that correct?" asked Cadmus.

"Yes." Eva caught a glimpse of a recording showing her arguing with Muthr in the dim light of her bedroom. Somehow this image was out of order form the others as she watched it play back in front of her.

"Hmmm . . . all Sanctuaries are marked as non-working, and yet here you are. How interesting."

Cadmus handed the electra-paper back to the aide. "I see you exited prematurely and explored some of the surface terrain accompanied by your Muthr?"

"Y-yes." Eva picked at her fingernails. "But . . . she's gone."

"Those older models were not designed for such extensive travel. I am impressed you were able to convince her to leave at all." Cadmus placed a sympathetic hand on Eva's shoulder. His focus darted about from screen to screen as if he were searching for something.

An electronic chirp pinged from the ceiling, and a large crab-shaped robot descended into the lab. Cadmus seemed to pay it no mind.

Eva backed away from the large robot. Its body reminded her of the temporary body Muthr had used while she'd repaired herself in the Sanctuary. "Muthr wasn't outdated," Eva said. "She was able to take care of me right up to the end."

"I understand your attachment, Eva. Truly I do," replied Cadmus. "The Muthr series performed exceptionally well at their given tasks. There are still some in operation here in the city."

"Please open your mouth and remain still," the robot instructed. In one of its wiry hands it held a test tube, while another brandished a cotton swab.

"Will it hurt?" Eva asked.

"No. Not at all," answered Cadmus, though his attention remained focused on a recording Eva had taken of Lacus. "My automedics are state of the art, able to move in one-angstrom increments."

"What's your name?" Eva asked the automedic.

"Name?" the robot replied. "We are a series 45 automated medical lab-bot, or 'automedic' for short, model number H3-1D1. Please open your mouth and—"

"That's what you are," Eva interrupted. "But what's your name?"

"Name?" the automedic paused and turned to Cadmus, appearing confused from Eva's questioning. "Sir?"

"The automedic team here is integrated into an expansive multilayered information database. It's a much more complicated system than what your Muthr and your Sanctuary was on, Eva," answered Cadmus. "Therefore, they view themselves more as parts of a whole working for a greater good."

"Oh," said Eva. Her mind swirled. As with the old program she had watched, it was hard keeping up with Cadmus's conversation.

"Hold, please," the automedic instructed, and

Eva kept her mouth held open. The robot swabbed Eva's mouth and plucked out a single strand of hair from her scalp. Each sample was placed in a test tube, and the robot returned to its perch in the ceiling. "Genetic tissue samples were successfully collected. We shall supply you with a full report shortly, Father Pryde. Thank you."

"Thank you," Cadmus said, showing Eva out of the medlab.

"About my Muthr," said Eva. "Can you—"

"All in due time, dear, all in due time," Cadmus said. "First I want you to relax and enjoy yourself. From what I see you've been through quite a lot." He led her through a bustling hallway, past a convoy of floating gurneys carrying patients, and into a side hall that brought them to his headquarters.

The spacious office was adorned with paintings on every wall. An expansive window looked out over the cityscape, while a detailed holographic miniature of New Attica floated in the center of the room. Two stoic authoritons guarded a closed pair of doors on the far side of the room.

Eva studied an ornately framed painting of a woman with dark hair. "I know this," she said, pointing at it. "It is one of the paintings I studied in my art programs."

"Yes." Cadmus joined her. "It's titled the *Mona Lisa.* It was actually painted by hand by a man named Leonardo da Vinci thousands of years before the Awakening."

"It doesn't move?" Eva waited for the woman to blink or a bird to fly by.

"The early paintings are static. Fixed images in time, filtered through the vision of the artist," Cadmus said, stroking his mustache.

"It seems awfully dark."

"Dark indeed, Eva. This was painted during a dark time in mankind's history. But if you look closely, you'll see the vision of a mastermind at work."

Eva studied the painting, still waiting for it to move.

"Leonardo has carefully chosen what he wants you to see and what he does not. There is no sickness here, no war, no famine, no death—though Leonardo's world was teeming with such scourges. In fact, he helped design weapons of war. But here he depicts beauty: both in the human form and in the developing landscape. His idyllic vision has become his legacy." Cadmus was now smiling under his snowy beard.

The double doors slid open to reveal a pristine robot identical to Muthr, save for the fine paint and polish. The number twenty-three was printed prominently on its torso. Like Muthr, it spoke in refined intonation. "Father Pryde, sir, you have completed your meet and greet at the registrar's, yes?"

"Yes," Cadmus replied. "Twenty-three, meet Eva Nine."

The robot tipped its head in greeting. "Welcome to New Attica, Eva Nine."

Eva waved at the robot but could not look in its warm amber eyes. They were too much like Muthr's.

"I have summoned an autoserver guide to begin Eva's orientation," said the robot.

"No, no," Cadmus said. "That will not do. We haven't had an imago here in years. I have something special planned for our newest arrival."

"Very good, sir," the robot said. "Marzug is waiting to deliver his report of the productive effects of the power rationing. Shall we begin?"

"In a moment, Twenty-three." Cadmus put a hand on the robot. "Is Gen here?"

"Yes, sir. She is waiting in the lobby. Shall I show her in?"

"Please do."

Eva tore her eyes from the robot as it rolled away. It was disconcerting how similar its movements and gestures were to Muthr's.

"I know you have questions, Eva Nine," Cadmus said. "Unfortunately, at this moment I've a city to run, so I shall reconvene with you later."

"Okay, sure." Eva didn't know whether she should shake Cadmus's hand, hug him, or just remain obedient and still.

"Very good. In the meantime I have someone special I'd like you to meet." Cadmus motioned to a teenage girl, a bit taller than Eva, sauntering into the room.

The artificial sunlight that shone in from the window played with the girl's iridescent hair, causing it to shift from deep emerald to sapphire blue as she approached Cadmus. Her extravagant frilly clothing and striking makeup gave her the appearance of a tropical bird in knee-high sneakboots. A collection of shiny charms hanging from her sleeve jingled with every step she took. *This is not a human girl,* Eva thought. *Not like me.*

The girl hugged Cadmus and kissed him on the cheek.

"Eva, I'd like you to meet one of my daughters, Gen," Cadmus said.

"Father, her appearance is . . . different." Gen looked Eva up and down.

"That is correct," replied Cadmus. "You see, Eva

is a newly emerged citizen delivered direct from her Sanctuary."

Gen's ice-blue eyes went wide with surprise. Her pupils were but pinpricks in the center. "Clone me! A reboot from the outside? You're remming!"

"I am not 'remming,'" Cadmus said with a smile. "Now, we haven't had an imago here for many years, so—"

"I'd say." Gen tilted her head and examined Eva. It reminded Eva of the way the royal taxidermist had looked at her before he'd attempted to embalm her. Alive.

"As I was saying, an event like this has not occurred in considerable time," continued Cadmus. "So I would like you to personally show Eva around the city and introduce her to some of your friends. In fact, today is Eva's day of genesis, making her only a year younger than you, Gen, so let's give her a special welcome."

"This is so jolt!" Gen said. Her dress shifted color from turquoise to a sapphire blue. With its intricate patterning the garment reminded Eva of the holograms she'd seen of an octopus changing hue. "Come on, Eva. Let's go. You're gonna love it here."

Eva nodded and smiled, mesmerized by Gen's ever-changing colors.

Cadmus's aide from the medlab entered the office and delivered Eva's Omnipod and an orientation pack to Cadmus. "The imago's full report, Father Pryde. Her Omnipod software has been updated, and her initial savings quota has been established. I have installed the quotacard on her O-pod," the aide said as he handed Cadmus an electra-paper.

"Ooo! You got a brand-new quotacard!" Gen squealed. "We are going to put that to work today."

"Go easy on her, Gen," said Cadmus, handing Eva back her Omnipod. "Return here before curfew at twenty-thirty. By then the city will have determined in what sector your home shall be located, and the fabrication crew will have it assembled and ready."

"Okay," Eva said, trailing behind Gen out of the office. "By the way, my friend, Rovender, will be coming soon to join me. Does he need to register as well?"

"Rovender—you mentioned him before." Cadmus followed the girls into his office lobby. Eva noticed several other people waiting in a row of hovchairs, including a man with a ridiculously wide frilled collar.

"Yes," Eva said. "He's a Cærulean from a village north of the Wandering Forest."

"The Wandering Forest?" Cadmus replied, raising an eyebrow. "You'll have to tell me about that when next we meet."

"You'd like him," continued Eva. "He knows a lot about sand-snipers and weeping bird-catchers and the Halcyonus."

The visitors in the lobby murmured among one another. Gen was talking into the palm of her hand, oblivious.

"Well, yes, then. I'd very much like to meet this friend of yours," Cadmus said with a smile. "In the meantime enjoy yourself. Till morrow's destiny."

"Till morrow's destiny," Eva replied, and shook his hand.

"Bye, Father," Gen said. "Will I see ya tonight?"

"Of course." Cadmus gave her a peck on the head. "Now go. Enjoy my city. Enjoy *your* city."

Eva glanced back over her shoulder as she exited the office lobby with Gen. Cadmus and the others were laughing and talking loudly as the door closed to his headquarters.

CHAPTER 11: ORIENTATION

I can't believe you're a reboot! And you have a fully stocked quotacard!" Gen led the way out of Attican Hall. "Wait till the other Gens meet you. They are going to completely short out!"

"What's a quotacard?" Eva asked.

"It's a card that records what products you consume. It regulates what you get, but only after it monitors you for a while to see if you're going to be a consumption freak. But you won't be, because—" Gen stopped and held her right hand up as if she were taking an oath. She recited,

"New Attica provides all that we want, because all that we want is all that we need." She burst out laughing and grabbed Eva's hand as they exited Attican Hall.

Eva felt something tickle her leg. She looked down to see a striped fuzzy tail swishing around from under Gen's ruffled miniskirt. "Do you have . . . a tail?" Eva asked.

"Isn't it rocket?" Gen giggled. "It's a robotail! They come in a million-zillion colors. We'll get you one at the Attican Galleria, my homecube away from home. It's not far. You can even get your lip done while we're there too." Gen pointed to her upper lip.

Eva realized that the cleft between Gen's lip and nose had been partially split, creating a felinelike smile. Eva winced. "Did it hurt?"

"Not at all. Father let me get it done for the Awakening celebration last year. My mother shorted out when she saw it."

Eva wondered if Muthr would have cared if she had her lip split—not that she would have asked to have it done.

"You didn't have any parents in your Sanctuary, did you?" Gen asked. "That is so jolt. Now that you're here, you can just come and go as you please and never answer to anyone. Just be your own person, right?"

"I guess," Eva replied. The independence to come and go as she pleased also meant not having anyone around to help or guide her. *I hope Rovee gets here soon,* Eva thought.

Gen and Eva walked along the bridge that took them over the central pond and toward the park. Eva noticed a group of locals, including several robots, feeding giant brightly colored fish from the bridge.

"Are they fishing?" Eva thought of how delicious the spiderfish platter had been at Hostia Havenport's home back in Lacus. The fish here under the bridge were the size of the Havenport's living room, large enough to feed a village.

"Fishing?" Gen seemed perplexed. "Oh, no. Not father's koi. Some of them are almost three hundred years old. But if you're hungry for seafood, there is a tiny synthsushi bar I know. They make the best pellet wraps."

At the park entrance a beeping gondola landed, and the bubble doors opened to reveal two other teenage girls. Both looked nearly identical to Gen.

"Is this her?" one of the new girls said.

"Yes!" replied Gen. "Girls, this is no holo. She is an actual reboot!"

"Clone me! Her hair is its natural color," the

second new girl said. "And her eyes still dilate."

"Just like a baby's!" the first girl said. At this point Eva could hardly tell who was who.

"So," Gen said, locking arms with the other girls. "These are my two darlings—Gen and Gen."

"We are known as the three Gens!" they said in unison.

"Look at her O-pod!" The second Gen pointed at Eva's Omnipod. "It's a handheld vintage edition! That is so jolt!"

"What do you mean?" Eva asked. "What does your O-pod look like?"

"Like this." They all opened their right hands to reveal small Omnipod-like eyes implanted in their palms. Under the skin delicate electrodes and wires could be seen like electronic blood vessels. "Carrying this thing must be so cumbersome," Gen said, running her manicured fingers over the tarnished device. "But I guess that's part of the mystique with antiques, right?"

Eva winced at the idea of having her Omnipod implanted into her hand, though somehow it now felt heavier in her grasp.

"And she's been on the outside. Can you believe it?" Gen said. She seemed proud, as if she'd rescued Eva herself.

"What a relic. A true treasure," another Gen said, stroking Eva's arm.

"It's like she's an actual time traveler." The third Gen played with Eva's hair.

Dizzy, Eva dropped down onto the cushy green turf. She felt numb and useless, like she was on the wrong planet. *How could Rovender go out exploring?* she thought. *I am seeing Muthr everywhere I look, and Hailey . . .*

You got what you wanted and I got what I needed.

"Beeboo, what is it?" Gen sat down and placed her arm around Eva. "Are you sick?"

"No." Eva concealed her emotion. "I'm fine."

"You are going to *love* it here. You're going to be one of us," Gen said.

"Yeah, you just need to fit in," another Gen added.

"And if anyone can help you with that . . ."

"It's us!" the three Gens said in unison.

"Come on." The Gens helped Eva up. "Let's grab some pellet wraps and get you upgraded."

The girls walked leisurely through the park toward the galleria, jabbering away with one another. Eva's eyes wandered about the meticulously manicured paradise. She watched children play games in the grass and picnic in the open field. There were adults around, but no one seemed to pay any mind to the children, nor were any Muthrs present to look over them. The girls strolled under the shade of a large tree.

"What a beautiful big tree." Eva stopped to stroke the rough crackled bark of an oak. "You must be glad it's the sort that doesn't walk. There's not much room for it to move around here."

The girls giggled. "A tree that walks?"

"You're funny, Eva. I like that," Gen said.

They continued along the shady path, passing by the entrance to the Attican Aviary. The sound of chirping birds sang out from the domed enclosure. *Wow, birds that I would actually recognize,* Eva thought. *Not some six-winged alien species.* "Hey, can we go in there?" she asked.

"Um, sure," Gen replied. "Why don't you go take a wander, and we'll wait for you right here?"

"It's okay," Eva said. "You guys want to go to the galleria, right? Let's do that."

"No, it's all right," Gen said. "If you want to see the birds, go on. I've seen them before."

"Yeah, they are so jolt." The second Gen tapped a beauty mark on her chin, changing the tint on the lipstick coating her pouty mouth.

"They are so beautiful," the third Gen said.

"Besides, I've got a million-zillion vidcalls to go through anyways," Gen added.

"Me too," the others chimed.

Eva watched people line up to enter the aviary. Among them she caught the glance of a woman with short ash-blond hair staring back at her. "Naw. Maybe I'll visit it later," Eva said. "Besides, I can come and go anytime I want to now, right?"

"That's right," Gen said, locking arms with Eva. "Come on. The Attican Galleria is just up ahead."

"You are going to short out on this place!" Gen said as the girls wandered along the promenade that took them past a variety of shops and eateries. "Even though you really don't need a store to get stuff, my dad wanted this place to be like an old-fashioned mall, where people could shop and meet."

"Yeah, by 'meet' she means 'meet boys,'" the third Gen said. The second Gen tittered.

Gen rolled her eyes and pointed to a clothing store. "First stop for you, Eva. The Duds Factory. You need some Emote-Attire like us."

"Yes, it will show your true feelings," the second added.

"Your true colors, for all the world to see!" all

three sang in unison, and then began to giggle.

The third Gen jabbed the sleeve of Eva's flight suit. "This old rag doesn't tell us anything at all."

"You're right," Gen said. "Is that what they gave you to wear at the medlab?"

Eva looked at the baggy blue garment that hung over her bony frame. "It's not even mine," she confessed. "It was one of Hailey's spares."

"Hailey?" The girls crowded Eva. "Who's Hailey?"

"The pilot who brought me here on his ship." Eva wished she hadn't mentioned his name. She didn't really want to think about Hailey right now.

"Pilot? Where is he? Why isn't he with us?"

"He's back home . . . I guess." Eva wondered when she'd hear from him with news of Rovender. "He lives outside of the city in the hills."

"You are completely shorting me out right now!" Gen said.

"Shoot me with a SHOCdart!" added the second.

"Are you telling me that you were brought here by a Toiler?" asked the third Gen.

Eva remembered the phrase that Van Turner had used. "Yeah. That's what he is. A Toiler."

"Disgusto!" Gen scowled. "Those Toilers are nasty."

"Yeah," the second Gen said. "My mother said they didn't know a good thing when they had it."

"I heard they steal children and eat them. Is that true?" the third Gen asked.

"I—I don't think so," Eva replied. "But Hailey *was* nasty. He traded me for ship parts."

"What! Oh, Beeboo, that's terrible." The three Gens huddled and hugged Eva.

This was a sensation Eva had never experienced before. These three human girls had taken her in as one of their own, as one of their flock. She felt safe in the huddle and clutched the other girls tight.

"Thanks, Gen," Eva said. "Now let's get me upgraded."

CHAPTER 12: VISION

It was early evening when the four girls sat down at a corner booth at Pel Palace, a busy restaurant with a fairy tale theme. Holograms of fairies floated here and there while dragons roared from the castle tops. The three Gens placed their right palms flat on the shield-shaped tabletop to activate the interactive menu. On the adjacent wall hung an ornate mirror.

"Welcome back, miladies," the mirror greeted them in a dramatic foreign accent. An amorphous smiling face floated in its center. "Will it be the usual gruel and ale?"

"Yes!" the three Gens chimed. "But wait a nano. We've got one more order to place."

"As you wish," said the mirror.

"Okay, Eva," Gen said. "What you do is pick your favorite foods from this menu, and then they custom make your order. They even have a million-zillion ice cream flavors."

Eva glanced down and caught her reflection in the monitor set inside the tabletop. With her dyed iridescent blue hair, makeup, and new clothing, she looked just like one of the Gens. The store's autoserver said she was a "true vision of beauty," despite the fact that she looked just like all the other girls she had seen shopping in the galleria. Though she had decided against getting her cleft split, Eva touched her glossy lips and marveled at the person looking back at her. She decided she liked her look. It made her feel just like one of the citizens here.

OPEN

"Oh, zappers! My quotacard is spent for the day," Gen said.

"Mine too," the second Gen added.

"Make that three," the third Gen said.

"Can you spot us, Eva?" Gen asked.

Eva shrugged her shoulders. "Sure."

"Rocket! Okay. We are going to order for you, too. I want to get you something really special." Gen tapped through the menu at a rapid pace. "There you go." Gen addressed the mirror. "All done."

"Your wish is my command, my lovelies," the mirror said. From the wall four empty test tubes—as long as Eva's forearm—rolled out onto the table. Eva grabbed one.

"Your feast is served, Gen," the mirror announced. Gen snapped the mouth of the tube into the wall dispenser and watched it fill up with pastel-colored pills and pellets. This action repeated three more times until the order was filled.

"Bottoms up!" Gen squealed, and the three girls filled their mouths. Eva picked one of the pellets out from her tube and tasted it. A sweet vanilla flavor coated her tongue as the pellet melted away. She could hear Rovender criticizing her for this, but he was not there. He'd had better things to do. She tilted the tube upward and filled her mouth with the entire contents. It tasted like chocolate fudge cake with vanilla crème icing and Neapolitan ice cream.

"My birthday," Eva said. "You remembered."

"No," Gen said, and giggled. "It's not your birthday, but it's—"

"Happy Arrival Day!" all three squealed.

"Aw, thanks." Eva smiled. She swallowed down her mixture of feelings and finished her meal.

"Clone me. Did you see Paige Trundle's new dye?" Gen asked the group.

"No, I missed it," replied the third Gen.

"Hold on a nano. You *have* to see it. I'll transfer it here so we can all look." Gen exited the main menu on the tabletop and brought up a hologram of a girl the same age as the Gens. "I snuck a shot of her when she was coming into the galleria."

"Liquid black with white weave-tufts? What a short-out," the second Gen said. "Her hair looks like a dud-cloned animal."

"Put her into Identicapture," the third Gen said.

"Oh, yes! Yes! Yes!" The second bounced up and down in her seat.

Eva watched the hologram rotate over the table. *Why would they open Identicapture? Are they really different species, after all?*

"*Homo sapiens neo*," the table reported. "Otherwise known as the new man, conceived by the—"

"No. That is incorrect," Gen said in a patronizing tone. "Please try again."

"It could be *Callithrix jacchus*, or the common marmoset. A species of New World monkey, originally indigenous to South America," the table announced.

The girls burst into peals of laughter.

"A monkey!"

"That is so jolt!"

"Isn't that hysterical, Eva?" Gen asked. She wiped the tear-smudged mascara from her eyes.

"Yeah, I get it." Eva faked a laugh. "That's funny."

The three Gens looked at one another and giggled.

"I am completely dehy. I need a Pow-R-drink," Gen said. "Anybody else?"

While one of the girls placed a drinks order, Gen led Eva to the back of the black-lit restaurant, which was fashioned after a castle courtyard and full of assorted games. Spectators huddled around a life-size animated chessboard while others engaged in a game of charades with a holographic dragon. A small gang of kids ran after a fluttering fairy with nets in hand.

"Oh, this is pretty rocket," Gen said, leading Eva

by the hand. She took her to the back of the courtyard, where the royal throne sat. As she stepped onto the dais toward the throne, Eva realized it was an old salon chair with colorful lights running up and down its sides. A dinged-up helmet was attached to the headrest, and the words "The Divination Machine" were printed under the armrests in fancy old lettering. On the large banner behind the chair read, "Your life—past, present, and future—at a glance."

"It's an old-fashioned fortune-teller," Gen said. "You sit in the throne, put the helmet on, and your future is projected on a window in front of you. This was really popular eons ago."

Eva looked over the bundled coils of wire snaking out of the helmet and the tattered armrests.

"Go ahead. Get in," Gen said. "You'll love it."

Eva thought of Arius prophesying through her cryptic chants and how uneasy it had made her feel. "I don't know," she said, picking at her newly painted fingernails.

"Are you afraid of this old antique?" Gen said. "Or is it what it may tell you about your future? Your future with . . . Hailey?" She let out a giggle.

"I guess it is just a machine, right?" Eva pretended she wasn't nervous and climbed up into the chair.

She wrangled her newly attached robotail and sat on the worn-out cushion.

Gen put the helmet down over Eva's new hairstyle and started up the machine. A holo-program flickered on, and an electronic fuzzy voice spoke from speakers within the helmet. "Welcome to the Divination Machine and your life, Eva Nine. Before we look into your future, let us take a peek at your past."

In the hologram window Eva saw images of her upbringing in the Sanctuary, similar to those that had been projected in the medlab. A scene of Muthr mashing up pellets for her to eat shifted to a scene of a young Eva playing with blocks, which changed once more into an image of Eva, obscured by shadow in her dimly lit bedroom, arguing with Muthr.

"Now let us look at today. The present," the machine said.

Eva watched the visions of her past evaporate into an image of her shopping and eating with the Gens. It stopped on a fixed image of her sitting in the Divination Machine with the helmet on.

"And now," the machine announced, "let us look into your future, Eva Nine." A scene materialized depicting Eva walking hand in hand with Cadmus.

Together they were leading a gathering a thousand people strong. The mass traveled through a rolling field of tall grass, and finally arrived at a vast lake. This reminded Eva of Lake Concors, where the towers of Lacus stood just offshore—but Lacus was nowhere to be seen.

"What happened to Lacus? Where's Hostia?" Eva asked aloud. The Divination Machine did not reply. The vision continued with Cadmus and Eva leading their followers around the lake's edge to the northwest, where the city of Solas lay. But in place of Solas there now rose a grand and wondrous human city, a clear-domed duplicate of New Attica. Eva scanned the area, searching for a familiar landmark. Poking out from the depths of the lake, the spire of Queen Ojo's palace could be seen, covered in clumps of wet algae. Eva's sweaty palms gripped the armrests tight as dread slithered its way into her.

The imagery concluded with Cadmus on a high balcony smiling and greeting his people, who were now flooding into the city. He looked down at Eva and said, "Now the air, water, land, and the earth itself are purified and reborn, thanks to you."

"No!" Eva yanked off the helmet, and the imagery in front of her vanished. Breathless and dizzy, she slid off the chair and onto the floor.

"Are you shorting out?" Gen knelt down next to her. "You can't eject from an old holo-machine like that until it is finished. Are you all right?"

"I'm—I'm fine." Eva stood on shaky legs.

"What happened? What did you see?" Gen helped Eva keep her balance.

Arius's words drifted into Eva's conscious. *And so one society flourishes as another one perishes.*

"I saw . . . um . . ." Eva noticed a woman with piercing green eyes watching her from across the crowded courtyard. The woman stood, unmoving, as children cavorted noisily around her. Her face, with dark mascara under choppy ash-blond hair, looked familiar.

"That lady. She was in the park today," Eva said, catching her breath. She moved to approach her, but staggered, still light-headed with visions from the Divination Machine. The blond woman disappeared in the throng of kids.

"Come on. Let's get you back to the booth so you can reboot," Gen said.

"How do I know that lady?" Eva shook her head, trying to clear it, and followed Gen.

"It was weird," Eva said in between sips of her Pow-R-drink. "It was like all the aliens no longer existed anymore." She leaned back in her seat facing the three Gens, who sat across from her in the booth.

"Aliens?" Gen exchanged glances with her peers. "What do you mean?"

"You know, like the Halcyonus or the Cæruleans," said Eva.

The three girls stared at her with blank looks on their faces.

"What?" asked Eva, confused by the Gens' reaction.

"What on earth are you talking about?" Gen said with a giggle.

"Oh, that machine definitely shorted you out," said the second Gen.

"You are seriously remming right now," added the third.

"Remming? I'm not remming at all!" Eva slammed her drink down. "You don't know what I am talking about? The aliens that live in Lacus? Solas?"

"I think she spent way too much time with those dirty Toilers," Gen whispered loudly to the other Gens. "They rewired her."

"Wait a sec." Eva realized something. "Have you ever left the city?"

"Um, no!" Gen said.

"It's filthy out there," the second Gen added. "Why would we?"

Eva watched the Gens whisper among themselves while keeping an eye on her. It was like Eva wasn't even there. She turned, scanning the restaurant to locate an alien that would prove she wasn't crazy. People of every sort enjoyed their meals, but there was not a single alien among them.

Anywhere.

She tried to remember if she'd seen any aliens today while she'd explored the city. It was hard. There had been so many colorful citizens in the park and on the promenade. *Have I seen any aliens here?*

Eva pulled out her Omnipod and activated Identicapture. She brought up a holo of Rovender. "Do you know what this is?"

The three girls examined the hologram as grimaces grew on their painted faces. "Yeah," Gen said. "It's a troll from a fairy tale program."

"Yes, from when we were three nanos old," the second Gen added.

"What? No. Rovee is not a troll or a mythical beast." Eva shut off her Omnipod. Her tone was serious, "Hasn't your father told you about Orbona? About the outside world beyond here?"

"My father is busy, just like my mother, so I don't

bother them," Gen replied. Her dress shifted to a dark mustard color. "He works hard for everybody here, to make life beautiful and safe for all."

"Your father is such a genius," the second Gen added. "I would never ever leave. We have everything we could ever possibly want here, right?"

"Right," the third Gen said. "But if your dad could order up a bigger galleria nearby, I wouldn't complain."

The other Gens giggled with glee. "Yeah, put it where those corrupted Toilers live!" All three of their dresses changed to an icy hue.

Eva stared at the trio of girls as if they were three sand-snipers. Her mind began to reel with worry for Rovender, when a chime rang throughout the restaurant. All the patrons began to gather their things and leave.

"It's nineteen-thirty," Gen said, looking at her palm. "Time to head to our cubes."

"Is it already?" the second Gen said. "I was having such fun with our Beeboo and her fairy tales that I forgot about the time."

"Let's hurry back so we can vidchat before we power out," added the third. The others nodded in agreement.

Eva followed the Gens out to a loading area and

into a line of people waiting to exit on gondolas. Above, the projected sky had turned deep lavender with a few stars twinkling in the cloudless heavens. *There are no rings,* Eva noted. *No Rings of Orbona.*

High above, on unseen speakers, Cadmus Pryde's warm voice broadcast throughout the city. "Good evening, my fellow Atticans. The time is nineteen-forty-eight. Please complete any tasks you may be enjoying and make your way home for the night. We'll power up first thing in the morning at eight o'clock sharp. The weather tomorrow will be . . ."

"Hey, you wanna share a gondola?" Gen asked while the girls climbed in.

"Sure." Eva scooted in next to Gen, and the gondola rose in the deepening twilight.

"Look!" Gen pointed out the window. "There's Paige Trundle!"

"Where! Let me see!" The other girls clambered over to the window, causing the gondola to sway.

"Monkey hair!" one of the Gens chimed.

"I don't know. I kind of like it," Eva said.

The three girls turned in unison and stared her down.

Eva shrugged her shoulders. "At least it's different."

The three girls all looked at one another.

"I wonder where she got it done," one of the Gens asked.

"The Attican zoo?" replied another.

This sent the girls into fits of laughter once again.

"So, am I coming home with you, Gen?" asked Eva.

"I think you have to go back to Attican Hall to find out where your cube is," Gen replied in a condescending tone.

"But you need to get there by twenty-thirty. That's the curfew," the second Gen added. "We all live in level one, but you should still make it there in time."

"Just do it before twenty-thirty," Gen said.

"Why?"

"Because the power shuts down," Gen said.

"And the authoritons will lock you in detention for the night with the other short-outs," the third Gen added.

"Yeah," Gen said. "You don't want to end up there. You want to be in your cozy new cube."

CHAPTER 13: EIGHT

Level one was the topmost level of New Attica, closest to the now twinkling atmospheric membrane. All around, citizens arrived home for the evening in glassy towering elevators and gondolas.

Bidding the three Gens good night, Eva directed her gondola to take her to Attican Hall. The craft swiftly glided over the darkening park toward her destination as a light rain drizzled down from the artificial sky. As she landed, Eva noticed an authoriton directing empty gondolas. Each craft parked in a perfect row outside the great gleaming pyramid. Eva's gondola set down at the end of the row, and she hurried toward the hall entrance.

"Excuse me, miss." The authoriton held out a large hand. "The time is twenty-twenty-three. Attican Hall is closed for the day."

"But I—"

"Please return to your domicile for the evening. The hall opens at eight o'clock tomorrow. We will see you in the morning," the robot continued in a firm tone.

"But, sir. Cadmus told me to come back here—"

"Thank you for your cooperation. We will see you at eight. Good night." The authoriton remained steadfast. High above him the beacon at the peak of the pyramid roved around the cityscape.

"Okay." Eva slumped her shoulders and left. "Good night."

Through the drizzle Eva trod across the bridge and into the park, pondering what to do next. *I need to find an elevator to take me up to level one if I am to make it to Gen's house in time. Hopefully Cadmus will be there.* Eva dashed across the wet turf and slipped in her new high-heeled boots. After standing up, she pulled the boots off and continued faster now on bare feet. She arrived at the lower level of buildings that ringed the park, and stopped to catch her breath. "Sheesa," she said, panting. "I didn't see what building Gen lives in." She pulled out her Omnipod.

"Greetings, Eva Nine," the device chirped. "How may I be of service?"

"Please contact Gen Pryde," Eva said as she wiped her dripping hair from her face.

"Attempting voice connection with Gen Pryde," the Omnipod said. "Please hold."

Eva looked up at the towering homes, each full of people. Each full of families.

"Cancel that," she said, yanking off her robotail. "Contact Hailey Turner. I need to find out where Rovee is."

"Call canceled. Attempting voice connection with Hailey Turner." The little lights flickered around the Omnipod's central eye.

Eva picked at the damp ruffle in her skirt. *Come on, Rovee. Where are you?*

"I am sorry, Eva Nine. I am not receiving a response from Hailey Turner. Would you like to leave a message?" asked the device.

Once more Cadmus's voice was broadcast across the city. "The time is now twenty-thirty. Please power down your homes to a minimum for the evening. You may all know that the power rationing has greatly improved our goal of lower consumption. I am proud of everyone's cooperation with this new directive. Sleep well knowing I am looking out and protecting each and every one of you. Till morrow's destiny."

The lights in all the homes dimmed, and the ambient music from the loudspeakers lowered. Below, a unit of authoritons patrolled the glistening street. Their bright red lasers scanned every nook and alley as they moved through the night. The steam rising from the ground level hid their details, giving them a shadowy, ghostly presence. Eva turned back toward the dense growth in the park and ran into the darkness.

As she searched for a tree to climb up for the night, a distant song warbled out from the depths of the park. "I know that song," Eva said to herself. "How do I know that song?"

"*Caprimulgus vociferus*," her Omnipod stated. "Commonly known as a whip-poor-will, a nocturnal bird of the family Caprimulgidae. Shall I continue?"

"No," Eva said. She remembered the birdsong now from the many survival simulations back in her Sanctuary. She thought back to the list of skills she had needed to memorize. *Find shelter,* she thought, and dashed off to the aviary.

Eva clung to the shadows as she snuck toward the well-lit entrance of the ornate biodome. As she neared, a sensor pinged and a hologram of Cadmus materialized, giving Eva a start.

"Welcome to the Attican Aviary and Avian Cloning Center," he said, "where the birds of yesterday take flight once again. Inside you will find more than six hundred species of birds incubated right here in . . ."

The acidic smell of guano assaulted Eva's nose as she slipped inside the humid aviary. Mixed with the whip-poor-will's call was a chorus of chirps and hoots. All about the dome birds fluttered to their nests and canopies to settle in for the night. The thick foliage that grew inside filled each and every exhibit. *I should be safe from the authoritons here.* Eva sighed, relaxing a bit. A white-faced owl alighted on a nearby tree. *This is just like one of my holographic simulations back home.* Eva pulled out her Omnipod and initiated Identicapture.

"*Tyto alba,* commonly known as a barn owl," the device said as it displayed a three-dimensional model of the bird. "*Ajaia ajaja,* or the roseate spoonbill. . . . *Goura victoria*, the Victoria crowned pigeon." On and on the Omnipod identified each and every specimen within the aviary. Eva was circling an indoor pond in the waterfowl annex when an abrupt squawk erupted, startling her.

She froze, unsure of the source of the squawking. Something large was moving through the undergrowth toward her. Eva ducked into the green veil of a weeping willow and hid among its feather branches. The squawks continued to become louder.

Closer.

Eva switched the Omnipod into lumen mode and scanned the area with her light.

A waist-high round gray bird, supported by two thick legs, waddled through the hanging branches. Though the plumage of its tufted yellow tail was striking, it lacked the majesty and brilliance of its neighbors. The bird stopped its loud call and regarded Eva with bright lemon eyes.

"*Raphus cucullatus*, commonly known as the flightless dodo," Eva's Omnipod said. "Extinct since the seventeenth century, the dodo became the archetype of extinction due to mankind's interference. Thankfully the Dynastes Corporation funded the Avian Cloning Project, which brought many extinct species, including the beloved dodo, back into the world. Shall I continue?"

"No," Eva said softly. She knelt down and studied the bird.

The dodo croaked at Eva. Its eyes blinked rapidly as it watched her in the Omnipod's light.

She held her hand out to the bird. *Don't worry,* she thought to it. *I won't hurt you.* On pigeon toes the dodo moved closer to Eva and nuzzled its hooked beak into her armpit.

"I'd rather sleep here with you birds than with those ignorant girls," she whispered to the dodo as she stroked its feathers. Tears welled in her eyes. Tears she blinked back.

Deep within the aviary another dodo called out, and the bird broke away from Eva, shuffling off into the darkness.

Eva scooted in close to the trunk of the willow. Wiping her eyes, she tapped her Omnipod. *I should call Hailey again, but it's useless,* she thought. *He's probably long gone already.*

You must sometimes disregard what one is saying and focus instead on what they are doing, Rovender had said. *That is when one reveals his true self.*

Eva stared at the Omnipod, waiting for it to chirp with news from her blue friend, but the device was silent. She looked out through the droopy branches of the willow, through the clear dome of the aviary, where in the fading light she could see all the homes with their families in them. Eva put her head down and curled up into a ball.

Happy Birthday. Muthr, I wish you were here.

A covey of birds burst out from the bushes nearby. Eva drew closer to the wide trunk of the tree. She held her breath and listened. *Have the authoritons tracked me in here?*

"Hello? Eva?" A woman's voice whispered from the shadows. "Are you Eva Nine?"

Eva remained still, saying nothing.

A woman draped in dark robes pulled apart the curtain of willow branches and ducked under the tree's canopy. Her elegant face was aglow from the soft light of the Omnipod in her hand. Peering around the trunk, Eva recognized her as the blond lady from the restaurant. Eva backed away to the far edge of the canopy, ready to bolt.

"Don't be afraid," the woman said. "And don't run. The authoritons will catch you for sure. They are beginning their patrol of the park by now. They'll be here soon."

Eva squinted at the woman through the shadows.

Somehow she seemed familiar to her. "Do I know you?" she whispered.

"You don't." The woman's eyes darted around. "But I know you, and I can help."

"Who are you?"

The woman smiled. "We come from the same Sanctuary, number five-seven-three. . . . I am Eva Eight."

End of
PART I

PART II

THE PAST SHALL
PRESCRIBE
THE FUTURE

CHAPTER 14: NON-TRACKERS

Eva Eight hugged Eva Nine tightly under the dark cover of the weeping willow. "I am so happy I found you, Nine," she whispered. "I can't believe you're here at last."

It was an odd sensation to be embraced by someone who knew Eva but whom Eva truly did not know; and yet she felt the warm feeling of security being with Eva Eight.

Eva looked into Eva Eight's sea-green eyes. It was like looking into a warped mirror. Aside from the shorter hair, Eva Eight looked like an older version of Eva, complete with perfect porcelain features.

The woman brushed back Eva's bangs and gently ran a finger over her cheek. "Muthr never told you about me?" she asked.

"No," Eva replied, her head spinning. It had never occurred to Eva that the process that had brought her into the world might have been carried out before her existence by Muthr. "So, wait," Eva said. "If you are Eva Eight, is there an Eva Seven?"

"There is much for you to learn." Eva Eight rose and peered out into the aviary. "But right now we need to focus on getting out of here." A radar image on her Omnipod showed a dozen red dots moving in perfect choreography, which Eva Nine assumed was a patrol of authoritons.

"Are you worried about us getting caught, Eva?" Eva Nine asked.

"Call me Eight. I do not hide the fact that I was Sanctuary-born. Neither should you." She gestured at Eva's attire.

"I like these new clothes," Eva replied. In the glow of Eight's Omnipod, she could see her dress shift to a liver brown. "Besides, this is the only thing I got for my—"

"Birthday." Eight cut her off. "I know. Today is my birthday as well."

"It—it is?" Eva said.

"Yes, all of us born in five-seventy-three were created in the generation room on this day," Eight said. "But the few reboots living here in New Attica have forgotten they were born in a Sanctuary. So nobody celebrates that sort of thing."

"Muthr used to make me a cupcake," Eva said with longing.

"With strawberries on top. I remember," said Eight.

Eva blinked at her. "I thought she'd done that just for me."

"It's okay." Eight knelt down and looked Eva in the eyes. "I know what you've been through. I understand *everything*. And now we are in this together, right?"

"Okay," said Eva.

"Good. Before we leave, Nine, there is something I need to do. Do you trust me?"

"What is it?"

Eight ran her hand up Eva's neck and touched her raised mole. "I need to remove the tracking chip inside you. If I don't do it, we will be captured by Cadmus's night patrol."

"Why? We aren't doing anything wrong." Alarmed, Eva backed away and rubbed the mole on her nape. She remembered Hailey mentioning the chip too, but he was hardly trustworthy. "Can't we just tell the authoritons we are going home?"

"Well, we are going home, Nine—but not here. Not this place. We have to leave as soon as we can." Eight pulled out a small plastic case from her satchel.

"Leave?" Eva was confused. "I just got here. I want to—"

"What? Stay? So you can be another one of Cadmus's mindless automatons?" Eight opened the case to reveal a kit of delicate medical instruments. "This isn't living. It's mind control. Domestication. Everyone is more programmed here than Muthr was."

Eva furrowed her brow. "I don't think so."

"You don't think so, huh?" Eight eyed Eva. "Okay, what about the machine back at the restaurant? The one that showed 'your life at a glance'?"

Eva realized it was Eight who had observed her on the Divination Machine. But the woman had not introduced herself then, nor had she stopped Eva from using it. "That machine was wrong," Eva said, crossing her arms. "It showed me a future that will never happen . . . that I would never be a part of."

"Let me guess. Was it a future with you and Cadmus hand in hand leading all the happy people to a rich, fertile new kingdom?" Eight looked up from cleaning the instruments and pulled out a small glass vial.

"It was!" Eva gasped. "How did you know?"

"Everyone sees the same image. That's what I am talking about, Nine. That's how he keeps control," said Eight. Then she gestured around them. "He does it in the programs and the games. He does it in the food. In the water . . . the air. *In everything.* And it starts the second you are conceived in that generator room back in the Sanctuary."

Eva remembered how the visions of her past on the Divination Machine had been similar to the images her Omnipod had displayed back in the medlab. She tried to conjure up some of Arius's fortune in hopes that it might help her see through to the truth here, but nothing came.

Eva Eight finished her prep on her instruments. "Ready?"

A nervous sweat ran down Eva's neck under her fancy dress. She squirmed in the dark-toned garment, uncomfortable. "Will it hurt?" she asked.

"A little at first," replied Eight. She pulled the cap off a syringe and tapped out the air bubbles.

"But it will be over quickly. We need to hurry."

Eva thought about what Rovender had told her. She closed her eyes and tried to listen to what her heart, her gut, was saying to her. She felt as if she were walking in her sleep—in a dreamy wonderland of ever-changing characters. Somehow, though, she knew that there was a truth to what Eva Eight was saying. There was sincerity and conviction in her voice.

"Okay." Eva sat with her back facing Eight. "Do it."

The sharp pinch of a needle soon became numb from the anesthetic that it administered into Eva's neck. The smell of burnt hair and skin wafted past her nose from the laser scalpel that removed the mole.

Eva tried to suppress a whine of anxiety.

"Almost finished," whispered Eight. "Just. Don't. Move. I've got to get all of it out."

A tingling sensation rippled up Eva's back as if a thread were being drawn from inside her body. This was followed by the trickle of blood running down her neck.

"Got it," Eight exhaled. She put a medical sticky bandage over the incision. "That medi-sticker will heal you up quick. You're good to go."

Eva rubbed her hand over the wound and watched as Eight dropped what looked like a coarse hair, with minute electrodes attached on either end, into the glass vial.

"Now you are a non-tracker like me. You are truly free to go as you please," Eight said with a wide grin as she packed up her instruments. "How do you feel?"

"I think I'll be all right," replied Eva.

"Good." Eva Eight studied the movement of the authoritons on her Omnipod. "Now we have to get rid of your tracking chip. Follow me and keep close!" She led Eva out of the aviary.

"Can't we just leave the chip there?" Eva asked as they scurried through a wooded area.

"No," replied Eight. "The city's central computer is monitoring it right now. Though the curfew is twenty-thirty, if you aren't in a home by twenty-one o'clock, the computer will send a squad after you."

"Then, let's just destroy it," said Eva.

"That won't work either," Eight said, checking her Omnipod. "If you were to suddenly disappear from the grid, the city would then send a patrol to investigate. I'm telling you, Nine, this is a controlled environment." Eva Eight stepped slowly out into the open green of the park, checking her surroundings. "This way. Hurry!" she whispered. The two darted to the edge of the park toward the lower level storefronts.

"This is level six," Eight said, pointing to the darkened buildings. "It's primarily shops and commercial use." She gestured to the topmost ring of homes overlooking the entire city. "And up there is level one. Most of those housing units are full of Cadmus's children and relatives."

Eva looked up at the cubic homes. "Cadmus has a lot of kids?"

Eight snorted. "Are you kidding? He has more than seventy. But if you ask him, he will tell you 'We are all his children.'" Eight opened up the door to a darkened storefront and ushered Eva in. Shelf upon shelf of sneakboots and other shoes lined the walls and aisles.

"Is this where you live?" Eva asked.

"No," Eight said. "However, the autoserver here is buggy and hardly ever online, so we can pass through unnoticed." She pointed out through the skylight to the ring of buildings above. "We need to get up to level five." With Eight's Omnipod lighting the way, they dashed through a maintenance room in the rear of the shop and into an access stairwell.

"Come on, Nine. Hurry!" Eight said, taking the stairs two at a time. "We are cutting this close."

"Can't we just take a gondola? Or an elevator?" Eva huffed behind her. She wondered if the gondolas would even recognize her now with her tracking chip removed.

"All Attican transit share systems are powered down for the night. The city CPU controls all that." Eight cracked the door on the stairwell and looked around. She checked the radar image on her Omnipod. "Twenty-fifty-seven. Just in time," she whispered, and led Eva out into a perimeter walkway on level five. Stacks of small cubic homes ringed the level, with a few streetlights glowing, lonely in the quiet neighborhood.

Eva Eight pulled out the vial with the chip in it. She removed a wad of putty from her satchel, which she then kneaded and wrapped around the glass vial. She winked at Eva, then hurled the putty ball upward. It clung to an overhang on the second story of a nearby home.

Eight kept her eyes on the putty to make sure it held. "Good. As far as the city knows, you're in a home and staying put."

"Wow," said Eva. "I had no idea."

"Like I told you, you have a lot to learn," said

Eight, heading back to the stairwell. "But let's keep moving. We'll go around to the eastern side of the city back on level six. It's easier to move around down there."

"How did you unlock these doors?" Eva asked, following Eight back down into the sneakboot shop.

"All the doors here are unlocked," Eight replied. "There is no crime, so no one has any reason to lock them. While we are here, do you want to get new shoes?"

Eva looked down at her dirty bare feet. "I guess so. I left my new sneakboots back at the park somewhere."

"Take what you need," Eight said. "That's what it's here for."

"What about my quotacard?" Eva held up her Omnipod. "Who do I give it to?"

Eight grabbed Eva's Omnipod and carefully removed the small card from its port. "No more quotacard. You're a non-tracker, remember?"

Eva nodded, saying nothing.

Eight continued, "Think of it as going to the supply room in our old Sanctuary. Okay?"

"Got it." Eva grabbed a simple pair of sneak-boots. They were similar to her old pair from her

Sanctuary and, for this reason, felt more comfortable.

"All right, Nine. Come on. I want to show you something." Eva Eight led her out into the night.

Eva Nine and Eva Eight snuck down the abandoned shopping promenade, traveling in the shadows of the perfectly trimmed trees that lined the street. After pausing at an abandoned intersection, they made their way along the perimeter road that rounded the entire city.

"This will take some time," Eight said in a hushed tone. "But there is something I want you to see." She led Eva to a darkened alcove between buildings.

The small alcove was dominated by a thick pipe, as big around as Eva Eight's body, jutting out of the quarry wall before arching down into the pavement. Eight squeezed under the elbow of the pipe. "Come here, Nine. Feel this," she said.

Eva did so. The pipe was warm to the touch.

"Get under here with me," Eight said.

Eva huddled next to Eight under the perspiring pipe. A whooshing sound of steam and water gurgled from within its thick cylindrical walls. Ahead, on the perimeter road, an authoriton rounded a building, scanning the area with a roving red laser. Frantically Eva Nine started to run.

"No!" Eight grabbed Eva by the sleeve. "Stay right here. Don't move and don't say a word."

The authoriton rolled closer. The sharp angles of its helmet-shaped head gave it a sinister appearance as it monitored its surroundings. Tiny lights flashed on its torso, which Eva knew from her time with Muthr meant that it was communicating with others.

"It's—" she started, but Eight's hand clamped over Eva's mouth. The authoriton's laser flashed over them and the pipe they hid behind but continued on its way without pause.

"Okay. The coast is clear," Eight said, removing her hand from Eva's mouth. "We've got about ten minutes before the next one comes by." She set the timer on her Omnipod.

Eva let out a breath. "I don't understand. How did it not see us?"

"These drainage ducts are about the same temperature as our bodies," Eight explained. "Thankfully, we were scheduled for rain tonight. The sound of the rushing water muffles our heartbeat and breathing. Authoritons use motion, body temperature, and sound to detect humans."

"But why are they even here? Why can't the people be out enjoying the night despite the power rationing?" Eva asked. She enjoyed being out in the dark, both in her Sanctuary and in the wilds of Orbona.

"You are questioning the rules, Nine. That's good," Eight said. "Cadmus wants everyone in their homes because there is something he is hiding that he does not want them to discover."

The duo stole their way around the perimeter of the city, moving from duct to duct and avoiding interference from the roving robots.

"So, how are we related?" Eva asked as she wriggled out from behind a duct.

"We are like sisters, you and I," Eight replied. "I shall take good care of you."

A sister! Eva thought. *A sister from the same home who has searched and found me. A sister who will understand me in ways Gen never could. I wish Muthr were here to see her daughters reunited.* Eva wondered if Rovender would like Eva Eight. "When did you leave the Sanctuary?"

"More than a hundred years ago. I've remained in this dreadful place waiting for you. Now that you are here, we can return as a family to live in the Sanctuary, as it should be." Eight turned to Eva and smiled.

"We—we can't go back." Eva stopped.

Eight turned and put her hands on Eva's shoulders. "I know you think that because you've been told that. But we *can* go back. I did it once before, and I'll do it again. Together we'll convince Muthr to let us stay."

"You don't understand," Eva said, her dress turning a drab olive. "The Sanctuary . . . Muthr . . . they're gone. Destroyed."

Eva Eight was silent for a moment as she studied Eva. "You're wrong. The Sanctuary is fine. It's a fortress. Practically impenetrable."

"No." Eva looked down, speaking softly. "I wish I were wrong. But Besteel, this big evil alien huntsmen, broke in and ruined everything."

Eva Eight's body began to tremble, and she dropped to her knees. "My home? *Our* home?" she said. "How is that even possible?"

"He had weapons." Eva knelt down next to her. "Weapons that were stronger than the Sanctuary was."

Eight clutched Eva's arm, squeezing it tightly. "Then, we will rebuild the Sanctuary. We'll take supplies from here. We'll make it even stronger. Then we'll find this Besteel and eliminate—"

"It's okay, Eight." Eva wriggled her arm free and

patted her sister's back. "Besteel's gone. I took care of him."

"Besteel's gone? *Thirteen years* are gone!" Eva Eight slumped down to the ground. "I've been waiting thirteen years for you so that we could put this plan into action. And now . . . gone. It's all gone!"

"We have each other, though," Eva said, feeling sorry for Eight. "That's a good thing, right? We can start again."

Eight sniffled and wiped her eyes, smearing her mascara. "Yes. A fresh start of it. I'll watch over you now as if you were my very own."

Eva gave her sister a hug and helped her rise. Up ahead the familiar red light of an authoriton scanned the storefronts.

"Come on," Eva said, and led Eight behind a drainage duct. They remained still as the robot rolled by.

Did she wait all this time for me? Eva thought. As they exited their hiding spot, she squeezed her sister's hand, and they exchanged smiles.

Eight composed herself and led the way. On the road ahead she pointed to a grand gate set in the quarry wall. "Now look. Over there is the eastern entrance. Is this where you entered the city?" she asked.

"I think so. Yes," Eva replied. "We came in here this morning." At night the majesty of the area was tinged by a permeating gloom.

"You were so close to the truth. Come. I want you to see this," Eight said. She approached one of a pair of drainage ducts that flanked the eastern gate. On the wall below the duct was a small door, hidden from view, which she wrenched open. A cloud of steam billowed out from within, escaping into the cool artificial night.

Eva could feel the heat as she ducked into the low cramped passage. Ancient pipes of every size ran along the grimy walls, sweating with water and hissing with electricity.

"Be sure to shut the door behind you," Eight said.

Eva pushed the door as hard as she could, for despite its small size, it was quite heavy. The door closed with a loud *CLANG*.

"It's okay," Eight said. "Even if that sound attracted any authoritons, they won't find us."

"So this is where you live?" Eva asked. The climatefiber in her undergarments activated, cooling her skin. Her hairdo, however, drooped in the humidity.

"No," Eight said, leading Eva down the hidden way. "I stay in several places. There are some abandoned cubes on level three where I don't have to deal with Cadmus's ridiculous rules and no one bothers me."

The humidity in the tight passage clung to Eva's brow. "So if you don't care for the rules, why don't—"

"It's not just that I don't care for the rules here, Nine. I don't trust Cadmus." Eight passed a hissing valve. "And he is supposed to represent the pinnacle, the leader of the humans. You should be able to trust your own leader, don't you think?"

"So, why do you stay?" Eva thought of Van Turner leaving the city with Hailey's father.

"I was waiting for you. Though I wasn't expecting you for another three years," said Eight.

"You really were waiting . . . for me? All this time?" Eva asked. Her Emote-Attire tinged a golden hue.

"Yes. Imagine my delight when I saw you today. I couldn't believe it was you standing right there in the park, yet I knew it as I know my own face," Eight said. "Then it was just a matter of waiting until you were alone so I could confirm it."

"And now what?" Eva rubbed her sweaty neck where her mole had been. Even under the medisticker the scar was tender.

"We are sisters now, and I am happy for it," Eight said, squeezing Eva's hand tightly. "You've brought light to my dreary life here."

These words made Eva think of Rovender. While she followed Eva Eight past more pipes, she wondered how she was going to find her blue friend.

"Eight." Eva spoke softly. "You said you'd take care of me as if I were your own daughter. Don't you have kids?"

Eight's face was dark in the shadows. Her voice was solemn. "I am not genetically pristine, Eva Nine, as I have a predisposition to certain incurable diseases. Therefore, by law, I cannot bear young."

"You . . . you can't?" Eva gasped in shock.

"No." Eight's voice was barely a whisper. "Early in my embryonic development I was made to be sterile."

Eva knew that "sterile" had something to do with not being able to have children. She thought back to the child-holograms that she had played with when she was younger. She'd even enjoyed being around Hostia's little son, Zoozi, back at Lacus. Perhaps she would be a mom one day, like Muthr, but that was a million-zillion years from now.

"I'm sorry," Eva said. It was all she could think

to say, even though she knew the words wouldn't fix anything.

Eight looked at Eva. "Thank you, Nine. I've lived with this for all of my life, and I wish it could be changed, but it cannot be undone. That is why I returned to our Sanctuary—*to get you.* I wanted to raise you as your mother and to provide you with the upbringing I did not have."

CHAPTER 15: BLACKOUT

Eva Nine followed her sister down the secret passage outside the city. Eva Eight's light flickered erratically as she moved, creating jumpy elongated shadows. Mysterious mechanical sounds murmured somewhere deep below them.

"We are here," Eight said, pointing to a round hatch mounted in the center of the floor. She grabbed a long steel rod leaning against the rough-hewn wall and hooked the rod into a notch in the center of the hatch.

"What is this place?" Eva asked. The hatch reminded her of the hidden door in the back of the supply room in the Sanctuary.

"It's a maintenance passage from when the city was still completely underground." Eva Eight grunted as she slowly lifted the hatch cover. "I stumbled upon it one night while I was hiding from the night patrol." She slid the hatch cover off and stood, catching her breath. "Phew! That thing is heavy!" she said. "Go ahead, Nine. Take a look."

On hands and knees Eva peered down the open hatch. The sounds she had heard in the passage were certainly coming from what she spied below her.

Far beneath, Eva saw a vast foundry. She quickly determined it was a manufacturing plant of some sort by the busy crew of laborbots performing various tasks. A great forge belched out vaporous breath and vomited hot liquid metal into labyrinthine molds. Out of these molds came strange mechanical components that were fed on a conveyer belt to a huddle of laborbots. Some laborbots welded while others wove cords, cable, and fiber-optic bundles through the parts.

Across the plant an impossibly large roll of plysteel steadily unfurled and fed a parade of pounding presses. These presses formed, trimmed, and stamped the ply-steel into heavy plates and panels, which were then welded together by more labor-bots.

As the welded shells were carried toward a painting room, it dawned on Eva what they were fabricating. "Robots," she whispered to Eight. "I don't get it. They are just making giant robots."

"Yes, but for what purpose?" Eight asked, her face aglow by the light of the forges below.

Eva shrugged. "Why don't we just ask our Omnipods?"

Eight scoffed. "Don't bother. Your Omnipod won't know and wouldn't tell if it did know, even if you overrode it with a password."

"So this is it? This is what Cadmus is hiding?"

"Don't you see?" Eight resealed the hatch. "The entire city is rationing its power for this—the manufacturing of these robots. Why?"

"I don't know." Eva stood and dusted off her hands. "And, honestly, I don't care. I just want to find Rovee and a place where we can all live together."

"Fine," Eight said. "Let us go then. We'll grab a few things, and—"

"Halt, civilian!" the firm voice of an authoriton rang out from behind them. A red laser shone brightly on Eva's face and chest. "You are in breach of statute twelve-thirty-nine, New Attica's mandatory curfew. Please surrender willingly."

Eva Eight grabbed Eva Nine by the hand and wheeled her around. "This way!" she said as they dashed back from where they'd come. At the end of the passageway two more authoritons emerged, each with their arms cocked. Eva froze, blinded by the bright lights in her face.

"SHOCdarts armed. Apprehension and immobilization to follow," an authoriton declared. "Please remain stationary."

"Go clone yourself!" Eight spat. "Come on, Nine, let's get out of here."

"Subdue humans orderly and carefully via SHOCdarts."

Before she could take a step, Eva felt the piercing jolt of several darts go into her leg and hip. She tried to reach down and remove them, but a searing electric charge caused her legs to buckle and give out. *I'm falling down . . . down. . . . No, up to the ceiling,* her mind whirled. Eva hit the ground, her head spinning from vertigo. Her last thought before she blacked out was how much she hated Hailey for bringing her to this horrendous place.

". . . Nine, Eva Nine, wake up," a voice drifted into Eva's consciousness. Eva's eyes fluttered open, and the tired face of Eva Eight came into focus. With her sister's help Eva slowly sat up.

They were on a cushioned floor in an artificially lit cell. A simple toilet was mounted on the cell wall next to a pellet and water dispenser. The cylindrical walls seemed to go up forever and appeared to be the source of light. Eva's ears buzzed from the low hiss of an electric charge coming from all directions.

"We've been captured," Eight said as she brought a cup of water to Eva's lips. "Right now we are in the detainment ward, somewhere below Attican Hall."

"How do you know?" asked Eva as she rubbed her leg. It ached where the SHOCdarts had stung her.

"I came to momentarily when they were bringing us in last night." Eight took a sip from the cup.

"How long have we been in here?"

"My guess—all night and most of the day," Eight replied. "I'm not sure how long the effects of the SHOCdarts last."

"So now what?" Eva looked around the cylindrical cell. It was smaller than her bedroom back in the Sanctuary.

"Now we wait," her sister said with a sigh.

"Hopefully they'll just kick us out of the city and that will be the end of it."

Eva couldn't believe that in a day's time she'd gone from a having a burning desire to be a citizen of New Attica to banishment. As she wondered if Rovender could help her out of this mess, she reached for her Omnipod—but her satchel was gone.

"Don't bother," said Eight. "They've confiscated everything."

Eva lay back on the cushioned floor and closed her eyes, trying to take her mind off the pain throbbing in her legs. She thought of the Halcyonus living peacefully back in Lacus and how wonderful Hostia and her family had been to her and Muthr. That seemed like such a long time ago, a different life altogether. . . .

The hiss of an opening in the cell wall stirred Eva from her light sleep. A thin man entered, flanked by two authoritons. He was dressed in a dark uniform, and his head was encircled by a wide white ruff that projected a cone with dozens of holographic newsfeeds around his face. Eva recognized him as the same man from Cadmus's office. His firm diction carried the weight of authority when he spoke. "I am Marzug, Attican magistrate and counsel to Cadmus Pryde. You are Eva Nine and Eva Eight, originally of HRP Sanctuary five-seven-three. Is this correct?"

Both girls nodded, saying nothing. Eva Eight stood defiantly and faced Marzug. The authoritons rolled in front of him, brandishing their thick padded arms. Eight said, "Besides roaming about after dark to find shelter, we've done no harm. If you let us leave, we'll be no more trouble."

"Not only have you violated our stated curfew, but you've removed your trace chips and therefore are deceiving the city's Centralized Individual Location Assistance, both of which are put in place for your own safety."

Eight tried to cut in, "But you don't—"

"You show blatant disregard for the few rules we have here, Eva Eight," the magistrate said, his bony arms crossed. "If it were up to me, you would serve the maximum punishment for your transgressions."

"But we—"

"However," Marzug continued, "it is not up to me. Cadmus would like to deal with you both personally, so I'm to take you to him immediately. Follow me, please." The magistrate exited. The click of his heels echoed through the detainment ward as he stepped down off the raised dais that housed their columnar cell. The girls followed him past rows of identical cells, under the watchful eyes of the accompanying authoritons.

They entered a large formal assembly chamber with a presentation stage centered under a high vaulted ceiling. Rows of seats radiated from the stage, each seat with an occupant. Eva recognized Cadmus's voice as he addressed the gathering.

". . . based on what the Prime Adviser has told me, this could be a considerable gain for our people if we are willing to take the risk. So I will present a detailed course of action to you, my esteemed council members, for your input, perspective, and wisdom."

Marzug pointed to both Evas. "Wait here you two, and don't make a sound," he said. With much pomp he walked down the center aisle toward the stage.

Eight leaned over and whispered, "This is the council that reigns over New Attica. Recognize anyone?"

Eva studied the aged faces of the people who sat in the circular chamber. "That looks a lot like

Albert Einstein." Eva pointed to a man with a gray bushy mustache and disheveled hair. "And over there I see Mahatma Gandhi. And there . . . Is that Abraham Lincoln?"

"Yes," said Eva Eight. "You remember your history well. I also see Adolf Hitler, Genghis Khan, and Napoleon Bonaparte."

Eva wondered how these world leaders from other times could all be sitting here in one room with Cadmus. "Are they clones?" she whispered.

"Holos," Eight replied. "This is the famed Chamber of Historic Thought, where Cadmus's façade continues. It's just a puppet show to appease the masses."

Eva thought back to the program she'd watched on Hailey's ship—historical figures brought to life via holograms by another man named Pryde. *Is he related to Cadmus?*

"The corruption and her apprentice, Father Pryde," Marzug said, and gestured to both girls. Cadmus dismissed the magistrate and approached Eva and her sister. His white silken robes billowed as he passed through a hologram of Ch'in Shih Huang Ti.

"Eva Nine, while I am busy securing a home for you, you're falling into company with this mischievous one. What are you two up to?" Cadmus put his hands on her shoulders.

"We were just leaving," Eight answered, stepping between Cadmus and Eva. "If you just return our belongings, we'll be on our way."

"Leaving?" Cadmus kept his gaze on Eva Nine. "But, Eva Nine, you just arrived. You can't possibly be bored by my fair city already, can you?"

"I think she's seen the *real* New Attica, in all of its splendor," Eva Eight retorted, her arms crossed in defiance.

"Really?" Cadmus continued evenly, though his focus remained on Eva. "So tell me, Eva Nine, what is the *real* New Attica?"

Eva shifted in her dress while it turned a sour green. She felt uncomfortable with the presence of the armed authoritons right behind her. And though they were only holograms, even the world leaders caused Eva unease. Cadmus had been amiable so far. He'd even asked his own daughter to show Eva around—though Gen had seemed a bit sheltered. From the recesses of Eva's mind drifted Arius's chant:

Illusion shepherds a flock just as a queen
protects her hive.

Eva asked, "Why is it that there are aliens and other creatures outside but the people here act as if they don't exist?"

"Ah! Answer a question with a question. I like that. I like that a lot. And this is quite a conundrum, to be sure." Cadmus put an arm around Eva and led her to the center of the chamber. Eva glanced back and saw the authoritons preventing Eight from following.

Cadmus spoke and moved about the stage, so that all eyes were on him. "Eva, as long as there has been civilization, there have been dangers that would infiltrate and upset mankind's desire for serenity and order—from Neanderthal clans fighting off saber-toothed cats to an ark full of alien life-forms encroaching upon Earth." The council nodded and murmured in agreement. "The irony is that people are aware that dangers lurk about on the fringe of their happy lives. But people by nature don't want to confront these threats. In fact, they'd rather not deal with them at all and exist instead in a blissful state of pure innocence."

"Perhaps you want them to exist that way," Eight called out from the back of the chamber.

"Oh, no, Eva Eight. It is the truth. Go out there and ask anyone on the street. They like life here.

They feel safe here. They want nothing bad to happen to them or their children, and they want to enjoy the luxuries of life their predecessors could never afford. I have provided this reality for all, including you."

"But bad stuff is out there. You can't stop it," said Eva Nine.

"The truth is always so pure when spoken by a child, is it not?" Cadmus addressed the council. "And you are correct, Eva. Bad things happen whether we like it or not. And so it is my responsibility as leader to take care of my people at any cost."

"Yeah, right!" Eight snorted.

Cadmus stepped off the stage and ushered Eva back to her sister. The council members watched as they walked past them. The holograms were more detailed and lifelike than any others Eva had ever seen. She watched as Albert Einstein, dressed in a collared shirt and casual sweater, lit his pipe with holographic matches that he pulled from his trouser pocket.

Cadmus addressed Eva Eight. "The truth is that we are running low on resources and the region surrounding us is not viable. It pains me to see my people, my children, be forced to remain in

this small space unable to enjoy *our* Earth's many splendors. But all of this will soon be remedied. You must have faith in me."

"I have faith," Eight said, pulling Eva back toward her. "But it is a faith in myself to steer my *own* life and control my *own* destiny. Not the one that *you* think Nine and I should have."

"And you, Eva Nine?" Cadmus said, looking down at her. "Do you feel the same?"

Why couldn't Rovender be here? This is not what I wanted. She looked away from Cadmus and whispered, "Yes."

Even though she was no longer looking at him, Eva knew that Cadmus kept his gaze on her.

"Fair enough," he said at last. "This paranoia has occurred in the past with some of the other Sanctuary-borns. We could certainly remedy it here, but I will not keep either of you against your will." He gestured to the magistrate. "Please retrieve their confiscated property, Marzug. Thank you."

"Of course, Father Pryde." Marzug swept from the chamber.

"Well, Eva Eight, I am sorry it did not work out for you here. Perhaps you will find it more agreeable with Eva Nine's friend Hailey Turner and his vagabond gang," Cadmus said, shaking Eight's hand in farewell. "And, Eva Nine, my Gen had taken a real liking to you. It's too bad she won't be able to say good-bye." Cadmus reached out for Eva's hand and noticed the glyph, the circle within the circle, on her forearm.

Eva quickly pushed her sleeve down to conceal Arius's symbol.

Cadmus appeared thoughtful for a beat. "I've an idea. How about I leave you both with a lasting act of my generosity? I'd like you to clean up and dine in one of the guest rooms here in the hall while I arrange for a small shipment of supplies that you can take with you."

"It's okay. We can manage," said Eight. "We just want our belongings back."

"No, really, I insist," said Cadmus, summoning an autoserver. "It will not take long at all, I assure you. I'll send it up with your belongings, and my escort here will see that you exit the city safely."

Eva shared the apprehension that she could hear in her sister's tone. Regardless, there seemed no other way out of the situation. She thought of Rovender going through Besteel's old belongings looking for items that might be of help to them. "Okay," Eva said to Cadmus. "We'll wait."

"Very good! This one is smart, Eight. You would do well to follow her lead." Cadmus grinned. "Now if you'll excuse me, the city needs its leader, so I must say farewell. Till morrow's destiny."

CHAPTER 16: PUZZLE

"I don't know why you agreed to this, Nine. He's up to something. I know it," Eva Eight murmured as they followed the autoserver to the guest suites on the upper floors of Attican Hall.

Eva was still sorting out everything that Cadmus had said about taking care of his people. "Let's just forget what he says and see what he does," she whispered back.

"Well, what *we* need to do is get out of here. And the sooner the better," said Eight.

"Your room is here." The autoserver extended an arm from its cylindrical body and typed in a code on the pad next to the door. The door slid open, and the robot led them in.

"Welcome to the suites at Attican Hall. You are in unit number thirty-nine-seventy-three on the thirty-ninth floor," the bodiless voice of the room greeted the arrivals. The sitting room had an airy feel to it because of a window that constituted the outer wall. Outside, the atmospheric membrane projected an azure cloudless sky. "If there is anything you need, do not hesitate to ask. There are call buttons located in every room for your convenience, or simply address the room directly. Thank you."

The autoserver opened the drapes and powered up the holographic music player. At the far end of the room, a life-size hologram of a lean man in a dark suit sat at an ornate grand piano. He adjusted his pince-nez spectacles and smoothed his thin mustache. He spoke with a foreign accent, "I am Igor Stravinsky, and I'd like to play for you one of my compositions, 'The Rite of Spring.'" An adventurous melody came from his piano over the room's speakers.

"Feel free to use any and all conveniences while you await your personal items," the autoserver said as it rolled past the hologram and fluffed pillows on the ornate couch.

As Stravinsky's melody filled the room, Eva explored the stylish suite. From the sitting room a small dining area led to a kitchen stocked full of bar and pellet dispensers. Beyond, a large cushy bed, covered in a heaping arrangement of multicolored pillows, dominated the bedroom, and a spacious washroom held an enormous Roman-style soaking tub.

"Is there anything else I can do for you?" asked the autoserver.

"No, thank you," Eva said. She caught herself in a floor-length mirror as her Emote-Attire shifted from an icy blue to a lovely shade of lilac.

"Till morrow's destiny." The autoserver disappeared through a small access hatch in the bedroom wall.

Eva joined her sister back in the main sitting room.

"Look at all those people." Eight leaned her head against the large window and gazed at the bustling metropolis below. "They are all robots under his command—each and every one of them. They have no desire to leave the safety of this place nor have a yearning to find the truth."

"Well, I am ready to leave," said Eva, "just as soon as they bring up our stuff."

"I don't want anything else from that fraud," Eight said. "I just want to start a new life. With you."

"Well, as soon as we get our O-pods back, I can contact the pilot who brought me here and he can tell me where to meet up with Rovee. He must be in the city by now, looking for me. I can't leave without him."

"You mentioned Rovee before," Eight said. "Does he work with the retriever who brought you?"

"No. He's a Cærulean and my best friend."

"Cærulean? You mean an alien? Is here in New Attica looking for you?" A look of alarm came over Eva Eight. "Why didn't you say so before?"

"Well, I know there's not a lot of aliens here, but—"

"There are no aliens here."

"But I saw—"

"Nine, listen to me when I tell you—there are no aliens living in New Attica." Eight was now aghast. "No one here knows of their existence *at all.* Didn't you listen to what Cadmus was saying? If your friend came here, he's probably been thrown into the detainment ward where we were . . . or worse."

"Why? Rovender could teach everyone about the outside . . . ," Eva started, but then the memory of the Gens having no idea who, or what, Rovender was flitted into her mind.

It's a troll from a fairy tale program, Gen had said.

The Divination Machine had shown her a future.

A future without aliens.

I could just send him over to meet you once they're back, Hailey had said.

"We have to leave now!" Eva rushed to the door, passing through the hologram of Stravinsky while he played furiously at his piano. "I have to find Rovee!" she said, activating the door's switch. The door did not move. "What's wrong! Why won't it open?" Eva's heart began to race.

Eva Eight joined her and punched at the buttons on the control pad. "It's locked," she said. "I knew it! Room Thirty-Nine-Seventy-Three, please open our front door."

"I apologize," the room responded in a relaxed tone. "I am experiencing a momentary system glitch with the doors on your level, which is causing them to malfunction. I shall have this remedied in just a few moments. Please hold. I am sorry for the inconvenience."

"There's no other way out of here?" Eva ran to the window and looked out. Even though the sides of the pyramid were angled, it was a long drop to the ground below.

"Hold on," Eight said. "I'll get us out of here. I just need to think." She paced through the rooms.

Eva calmed herself and cleared her mind as she followed her sister. *I've been presented with a puzzle,* she thought. *What would Rovender do?* She examined the ceiling and the floors, looking for a clue to aid in their escape. "Eight, what about this?" Eva pointed to the sealed hatch where the autoserver had exited.

"That's a maintenance hatch for service robots," Eight said.

"Let's call one up." Eva ran over to the main keypad for the room and pressed the call button.

"I apologize. Your main door is still malfunctioning. May I help you with something else?" the room asked.

"Yes," Eva said. "I'd like to order some . . . um . . . more food, please. Some synthsushi."

"Once again, I must apologize," the room replied. "There is a temporary hold on the autoservice on your floor because the malfunctioning doors are causing a backup of deliveries from our kitchen. Please contact us again in a few moments. Once again, I apologize . . ."

Eva ignored the rest of the message and rushed back to the hatch. She ran her fingers around the tight-fitting seam but could not pry it open. "How do we get this to open?"

"I dunno." Eva Eight knelt alongside her. "Usually these robots just come in and make your bed or clean up any messes you make."

Eva ran out to the dining room.

"Where are you going?" asked Eight.

Eva returned, a hovchair in her hands. "If there is one thing I know how to do, it's make a mess." She ran into the washroom and hammered the sink faucet with the chair. After three loud clangs the faucet broke off and water spewed into the room.

"Good afternoon," the room greeted them. "Our sensors indicate that you may have a leaky faucet in your washroom. May we send up an autoserver from maintenance to address this?"

"Yes, please," Eva replied as calmly as possible.

"One moment," said the room.

Eva grabbed another floating hovchair from the

dining room and slid it over to Eva Eight. "Get ready," she said, and sidled up to the hatch.

There was a rush of air followed by a hiss of the hatch as it slid open. The waist-high autoserver rolled out. "Greetings," it said. "I am autoserver forty-two, and I am here to—"

Eva whacked the robot across the room with the hovchair. "Jam the door with the chair!" she yelled to Eva Eight. She rushed over to the robot and pushed it into the flooding bathroom. Eva closed the door behind it and locked it.

"No. He'll warn the others!" Eight wedged her chair in the opened hatch.

"It's okay." Eva hurried toward the hatch. "We'll be gone before anyone comes. We don't need to hurt him."

Eva Eight brushed past Eva Nine, snatching the chair from her hands. "He's a robot, Nine. They'll fix him." She opened the bathroom door and began pummeling the autoserver with the hovchair.

Eva blocked out the sound of the robot's demise and tried to keep her focus on escaping. She peered down the vertical channel that the autoserver had come up. It was brightly lit by rows of recessed lights and was about as wide as the kitchen exhaust shaft she had used to escape her

Sanctuary. But, unlike the exhaust shaft, the vertical channel had no rungs to hold on to for climbing. Eva crawled in, keeping herself in a crouched position. Using her legs, she pressed her back against the wall of the duct and began to scuttle downward. "Come on! We need to go!" her voice echoed up to Eva Eight.

Her sister scrambled in and kicked out the chair that was jamming the hatch to their room. The hatch slammed shut, which caused the lighting to extinguish, leaving the two sisters alone in the dark.

"We have to move fast before they send up another service robot." Eight's voice bounced down to Eva as they continued their steep descent.

"There is a junction just a little farther," Eva said. "I can see a light coming from it." She crawled into the adjoining horizontal duct and poked her head out to watch her sister's progress.

"I'm almost there," Eight said. The lights in the channel flickered back on, and a whooshing sound could be heard from the bowels of the pyramid. A strange clanging reverberated up the vertical duct. Eva looked down to investigate.

Below she could see the duct junctions sealing shut in ascending order. "Hurry! They're sending up another robot!"

Eva Eight began moving faster and lost her footing. She shrieked as she tumbled down the cramped duct toward Eva.

With arms outstretched Eight caught the lip of the opening as she fell past it. Eva seized her sister and yanked her into the horizontal shaft. Eight slid her feet in just as the junction opening sealed shut. There was a rush of air outside as an autoserver shot past them.

"The channels are pneumatic," Eight said as she caught her breath. "They use air to push the robots around."

"We're going to have to be careful," Eva said. Far above she could hear the faint sound of their room hatch sealing shut. The lights dimmed once more.

"I'll say." Eva Eight squeezed Eva's hand in the dark. "Thanks for helping me. I don't think that would have ended so well."

"No problem." Eva smiled. She curled her small lithe body into a tight ball and turned around in the cramped space. "Let's go."

"Where?" Eight asked.

"Back to the detainment ward. If Rovee is there, I have to rescue him." Eva crawled on hands and knees. The lights flicked back on and air rushed through nearby ducts.

"Nine, that's not a good idea. We need to get out of here. Cadmus will find us."

"I'm not leaving until I find Rovee." Eva's voice was resolute. "I knew something was wrong. He would have found me by now."

"He's just an alien. I can take better care of you."

"He is NOT just an alien!" snapped Eva. "You don't know him. He'd do anything for me."

"I'm sure he would," said Eight. The lights darkened and the channel became quiet once more. "But no one knows you like I do, Nine. We are from the same birthplace. We were raised identically. We have experienced many of the same things. I understand what you're feeling."

"If you understand, then you know I have to go and rescue Rovee," Eva countered.

"I am glad that this alien helped you. You've clearly been through a lot. We all have, but—"

"You don't know what I've been through!" Eva said. "You don't know me!" Tears pricked her eyes. "If you want to leave, go ahead. But I have to find my friend." She began moving faster now.

"No!" Eight reached out and seized Eva's foot. "Don't do this. We have to escape together. I've waited so long for you to come."

"No! Let go of me!" cried Eva. "Let go!" She kicked wildly. Eight let out a yelp and suddenly released her sister. Eva scrambled away from Eight as fast as she could, and then she stopped after several meters and stifled her tears. *Why can't Muthr be here? She'd agree to go after Rovee.*

In the darkness Eva heard a hissing sound echo throughout the shaft. The hatch below her opened and she tumbled down into the darkened labyrinth of ducts.

DYNASTES

CHAPTER 17: TESTS

Eva rolled down an angled shaft and slammed into a closed hatch door. She lay crumpled at a bend created by the angled duct joining with a horizontal one. A blast of air surged past her, followed by a rising whine. The lights in the horizontal duct flashed on, and Eva could see an autoserver barreling down the channel directly toward her. Frantic, she kicked hard on the hatch door, trying to knock it open, but to no avail.

The zooming robot was almost upon Eva. She scooted up the angled shaft just as the autoserver slowed and exited through the maintenance hatch. Eva dropped down and followed the robot out into the room.

She entered a white, dimly lit atrium devoid of any décor. The autoserver paid Eva no mind as it rolled through one of the many doorways that ringed the room. Eva moved to follow the robot, but the door slid shut quickly behind it. As Eva neared the door, the solid material that it was constructed from became transparent. Though the door remained closed, she could see the autoserver continue down the hall and into another room. It was the same hall Cadmus had led her down earlier from the registrar's office.

I'm near the medlabs, she thought. Eva backed away from the door, and it became opaque again. *I have to find Rovee. How do I get out of here?*

Eva approached the next door on the right. Inside the room, a robot, similar in appearance to Muthr, lay on a gurney with its head and braincase opened up. A duo of crab-shaped automedics hovered around the patient, one holding a large liquid-filled beaker with a pink brain suspended within. Wires and electrodes hung limply from the dripping brain tissue as the other member of the surgical team removed the organ from the jar and placed it in the patient's braincase.

Eva shuddered and moved on. The next room appeared empty, save for a disassembled robot lying in pieces on a worktable.

The atrium door hissed open again, and the autoserver rolled back in. Eva ducked into the room with the disassembled robot.

From inside she watched the autoserver approach the maintenance hatch, which opened, dispensing a parcel of pressed and folded exam gowns. The robot grabbed the bundle and wheeled to a supply closet. Eva spied on the robot, which continued to load the shipment of medical supplies into the closet.

Deciding it was best to stay hidden from the autoserver, Eva remained in the room and inspected the fragments laid out on a surgeon's table. She realized that these were not pieces of a broken-down robot as she had assumed, but a collection of alien artifacts and components. *Those are vocal transcoders . . . and that's a boom-rod charger just like Besteel carried.* She picked up the heavy battery pack. Coiled nearby was the connecting charge cable. In another pile was a rifle-size boomrod with the handle removed. *What would Cadmus want with Dorcean weapons?* She scooped up a handful of transcoders.

Eva checked on the autoserver's progress out in the atrium. The robot unloaded the last of the shipment, entered the maintenance hatch, and zoomed off down the duct. The hatch sealed shut behind it, leaving the atrium vacant. Eva slipped out of her room and into the supply closet. The lights in the closet flickered on, and the room greeted her, "Hello . . . I'm sorry. I am having trouble identifying you. I need an identification before I can help you."

"Oh, it's okay," Eva replied, her eyes scanning the room. The walls were lined with shelves containing a variety of medical and surgical supplies—dissecting scissors, forceps, and clamps. On the back wall she spied a rack with blue uniforms similar to what Cadmus's aide had been wearing when she'd arrived in the medlab. "My tracking . . . er . . . identification chip has been malfunctioning. My name is Van Turner. I am a new aide to Cadmus Pryde. He sent me here to get outfitted."

"Welcome, Van Turner," the room replied. "Please stand on the lighted pedestal here." A glowing tile rose from the floor, and Eva took her position. A red laser scanned over her body. "I apologize, but your size is smaller than the majority of our staff," reported the room. "However, I have attire that will suit your needs temporarily." A thin rod extended from the wall. From the rod hung a pressed uniform, which included a lab coat and skullcap. "I have placed an order matched to your actual measurements. Please check back with me in twenty-four hours, and I will have it pressed and ready."

"Thank you," Eva said, and changed out of her garish garment. She pulled her iridescent hair back into a bun and then tucked it into the skull cap. Eva balled up her Emote-Attire and threw it into a trash receptacle. She then looked out into the atrium for any sign of activity.

The medlab hall door opened, and a hovering gurney floated into the atrium. Lying unmoving on the gurney was a human patient with a large respirator strapped to the face. A neighboring door opened, and the gurney floated in. Eva slipped out of the closet and peered into the patient's room.

It was hard to see any facial details from her vantage point at the door, but the unconscious individual was dressed in an exam gown. Pale human feet stuck out from the gray gown, and a variety of medical apparatus were attached to the hands and head. Over the gurney flickered several holographic charts detailing the patient's vitals.

A low bleep sounded in the room, and an automedic descended from the ceiling. Its movement reminded Eva of the holograms she'd seen of a spider dropping into its web to eat its entwined prey. The robot spoke to the gurney, and the bed turned to float back out of the room. To avoid detection Eva dashed from the doorway and into the abandoned room with the alien artifacts.

Huddled near the closed door, Eva now had a clear vantage point as the automedic followed the gurney across the atrium and into an adjacent room. Though the patient's face was partially covered by the respirator, the brown and blue hair was unmistakable.

It was Hailey.

As soon as the door slid shut behind the gurney and the automedic, Eva slipped back into the atrium. Peeking into Hailey's room, she watched as the robot pushed the pilot's bed next to an empty gurney on the far side of the large lab. In the center stood an examination chair with its back to the door.

The automedic turned from Hailey and tended to the chair. Eva realized there was another patient that she could not see.

Van Turner?

What she could discern was a series of wires and electrodes going into the chair and patient, likely for monitoring. The robot removed several of the electrodes near the patient's head and set them in a jar of fluid. Crimson blood ran off the electrodes and swirled around in the jar, tinting the fluid pink.

The robot dressed the patient's head and then picked up an Omnipod and spoke into it. Through the door it was hard to hear what the robot was saying, but it sounded like abrupt commands. Eva longed for her Omnipod so that she could eavesdrop. She gave a start of surprise when the mysterious patient in the chair began to convulse violently. Eva's eyes darted around the atrium. She was half-waiting for the commotion to attract other robots. When it did not, she looked back into Hailey's room. The automedic gave a quick injection to the convulsing patient, stopping the seizure.

Eva gasped as a familiar arm hung limply from the armrest of the chair. Thick blue fingers twitched in erratic spasms from a spiderweb of wires and electrodes snaked under pallid blue skin.

"Rovee!" Eva shrieked, and the door to the lab hissed open.

CHAPTER 18: SUBJECTS

"May we help you?" The automedic rushed over to the door. "Your identifier is not responding. Therefore, you must have an authorization code before entering."

Eva froze, unsure of what to do. *Cadmus is going to catch me for sure,* she thought. *He's going to catch me and put wires into my body and brain.*

"Please identify yourself with an authorization code within ten seconds or we shall summon security," the automedic said. It then began to count down, "Ten . . . nine . . . eight . . ."

"An authorization code?" Eva's mind reeled.

"Seven . . . six . . . five . . . four . . ."

Somehow that term rang a bell. She remembered being locked out of her Sanctuary and needing a code to reenter.

"Three . . . two . . ."

"C-P-zero-one. Password: omniscient," Eva replied.

The automedic withdrew from its position and returned to its patients. Eva followed with trepidation, and the lab door slid shut behind her.

"You are here for a progress report?" the automedic asked.

Eva stood tall and nodded. "Yea—yes. For Cadmus. Father Pryde."

"Very good. What we have determined is that the physiology of this alien species is quite similar to fellow terrestrial organisms, despite the rearrangement of the internals," the automedic reported. "We feel that cerebral manipulation will be attainable, though we are not certain that any Tech we devise in the short term will have an all-encompassing effect on the spectrum of beings present at the touchdown site."

Eva glanced at the Cærulean. Now that she saw his face, it was clear that the unconscious patient was not Rovender but another Cærulean. She let out a small sigh of relief. "And him?" She pointed to Hailey.

"As Father Pryde has consented by consultation with his Prime Adviser, similar tests on this corrupted subject will be performed this evening, as scheduled, in his personal medlab. Please tell Father Pryde we are preparing the patient now," said the automedic. It removed the cap from Hailey's head and grabbed a laser hair trimmer.

Mind control? On aliens and humans? A chill shivered down Eva's spine. Hailey deserved to have wires shoved into his brain after dropping Eva off without telling her the truth. *But no one should be made to suffer in Cadmus's cruel experiments. If only Rovee were here to help me devise a plan.* "So this subject is set to be operated on?" she asked aloud.

"Yes. All corrupted specimens in the ward must be studied and analyzed for treatment. However, Father Pryde was specific about this one's immediate attention," replied the automedic as it shaved off Hailey's brown and blue hair.

"He is a corrupted specimen?" Eva asked.

"Yes. As you know, all corrupted specimens of *Homo sapiens neo* are individuals with a predisposition to free thought due to unmanaged neurochemicals in the brain. Such individuals can be prone to dissension or hostile acts toward authority and need to be treated before they are naturalized into the general populace."

"Are there any more specimens like this one?" Eva gestured to the Cærulean.

"There is one more, brought in yesterday morning by the outsider that we are currently prepping."

Rovee!

The automedic brought up a hologram of Hailey's brain and superimposed it over Hailey's shorn head. The robot then made tiny ink markings all around his skull.

Eva tried to appear nonchalant. "And any other humans?"

The automedic swabbed Hailey's head with iodine. "Yes. There are two more that were brought in from the night patrol. They are also genetic corruptions, like this one, but they have been contained. Please report to Father Pryde that our purebred stock in the city will remain intact."

Eva went numb down to her fingertips. *Eva Eight was right.* She swallowed hard and tried to control the shaking that was fast overtaking her. It was like being in the taxidermist's lab all over again. She squeezed her eyes shut and focused her thoughts.

Rovee is in the detainment ward. That is where I have to go.

"Well, I am also here to inform you," she said in a firm tone, "that Cadmus wants these two here swapped out for the . . . uh . . . two girls."

The automedic stopped its surgical preparations. "The two corrupted females?"

"Yes," Eva replied. "Down in the detention ward." *Keep calm.*

A warning ping sounded in the room. Holograms of both Eva and her sister were projected onto the far wall. Eva tried not to pay any attention to the images.

Keep calm. Keep calm.

The automedic looked up at the holograms, setting down the iodine swab. "We never said that the other two subjects were females. Who exactly did you say you were again?" The robot crawled closer to Eva.

"V-Van Turner," Eva said, stepping back. "Cadmus's new aide." She nudged closer to the door. The Cærulean patient in the chair began to stir.

"We are receiving word that we have no record of a new aide by that name in our database." A fine red beam issued forth from the robot's face and scanned Eva. "And there is no trace of an identifier, malfunctioning or otherwise, within you. Please provide proper identification immediately."

Eva could see the blinking light on the robot's torso. It was communicating with others.

"I told you." Eva was now backed to the door. Behind her back she fumbled for the controls. "I'm Van Turner. I told you the code."

"You told us a basic authorization code that few have. However, your behavior is nontypical for a medlab assistant." The automedic was now almost upon her. "You are one of the fugitives. You are Eva Nine."

The automedic lurched forward to snatch Eva, and it would have succeeded, but the Cærulean still bound to the exam chair grabbed on to one of the robot's many legs. This bought Eva a few precious seconds to dash out of the room. She scrambled across the atrium and into the room with the disassembled boomrod, closing the door behind her.

Okay. How does this work? With trembling hands she grabbed the components and began fitting them together. Outside, the click of the automedic's feet could be heard as it scuttled from door to door in search of its quarry. "Please work. Please," Eva whispered as she plugged the charge cable into the back of the boomrod. "How do I turn this thing on?" She looked at the battery pack. The dials, buttons, and switches were labeled in an alien language.

The muffled voice of the supply closet could be heard greeting the automedic. The robot was two doors down from Eva.

"Come on! Come on!" Her mind raced. *How did Besteel do it?* She squeezed a lever set in the middle of the rod, and the device began to hum.

The door to the room slid open, and the automedic burst in. "You cannot escape, Eva Nine. Let us treat the corruption within you. Let us remove all violent tendencies. It is for the greater good of your kind."

"I don't need your help." Eva released the lever and tripped the trigger. The distinct sound of a *WOOM* erupted from the boomrod, throwing Eva backward. The sonic blast hurled the automedic across the atrium and into the wall, where it collapsed in a heap. An electronic alarm pinged in a steady rhythm. Eva scrambled to her feet and dashed back toward Hailey's room.

The other two automedics were drawn out from their lab by the alarm. Eva fired the boomrod and quickly dispatched them.

"Hailey!" Eva burst into the room. She pulled the aspirator off and lightly slapped his face. "Come on. You need to wake up! Now!"

"Please, help me," a soft voice creaked from behind. Eva turned to see the Cærulean struggling with his binds. She hurried over and helped free him from the examination chair. "Thank the stars for you, little one." The alien patted Eva. He was smaller and less scruffy than Rovender—possibly even younger, though it was hard to tell beneath all the bruising the poor creature had sustained from experimentation. "I knew you were not like the others when I could understand your words. Since my imprisonment I have been unable to communicate with my captors."

"I am sorry for that," Eva said, helping him up. "Can you walk?"

"I shall try." Unsteadily the Cærulean stood. "I am Nadeau of the Kitt clan from the village of Faunas. I need to return to my people immediately and warn them of this fate."

"I'm Eva Nine." Eva checked on Hailey. He was still anesthetized. "The Kitt clan?" she wondered aloud. "Do you know—"

On weak legs, Nadeau tripped and fell, upsetting

a tray of equipment. Eva dashed over and helped him up once more.

"I am afraid . . . my time, my journey, is near its end." Nadeau huffed as he pulled himself up.

"No, it's not." Eva guided him over to the empty floating gurney. "Get on."

As Nadeau climbed onto the second bed, Eva instructed Hailey's gurney to return him to the detention ward. The gurney floated out of the room and down the hall.

Eva crawled onto the gurney with Nadeau and repeated the instructions. She pulled a sheet over them and readied the boomrod as the gurney drifted out into the atrium.

The hall leading away from the medlab was now bustling with alarmed robots, patients, and other medical staff. Eva lay perfectly still and peeked out from under the sheet as the gurney joined other hovering gurneys and navigated its way through the mayhem. Cadmus's aide flanked by two authoritons rushed passed her. "I am told she is in lab C and is armed and dangerous," the aide told the robots.

Eva flattened herself next to Nadeau. The Cærulean was so still that his shallow breathing was the only clue indicating that he had not perished.

Their gurney hovered next to Hailey's in a large lift, and the doors slid shut behind them. The elevator then began its descent to the detainment ward. With the trio alone and safe for a moment, Eva reached out and nudged the pilot. "Hailey! Hailey, wake up!"

The boy groaned while his eyes fluttered open. Using the intravenous pole mounted to the side of his gurney, he pulled himself up. "Where am I?" he said.

Eva slid out from under her sheet and sidled up next to his gurney, handing him a transcoder. "You were about to have your brain rewired by an evil automedic . . . but you didn't, thanks to me. Not that you would have done the same."

Hailey blinked in astonishment and ran his fingers over his now shaven head. "Eva? What are you doing here?"

"I'm trying to get us out of here—all of us."

"I'm sorry," the pilot said. "I didn't know. Cadmus tricked me when I returned with the *Bijou*. He said—"

"Whatever. We've gotta get out of here." Eva pulled off her skull cap and began undoing her lab coat. "Now do exactly what I tell you, and hurry!"

CHAPTER 19: REUNITED

Reaching its final destination, the lift stopped and its doors parted.

The two gurneys floated out, each carrying a patient, and Hailey followed them into the detention ward. He was now dressed in the aide's lab coat.

The elevator had delivered them to a back entrance of a round control room, which overlooked the two wings of cell blocks in the detainment ward. Both wings were dark, save for the glow given off by the orderly rows of columnar cells. At the elevator a pair of authoriton guards greeted Hailey, still standing behind the gurneys.

"I . . . um . . . have a patient transfer request from the medlab," announced the pilot. "We need the other blue alien that was brought in yesterday."

"We have received no record of this request," one

of the authoritons said, remaining steadfast in front of the gurneys. "Please wait while your transfer request is authenticated." The second authoriton rolled toward the central hub of the control room.

"Um, wait. We have our transfer clearance here." Hailey grabbed the intravenous pole of the closest gurney. He pushed down hard on the pole, causing the gurney to flip up onto its side, making a barricade. Eva dropped out from the bottom and blasted the authoriton with the boomrod. Before it toppled back into the second robot, the authoriton sent out a volley of SHOCdarts, which rained down onto the flipped-up bottom of the gurney.

Nadeau crawled out of his gurney and ducked under for protection. Hailey dodged more SHOCdarts while Eva finished off the authoriton guards.

"Let's get to those downed guards!" Hailey pointed to the felled authoritons.

"Why?" Eva blasted a third authoriton with the boomrod.

"I have an idea." Hailey yanked the IV pole off the gurney. Under the cover of the gurney, Eva and Hailey made their way over to the fallen guards. Using the pole, Hailey wrenched one of the arms loose from the destroyed authoritons.

Eva gasped as Hailey pulled the armor plating

from the limb to reveal a pale atrophied human arm within. "Is—is there a person in there?" she asked.

"Naw. I think it's just cloned parts," Hailey replied. "Don't think about them as people. They're just robots." He slipped the armor over his own forearm. "Now the odds are a little more even," he said as he studied the complex arsenal of wrist weapons. A high-pitched whistle squealed from Hailey's newfound firearm, and a large, serrated SHOCdart rocketed in Eva's direction. Eva ducked as the projectile shot over her head. She turned and glared at Hailey.

"Sorry," he said with a lopsided grin.

Eva charged her boomrod and blasted the thick doors of the control room. The transparent ply-steel buckled but did not give. From the wings on both sides, squads of authoritons closed in and took aim at the fugitives. Hailey exhausted the various weapons of the authoriton armor on the attacking robots while Eva recharged the boomrod once more.

A canister clunked down next to them with a red blinking light. "Take cover!" Hailey shouted, and the canister exploded with an angry swarm of mini-SHOCdarts. Eva released the trigger on the boomrod, and the walls to the control room ruptured under the sonic blast.

As the dust settled, Eva found Hailey had been immobilized by a slew of buzzing SHOCdarts that had pierced his body. She crawled through the rubble of the control center and pulled herself up to the main console. She began charging the boomrod, keeping it aimed at the console.

"Halt!" The squadron of authoritons surrounded the blasted opening. "Put your weapon away or we shall—" A bolt of electricity danced over the squad leader's metallic shell. As his squad fell one by one, Eva could see Nadeau behind them holding the firearm of a fallen authoriton. He had electrocuted the entire squad from behind in one shot.

"Help Hailey!" Eva pointed at the fallen pilot still twitching on the floor. She fired the boomrod at the console, and it exploded in a shower of sparks, sending Eva ducking for cover.

As she rose, she could see the effects of the damaged console. Each glowing cell in the ward lost its power. The lights flickered out, rendering the cell walls transparent. Eva hopped down the steps from the control room and ran through the rows of empty cells. In the third row she sprinted by, she discovered a pair of cells, each holding a prisoner.

The first contained an emaciated Halcyonus who lacked any of his usual brilliant coloration and did not stir at all when Eva tapped the cell wall with the muzzle of the boomrod. The prisoner in the second cell startled Eva because of the creature's remarkable height. A gawky alien in a flight suit stood on four thin rubbery legs watching Eva's every move.

"Get back!" She motioned for the alien to back up, and blasted the base of the cell wall with the boomrod. The smiling alien wriggled out through the hole and patted Eva on the head.

"Well, aren't you a little bayrie, come to rescue me! Name's Huxley, Royal Beamguide Scout for the queenic," he said. "Don't bother with that poor fishy." He pointed to the Halcyonus. "I don't think he's with us any longer, if you know what I mean. What's the best route out of this trap, little one?"

"I've got to find Rovee first." Eva started down the next row of cells. "Have you seen a Cærulean anywhere?"

Huxley kept up with Eva, though it seemed as if he'd trip over his own feet at any moment. "Eh? A blue, you say? Here in lockup?"

"Yes," Eva said, searching through the empty cells. "He's my friend. I have to find him."

"Well, it's no use running around in this maze. Let ol' Huxie have a quick look-see." Huxley leaped up

onto the outer wall of a nearby abandoned cell. With his padded fingertips and rubbery legs, he scaled it in seconds. "Over there's the little nip!" He pointed. "One row up and several cells down. Can't miss 'im."

Eva dashed off in the direction Huxley had indicated and came to a halt at the cell holding Rovender Kitt.

"Rovee!" squealed Eva.

Rovender stood and placed his palm flat on the glass. Around his wrist hung the tattered friendship bracelet Eva had made for him.

"Back up!" Eva shouted.

Within moments Rovender was out of his cell. He embraced Eva warmly. "You shouldn't have risked coming after me. But I am so glad to see you," he said with a smile.

"Me too," replied Eva.

"Did you molt on your birthday?" He tousled her hair. "Your color has changed."

"It has . . . but I haven't," Eva said.

"Oh, but you have, Eva. I can see it in your eyes."

Eva hugged him once more. The familiar feeling of Rovender's worn brown jacket pressed against her face.

"I am happy that you are okay," he whispered. "I was worried."

"You were right to be cautious," she said, and sniffled. "We shouldn't have come here."

Rovender held on to her. "It's okay, Eva. You are safe, and that matters most to me."

Huxley called from his lookout high on the cell wall, "We best hurry up, little bayrie. There will be reinforcements here very soon."

"Come on!" Eva said. "We have to get out of here."

With Rovender and Huxley, Eva met with Hailey and Nadeau at the control room. The pilot was still lying on the ground while Nadeau plucked SHOCdarts out of his leg.

"Nadeau?" Rovender said, clearly stricken by the Cærulean's deteriorated appearance.

On shaky legs Nadeau stood and held up both palms in greeting. "Rovender? Rovender Kitt? Is it you?"

Rovender embraced his fellow tribesman. Eva could see tears well up as he examined the scars, evidence of the horrors his friend had been through. "What . . . what have they done?"

"I feel no pain when I see you, lost brother of my tribe." Nadeau looked at him directly. "Just help me home, Rovender. So that I may see our clan once more."

"Give me that!" Rovender snatched Eva's

weapon. He charged the boomrod and aimed it at Hailey.

"What are you doing?" yelled Eva.

"I am ridding us of this traitor. He tricked us. All of us!"

"What do you mean?" Eva asked. She watched Hailey crawl under the overturned gurney.

Rovender kicked the gurney away. "He tricked me into coming here while you were still asleep, in order to separate us and sell us off one at a time. He will never again deliver anyone to their death."

"No!" Eva pushed the muzzle away. The blast fired off into the ceiling.

"Don't kill me! I didn't know!" pleaded Hailey. "I just thought you would both be admitted into the city. Not made into lab rats."

"Come on, Rovee," Eva said, taking back the weapon. "We have to get out of here. We'll kill him later!" She made for the elevators.

"Wouldn't want to be you, hero," Huxley said, rubbing Hailey's bald head. Hailey swatted the alien's hand away.

The elevator pinged. The door slid open, and a squad of authoritons poured out.

"Get back!" Eva fired at the squad with the

boomrod while the others retreated under the floating gurneys.

"There's got to be another way out!" Rovender said as he supported Nadeau.

"What if we take cover behind the cells?" asked Hailey.

"No good, hero," Huxley replied. "They'll catch us in there for sure. Like spiderfish in a pen."

"We need more weapons." Hailey limped across the control room toward the front offices that ringed it. The other fugitives followed while Eva covered them.

"Think of something fast! They are closing in!" she shouted over the fray.

"All doors are locked." Rovender pushed his shoulder against a closed door. A spray of SHOC-darts peppered the wall next to him.

"Hold on, blue. Old Hux'll get it." The large alien bounded over and beat the door in. "Nothing here. Next one."

"We could try the front exit of the ward," Hailey said.

"Wrong again." Huxley moved to the next office door.

Rovender added, "There will be more waiting. They are corralling us as it is."

"It doesn't look good. But at least we'll go down fighting," added Huxley.

The office door blew open from the inside, sending the fugitives scattering in all directions. Out of the dusty debris stepped Eva Eight wielding a large ElectroRifle. "There you are, Nine," she said with a smile. "I was starting to worry I'd never see you again after our little tiff."

Eva Nine smiled back as she fired shot after shot at the fast-approaching squad.

"I thought you only had one alien friend." Eight sidled up next to Eva and fired her rifle at a nearby authoriton. Its helmeted head exploded and its body fell to the floor. "It looks like you're liberating every prisoner in here."

"Eight, meet Huxley, Rovee, Nadeau . . . and Hailey." Eva fished around in her pockets while the boomrod charged. She pulled out a vocal transcoder, pilfered from the medlab, and gave it to her sister. "Press the button here and talk into this, then everyone will understand you."

Eight took cover and did as she was told.

"We need to get moving." Huxley pointed at the fast-growing squadron of authoritons. "Any ideas?"

Eight spoke into the transcoder. "There is

a maintenance shaft over here. Let's go!" She directed everyone into the room and toward the hatch. It was held ajar with the remains of a battered autoserver.

Eva Eight scooted into the shaft first and helped Rovender with the weakened Nadeau. Hailey then entered, followed by Eva.

"Oh, no," said Eva as she scrambled through the hatch. "Huxley, you won't be able to fit. We have to try to escape another way." She began to crawl back out.

"Too big? Nonsense!" Huxley laughed, patting his paunch. "Huxie can fit all this beauty into any space that my noggin can fit in." Playfully he pushed Eva back into the shaft. "Now get going!"

Huxley ducked his head in and wriggled his entire body into the shaft. Once in, he began to move through the duct like a giant slithering snake. "Let's move!" he said.

Eva heard the hatch slam shut, and the duct went dark. "They're going to figure out where we are," she called ahead as she crawled on hands and knees. "Where do we go?"

"We are underground, below Attican Hall," Eight replied. "We've got to get up to the ground level."

"We can't go up," said Eva. "They'll expect that."

"Do these shafts go everywhere?" asked Hailey.

"Pretty much," replied Eva. "These are pneumatic ducts for the autoservers that tend to the building. Why?"

"The western hangar is also underground," Hailey said.

"Hangar?" said Eight. "You want to get to the airship hangar? I came across it looking for you, Nine." The lights in the shaft flickered on for a moment. There was a loud whoosh as an autoserver zoomed by in a nearby duct.

"Is that where you brought the *Bijou*?" said Eva.

"Yeah," Hailey said.

Eva was afraid to ask, but it was the only chance they had. "Can you fly us out of here?"

"If I can get to the ship, yes." The pilot looked back over his shoulder in the cramped duct. He looked more like himself with dirt and grime smeared on his face. "I'll get you and your friends out of here, Eva. I promise."

Rovender grumbled loudly.

"You better help us," Eva hissed.

"I will," Hailey replied. "You have my word."

Still looking at Hailey, Eva called out to her sister, "Eight, lead the way."

CHAPTER 20: GERMINATION

Following her sister through the zigzag of pneumatic ducts, Eva tried to keep from panicking. *Cadmus could have an army of authoritons flush us out of these pipes at any moment. Where would we all hide? What would Cadmus do to us?* "Hailey, how is Nadeau holding up?" she whispered. There was a murmur as Hailey spoke with Rovender.

"Rovender says he'll make it," the pilot relayed back to her. "I don't know, though. He's been through a lot."

"That could have been you," retorted Eva.

"Honest, Eva. I had no idea Cadmus was doing crazy stuff like that." He looked at her over his shoulder. "I should have listened to Vanpa. He warned me to steer clear of Cadmus when I dropped you off."

"He warned you?" Eva scuttled forward and punched Hailey in the back of the leg.

"Ow! What the?"

"You knew that all along and you still delivered Rovee and me directly to Cadmus?"

Rovender called back, "Eva, not now. This is neither the time nor the place. We need to focus on getting out of here."

Eva cocked her fist, ready to punch the pilot one more time for good measure, but Hailey stopped her.

"I'm sorry," he said.

"Well, get us all out of this mess and I'll *consider* forgiving you."

"Deal," he replied. "I just want to get to the green

spot. I'd rather take my chances there than die slowly out in the wasteland."

"What's this about the green spot, little bayrie?" asked Huxley.

"You know," Eva said, "the green spot, where the Wandering Forest is . . . and Solas."

"Oh, you're talking about the Germination Zone, where the Vitae Virus generator was dropped," Huxley said.

"The what?"

"The Vitae Virus generator. How do you think King Ojo got this rock breathing again? He didn't use a magic monocorn's horn, I'll tell you that," said Huxley.

"So this generator is what did it?" Eva slowed her crawling, intrigued.

"Yup," Huxley replied. "Old kingy brings his big ship full of us colonists into Orbona's orbit and drops the generator down to the surface. Then he tells us we have to wait . . . How long was it, blue? Do you know?"

"About four trilustralis," Rovender answered from up ahead.

"That's it. *Four* trilustralis for that clunker to get working," Huxley said with a chuckle. "But work it did, and here we are. Little did we know there'd be natives who were none too happy about it."

"I'm sorry about that," said Eva. "I am not like Cadmus or his people."

"I see that, little bayrie. You don't need to explain."

"We're here!" Eva Eight's whisper reverberated through the duct. "I kept a wedge in the door, just in case." She pointed to the severed head of an autoserver, which held the hatch door ajar.

A series of ducts intersected at the maintenance hatch, allowing Eva and the others to huddle close and get a view of the vast underground hangar.

"This is it." Hailey spoke in a hushed tone. "The *Bijou* should be over there somewhere." He pointed past a fleet of gigantic polished airships parked in perfect rows. All around them crewmen and robots worked on the ships at a hectic pace. Sparks fell from giant welders as rounded gunner stations were attached to outer hulls, while cases of ammunition were loaded into cargo holds.

Gigantic gunmetal robots, almost as tall as the aircraft, strode into the hangar on thick gear-jointed legs. Their glowing orb eyes and downturned radiator grills gave them a gaunt skull-shaped countenance. A crewman directed the robots to different airships. As the robots approached the designated ships, they retracted their legs into their bodies and rolled on board.

"Those are the robots we saw at the plant, Eight," Eva said.

"And those are giant luxury transcarriers," Hailey added. "Boy, are they impressive. Look at the size of those engines!"

"But they don't usually have weapons on them," said Eight.

"That's because they are being outfitted for battle," Huxley replied in a grim tone.

Rovender grumbled, "This is not a good sight to see."

"I told you, Nine," Eva Eight said. "Cadmus is not to be trusted. He is rationing energy to build these warbots."

Eva thought about the vision on the Divination Machine. She thought about the ancient ruins and wondered what had become of Earth.

And so one society flourishes as another one perishes, Arius had said.

"Cadmus is going to invade Solas," Eva said. It seemed a horrible thought, an unbelievable thought, and yet there was no other explanation.

Quietly everyone watched as the humans and robots prepared the fleet of airships for war.

"Do you think you can get to the *Bijou*, Hailey?" Eva asked.

"I think so," he replied. "But I don't know how we are going to get a bunch of aliens through this hangar without Cadmus's entire army coming down on us."

"We'll figure something out," Eva said.

"What about once we are on board? Can you fly us out of here?" asked Rovender.

"If the hanger doors remain open, yes. I can fly through the narrowest ravine without getting a scratch," Hailey replied with a proud smile.

"How about with weapons firing at you?" Rovender said. "They have likely been alerted to our escape and will be expecting this."

"Rovee's right," said Eva. She ducked as a trio of crewman walked by and began to load crates onto the flat forks of a battered yellow robolift.

"None of these other ships look like they are airworthy yet," replied Hailey. "If we can get to the *Bijou*, I can get us out."

"What about the parts you needed so badly?" Eva asked.

"Hopefully they've fixed the *Bijou*," said Hailey. "After all, I don't think they were expecting me to come and steal her back."

"Okay." Eva charged the boomrod and aimed it at the three nearby crewmen. "I think I can get us onto the ship."

"Hold on. Don't charge it too much." Huxley turned a dial on the boomrod's charger pack. "You just need a quiet little wallop to knock 'em out."

CHAPTER 21: PRIME ADVISER

Hailey dragged the third unconscious crewman over to the hatch, where the others pulled him into the duct.

"Hurry up!" Eva whispered as she watched Hailey pull off his lab coat and don a crewman's drab coverall and cap. He ran to join Eva and her sister, already in disguise.

"Eva Eight and I will empty these," Eva said, depressing the open button on one of the ply-steel crates. The lid popped open. Inside were rounds of SHOCdarts, much larger than the sort the authoritons used. "Can you operate this lift, Hailey?"

"It shouldn't be too hard." Hailey stepped onto the dented hull of the robolift. He climbed up to a simple seat with controls set on a short tower overlooking the lift's rounded base. This base held an array of robotic arms and forks to heave and haul any load. The robolift lurched forward, then spun around uncontrollably, nearly toppling a towering stack of crates.

"Hailey!" Eva finished emptying her crate.

"Sorry, sorry," Hailey called down to her. "I got this. I'm good."

"You'd better," replied Eva. "Eight, help Nadeau into this crate here."

In moments Rovender and Huxley snuck out from their hiding place and climbed into their crates. With the robolift's arms Hailey hoisted and stacked them onto the forks of the lift and turned the vehicle toward the main hangar. "Climb onto the back," he called down to Eva, pointing at rungs affixed to the hull of the robolift. "The lift knows where the *Bijou* is and will take us there."

Eva and her sister climbed up, and the robolift entered the stream of bustling traffic in the open hanger. Traveling down the aisles, Eva looked up at the colossal warships. Their immense bulk blotted out the overhead lights as the lift passed underneath them. The polished ships were adorned with angry eyes and jagged teeth, making them appear even more foreboding up close. *Solas won't stand a chance against this,* Eva thought.

"Psst!" Hailey called down. Eva looked up and saw that he was pointing toward the far end of the hangar. There she could see a densely packed fleet of cargo ships all similar in size to the *Bijou.* The robolift carried them toward the airships, passing a knot of people and robots gathered around none other than Cadmus Pryde himself. Eva turned away, concealing her face, as the robolift rolled in front of Cadmus.

In the back row of the fleet sat a familiar battered ship. As the lift neared, the *Bijou* beeped and the entry ramp opened from its belly. Hailey took over the controls of the robolift and carefully unloaded the crates with the aliens in them. Eva turned back toward Cadmus and his gathering.

"Nine? Is everything okay?" Eva Eight lined up a crate on the ramp. The floor of the ramp began to move, like a conveyor belt, carrying the crate into the cargo bay.

"Yeah, I just want to see something. . . ." Eva peered through the docked ships at the throng out in front of the open hangar door. People and robots were leaving as if being dismissed. She could now see Cadmus clearly. He was standing with his back against a stack of crates conversing with a floating being.

It was an alien. The only alien Eva had seen in all of New Attica that wasn't being held in a cell or experimented on.

"I'll be right back!" Eva scurried through the airships toward Cadmus and the alien. Its shape and form looked just like Arius and Zin.

She rounded the duo and approached the stacks of crates behind them. Eva nodded at another crewman and opened one of the crates. From the other side of the stack, she could hear Cadmus's conversation.

". . . even if we don't retrieve her, I am certain of what I saw, Prime Adviser," he said to the alien.

Prime Adviser?

"A circle within a circle?" the Prime Adviser asked. His voice sounded like two voices saying the same thing at the same time.

"Yes," Cadmus said. "Set into her skin as if it were a birthmark."

"And the Omnipod's memories?"

"Shows that she went through the green spot to get to Solas. It was this clip recorded in Lacus that, I believe, has what you are looking for," Cadmus said.

Eva peeked through the cracks between the crates and saw Cadmus holding her Omnipod. A cinematographic hologram of Lacus appeared—the one taken by Eva the morning she was captured by Besteel. From the Omnipod's speakers she heard a familiar singsong voice. "Human child. Eva the Ninth. Nine Evas. The child human."

"That's it!" the adviser exclaimed, waving his stumpy arms. "Our first stop is Lacus. We shall start there."

Lacus? Eva thought. *What do they need in Lacus?*

"Hey! Who ordered you to open this cargo?" A crewman approached, pointing directly at Eva. "These are supposed to be sealed and loaded." As he neared, it was apparent that he was puzzled by Eva's small stature. "I'm speaking to you. Please identify yourself immediately."

"Sheesa!" Eva jumped up onto the stack of crates. On the other side the Prime Adviser rose. Eva gasped, realizing that the adviser was not like Arius or Zin, after all. The creature that faced Eva looked like a piece of rotten fruit as it glared at her with *two* pairs of slit eyes. Over a dozen of his short arms reached out to her, like an anemone trying to grab its prey.

"It's her!" the Prime Adviser said, though his mouth did not move.

"Capture her NOW!" Cadmus said. "I want her alive!"

Eva scrambled to the summit of the towering mountain of crates. As she was clambering up, her foot banged against the controls of a crate, and the top opened. It was another crate full of ammunition. A trio of nearby authoritons rolled close and took aim. With extreme effort Eva shoved the open crate off the top of the stack. It crashed down upon one of the authoritons, crushing it and sending a volley of giant SHOCdarts off in every direction.

Eva leaped toward the next stack of crates while darts shot up from below. She recognized the whine of an airship's engines rising in pitch. There was little doubt in Eva's mind for whom the ship was coming.

"Little creature, your past will serve my future. You will belong to me," two voices said behind her. As Eva jumped from one peak to another, she glanced at the Prime Adviser rushing behind her. The shreds of his dark tattered cloak flapped about like the wings of an ominous black bird. In moments he would be upon her.

The engine of the airship rose to a deafening

level as it closed in. The blast of its exhaust sent the Prime Adviser spiraling off Eva's trail. She scuttled to the topmost crate and took in her situation.

There was nowhere else to go.

On the ground below, swarms of authoritons encircled her while the Prime Adviser rose back up toward her. Above, the hovering airship lowered its ramp, revealing more armed authoritons. "You are surrounded, Eva Nine," the pilot's amplified voice broadcast over the loud engines. "Please surrender immediately or—"

A second airship rammed the first, sending it sideways into one of the docked warships. The battered *Bijou* swung around toward Eva, deflecting a flurry of SHOCdarts from below. The entry ramp lowered and Rovender Kitt stood there, holding out his hand. "Jump!" he cried.

Eva hurled her body toward the ship. She flopped onto the ramp hard, knocking the wind out of herself.

"Go! Go! GO!" Rovender yelled.

The ship jolted forward at amazing speed, sending Eva tumbling backward over the edge of the ramp. She grasped the ramp's edge tightly as her body dangled below. SHOCdarts fired up all around her from the authoritons down on the ground. Rovender flopped down next to the edge and seized Eva. He pulled her up and into the *Bijou* as the ship rocketed through the closing hangar doors.

Bright sunlight beamed into the cockpit window as the airship zoomed upward toward the cloud cover.

"Is she okay, Rovender?" Hailey turned from the controls, which included a diagnostic diagram of the ship, as the *Bijou* flew into billowy dense clouds.

Eva rushed up and punched the pilot in the shoulder as hard as she could.

"Agh! What the? Again with the hitting?" Hailey spun around and held his hands up in defense.

"That's for selling us off for parts. I could have died back there, you jerk! We all could have!" Eva spat. "Why didn't you tell us the truth?"

"I told you I was sorry." Hailey grabbed the controls while the ship rumbled through some turbulence. "Look, they almost lobotomized me, too. I didn't know what they were doing. You guys wanted to go to the city. I took you. It's as simple as that."

"But you left me there, alone. I thought we were friends."

"Friends?" Hailey put the ship on automatic pilot and turned from the controls toward Eva.

"What did you want me to do? Hold your hand through all of New Attica?"

Eva clenched her fist, ready to strike again.

"It is okay, Eva. You are safe now." Rovender put his arm around her. "We all are."

"Look, I wanted to help Vanpa and his friends. They're like family to me. I'd do anything for them. I wanted to change my life. Cadmus said he could *help.*" The pilot spoke softly. "It all happened so fast that I just didn't think it all through. Especially how it would affect you or Rovender . . . I didn't think at all."

Eva relaxed her fist, remaining quiet. The truth was she understood Hailey's motivation. But Eva had been so eager to get into the city that she had disregarded the pilot's odd behavior and the warning that Van Turner had given. *Don't let 'em rewire all your thinking.*

"Nine, I'm sorry you had to learn the truth the hard way, but I wouldn't have found you if you hadn't come." Eva Eight stroked Eva's hair.

"And who would have rescued ol' Huxie? Not blue here. He was bottled up like me," Huxley added with a grin.

"You're . . . right," Eva said. Her bright green eyes pierced Hailey.

"Are we all good now, Eva? Just tell me where you guys need to go, and I'll take you there," the pilot said.

"We need to get to Solas immediately and warn the queen," said Huxley.

"No," Eva said. "We need to head to Lacus. That's where they are planning to attack first."

"Lacus?" Rovender's face was one of confusion. "Why?"

"They need Arius, the soothsayer, for some reason," said Eva. "There was another like her and Zin working with Cadmus." Eva wondered if Arius could see her own future. Zin had said his other sister was dead. Was there another like them on Orbona?

"Where is Lacus? What will we do when we get there?" Eva Eight asked.

"Hostia . . . Fiscian . . . Zoozi," Rovender whispered.

"It's a little fishing colony," Huxley said. "They've no arsenal there, little bayrie. We'd be better off going to Solas to let the queen handle this."

"No. Lacus first," Eva said. "We need to warn the Halcyonus and Arius."

"Okay. Lacus it is," Hailey said. "Someone just tell me how to get there."

"Head toward the big lake east of the green spot, hero," Huxley said. "And I'll guide you from there."

CHAPTER 22: GIFT

"I'm still not sure why Cadmus would want to visit the soothsayer before he invades Solas," Rovender said. He was helping Nadeau into a cot on the cabin deck of the ship.

"Perhaps to find out the future? To see if he will successfully take over?" Eva said. She handed a bottle of water to her sister sitting next to her on the opposite bunk.

"But why? What have any of the 'newcomers' done to his people?" Rovender said. "Look at what he does to us. What he does to his own kind."

"I don't know why, Rovee." Eva put her head in her hands. "But even his fortune-telling machine showed me a vision—"

"Of a human city set next to a large lake." Eva Eight finished the thought. "Every citizen of New Attica has seen that vision since they were children. That's how he's preparing his people to support his actions. They are accustomed to it already and don't even know it."

"But a city by a lake," Huxley said. "It could be anywhere. We've encountered a number of lovely lakes while charting the terrain as the Royal Beamguide crew. There are many that look just like Lake Concors."

"No." Eva looked up at Huxley. "It was Solas. I know that lake . . . and Queen Ojo's castle was sitting at the bottom of it."

"Well, he could certainly expand his little kingdom if he had plenty of fresh water and fertile land. The desert he's in now has him confined for sure," Eight said.

"Agreed," Rovender said. "I don't know how Hailey's people have survived so long on the outside."

Eva remembered Cadmus's words. *It pains me to see my people be forced to remain in this small space unable to enjoy our Earth's many splendors. But all of this will soon be remedied.*

"That's it!" Eva sat up as she put the pieces together. "Huxley, you said there was a machine that created the green spot."

"That's right, the Vitae Virus generator," Huxley said.

"If Cadmus were to get his hands on that . . . ," Eva said.

"Then he'd control the natural resources," said Rovender.

"Well, he isn't going to find it in Solas, I'll tell you that much!" Huxley rose to his full height. "And why would Queenie hand it over to him anyway?"

"She won't," Eva said. "He'll just take it."

"And enslave us," Nadeau whispered.

"And us, too," Eva Eight added.

Everyone was quiet for a moment. Eva listened to Nadeau's shallow breathing in the cot opposite her. *How could Cadmus do this?* She looked at the Cærulean. *The Cadmus that created the Tech that brought me into the world can't be the same Cadmus who's in charge now. Do people change when they get older? Will I change when I am older? I don't want to.* The more Eva thought about it, the more confused she became. She felt dizzy.

"I've got to get some more water." She went down to the galley. Eva was filling her bottle from the ship's dispenser when the cockpit door slid open. Hailey walked into the galley.

"Eva—," he started.

"Don't." She cut him off. "The only reason you are even here is because you are the only one who can fly this ship."

"I know you're upset, but . . . well . . . It's hard to explain." Hailey let out a frustrated sigh. "Have you ever felt trapped? Like you couldn't escape your reality no matter how hard you tried?"

Eva snorted. "Try growing up in an underground bunker for twelve years. That's all I thought about."

Rovender entered the galley. "Nadeau needs more water."

"Wait, Rovee . . . Rovender," Hailey said, pulling something from his pocket. "I wanted to give you guys these." He handed him the blue painted decal from the nose of the ship. To Eva he gave the unpainted cutout of the human. "I wanted to be a retriever, just like my dad. But you both are more than stickers, and I know my dad would never have delivered his passengers to a dangerous place."

Rovender gave his decal to Eva and took the water bottle from her. Without a word he returned to the cabin.

"I trusted you." Eva looked Hailey in the eyes. "I will *never* trust you again." She placed the decals on the table.

Hailey looked more struck by Eva's words than by the punches she had given him. "Fair enough," he whispered, and returned to the cockpit.

Eva tried to rest in her bunk, but her mind could not stop replaying the events from the past couple of days. She could not stop thinking about the possible outbreak of war between the humans and the aliens.

Suddenly the *Bijou* pitched sharply. Everyone tumbled to one side of the cabin.

"What was that?" Eva asked. A look of alarm drew over her face.

There was a rumble from somewhere deep within the ship, and the craft rolled steeply in the opposite direction. A sharp pelting sound pummeled at the roof of the cabin. The door console exploded in a spray of sparks, sending everyone for cover.

"Are we under fire?" Huxley asked, crawling out from under a cot.

"Eva! Rovender! Get down here!" Hailey's voice crackled over the intercom. "We've got trouble."

The group scrambled into the cockpit. Eva held on to the doorway as the ship shuddered and swayed. A dark ominous cloud filled the cockpit windshield, giving the impression of night.

"A storm?" Eight asked.

"No," Hailey replied. "Worse."

From within the cloud a spray of bullets fired toward the cockpit.

"Hold on!" Hailey said, and pushed the ship into a steep dive. Eva could feel her stomach rise into her throat as the gray landscape below drew closer and closer. Hailey leveled the ship and then veered it sharply to the starboard side.

"Look!" Eight pointed above them.

The dark cloud was not a storm at all but a monstrous airship. An airship outfitted for war.

"Cadmus," Eva whispered.

"Yeah," Hailey replied. "I didn't think any of those ships back at the hangar could catch us, but he may have had a few deployed already."

"A few?" Huxley asked in a surprised tone.

"Yup." Hailey pointed to a radar image on his instrument panel. Several large dots pulsed in a cluster closing in on the *Bijou*. Bullets rained down on the hull of the ship, cracking the windshield. "This is not good," said the pilot.

Eva felt numb. Cold. Useless. From the window of a ship that she couldn't fly, she watched her pursuers close in. At least with Besteel she'd been on the ground. "Can't you get us out of here?" she asked.

"I'm trying!" Hailey gritted his teeth and sent the *Bijou* into an impossible climb straight for the clouds.

"They're gaining on us!" Eight said, clutching the back of the pilot's chair.

"This is a compact transcarrier." Hailey rolled the ship to avoid more fire. "It's not designed for this sort of flying."

"We have to get onto the ground!" Eva fought to stand while gravity tugged at her.

"We're flying over the Northern Wastelands, by the looks of it," Huxley said, grabbing on to the cockpit walls as the ship banked hard. "If we land here, we'll be sitting turnfins for sure."

A loud *BOOM* erupted from the side of the ship, and alarms pinged on the cockpit dash. The *Bijou* began to spin madly, out of control, and the passengers tumbled to the floor of the cockpit. Eva's head swam as the spinning became faster and faster. Eva Eight's hand clutched Eva's tightly.

This is it, Eva thought. *We are going to crash and I am going to die.*

Muthr.

The ship came out of the spin and hit the ground, then blasted over a valley of sand and rock before returning to the sky. Eva wiped her face, but her clammy shaking hands did little to dry the perspiration that coated her. Nausea crept up her throat and tried to squirm its way out.

"They foam-bombed the topside hover-thrusters near the stern," Hailey said.

"You've lost thirty percent maneuverability," the dashboard reported in a calm tone.

"Can we clear the thrusters somehow?" Huxley asked.

"Not without docking, no," Hailey replied, looking up. The shadow of a warship engulfed them. "They are trying to force us to land. Grab on to something!"

The *Bijou* tore away from its current course and came up the side from under the gigantic warship. Bullets battered its hull as Hailey pushed the ship to its limits. Once more he steered it upward toward the clouds.

Eva glimpsed a large bay door opening on the warship. "What is that?" She pointed at a trio of cones rising out of the hatch.

"I don't know," Hailey said, struggling with the controls. "Missiles of some kind."

"My guess is they're trackers that home in on our heat signature," said Huxley, grim. "They're done messing around."

"They will take out our engines," added Hailey.

"Not if I can help it." Huxley jumped to the ladder that led down into the cargo hold. "Come on, little bayrie," he called up. "I'll need a hand."

"What are we doing?" Eva asked as she climbed down.

Huxley unstrapped Besteel's glider from its mount in the hold. With ease he lifted the glider and set it on the entry ramp.

"Get that ramp open. And quick!" Huxley hopped onto the glider and fired up the engines.

"What are you going to do?" Eva asked. Anxiety trembled through her.

"I'm gonna draw those missiles away from the ship."

"No!"

"Aw, don't you worry about ol' Huxie." He smiled at her. "I've gotten out of worse scrapes."

"We've got trackers!" Hailey called over the intercom. "Whatever you're gonna do, do it quick!"

"Open it!" Huxley said.

Eva activated the ramp. Her ears popped as the air was sucked from the hold. Outside, three fiery stars approached from below.

"I wonder," said Huxley, "do you think ol' Queenie will have songs written about my bravery?"

Eva didn't know what to say. She rushed up and hugged the alien.

"Don't change," Huxley said with a smile, and rocketed out of the *Bijou* toward the missiles. As he neared them, he twirled the glider and dropped down. The missiles changed their course and followed him.

As the ramp closed, Eva could see the glider heading straight toward the warship.

Straight toward its engines.

Eva wiped her eyes with her sleeve as the warship exploded.

Good-bye, Huxley.

A blue hand patted Eva's shoulder. "Come on," Rovender said in a soft voice. "We've got to go."

As they climbed up to the cockpit, Eva could see that they were once more in the cover of the clouds. In the cockpit Hailey tapped a few buttons on the dash and took Eva by the hand. "Okay. Let's move!"

"Where is everyone?" Eva asked, following the

pilot up to the cabin level. More bullets peppered the ship below them.

Hailey led Eva and Rovender to the back of the crew's quarters to where a portal was now open. Inside a cramped life capsule sat Eva Eight and Nadeau. Rovender climbed in and joined them. "Get in. Hurry!" Hailey pushed Eva inside. "There is a week's worth of water and enough pills to last a month."

Eva sat down and strapped herself in. She realized there was no more room inside the tiny capsule. "Wait!" Eva said. "Hailey, where are you going to sit?" The *Bijou* trembled, and an alarm rang throughout the cabin.

Hailey remained on his ship and punched a code on a keypad. A timer in the capsule began to count down.

"Get in, Hailey!" Eva said. "What are you doing?"

"I'm giving you your birthday present," he said with a forced smile. The airlock slid shut, and the life capsule jettisoned away from the *Bijou*.

Eva Nine pressed against the small portal as the capsule plummeted toward the ground below. Far above, the *Bijou*, now smoking from its sides, emerged from the clouds and flew away in the opposite direction. Behind it two massive warships gave chase.

Small hover-thrusters on the capsule fired, slowing the descent.

"I can't believe he did that," Eva Eight whispered.

Eva watched as the airship and its pilot disappeared on the horizon. "I will still never trust you, Hailey Turner," she said.

"I think we can from now on," Rovender replied. In a cloud of dust the life capsule touched down on the sandy plain below.

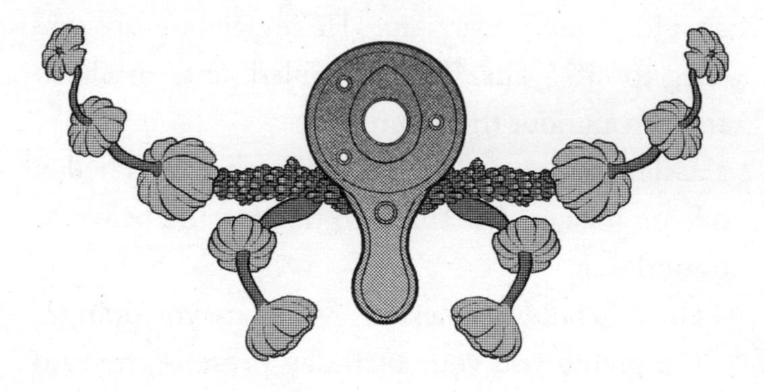

End of

PART II

PART III

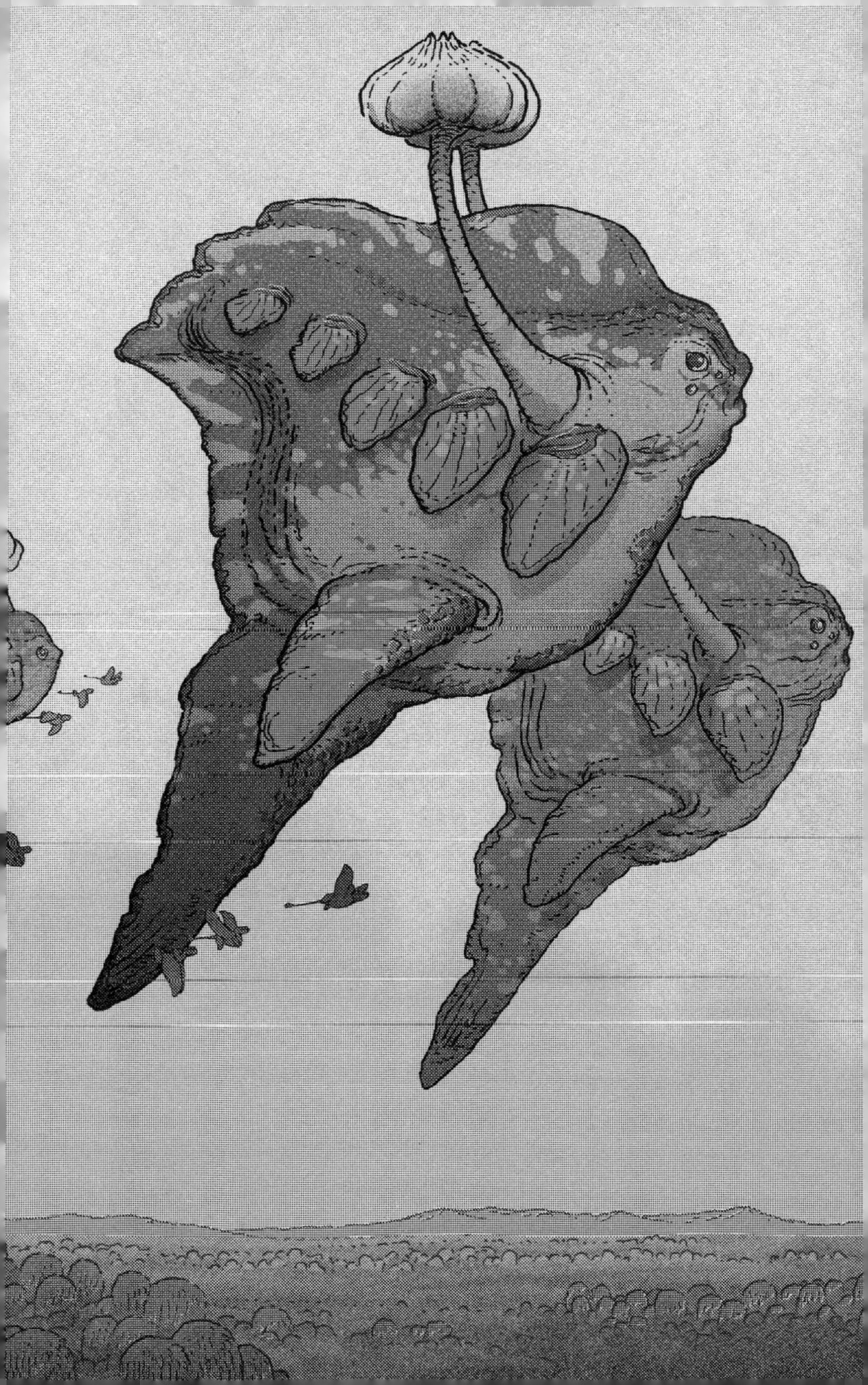

CHAPTER 23: CLAN

Eva Nine kicked open the hatch of the life capsule. She stepped out onto a vast dusty plain and helped everyone debark.

"Are you okay?" Rovender asked, supporting Nadeau.

Eva stared up at the hazy sky. Where the *Bijou* had once been, there was now only smoke and vapor trails crisscrossing the low clouds. "Yeah," she said. "I'll be okay."

"Good. Now we must hurry," Rovender said. Eva could hear Nadeau's shallow rasping breath as he clutched Rovender tightly. Together the two Cæruleans staggered away from the capsule. "We are out in the open, and you know what that means,

Eva Nine," Rovender said over his shoulder.

"Sand-snipers," said Eva, pulling out a bag of supplies.

"Sand-snipe? What's a sand-snipe?" Eight asked, grabbing a first aid kit.

"You don't want to find out," replied Eva. "So the sooner we get out of here, the better." She rummaged through loose supplies that had spilled out onto the floor of the life capsule. She threw everything she could grab into the supply bag.

"There are no Omnipods. That's just great!" Eight exclaimed.

"We don't need one," Eva said as she strapped the supply bag onto her shoulders. "Come on. Let's go."

"Hold on, Nine." Eight pointed to a pinging light on the life capsule's instrument panel. "Don't you think we should stay here? In case Hailey returns for us?"

"He's not returning," Eva said, and set off. "We are on our own now."

"There is shelter this way," Rovender called back. He was already far ahead with Nadeau, hiking across the wide plain toward a distant stand of wandering trees.

Eva was thankful to be on the ground and under actual overcast skies once more. Sitting cross-legged against the trunk of a large wandering tree, she closed her eyes and inhaled the cool earthy air. New Attica and Cadmus's plan felt like they were a million meters away from here.

"Here's an extra utilitunic if you want one." Eva Eight tossed the garment to her. "I don't think these coveralls have climatefiber. It feels like it may get cold out here."

Eva changed her clothes, comforted by the familiar feel of the utilitunic. She deactivated all of the life monitoring patches and discovered a rainbow-hued strip along the breast pocket. "My old tunic didn't have this. What does this do?" she asked Eight.

"Touch it."

Eva touched the strip, and her tunic changed from its usual buff tone to a bluish green. "Oh, it changes color. Like my Emote-Attire."

"Not exactly," Eight said. Her tunic was a midnight blue. "It's thermotinted climatefiber. According to the tag the fabric color shifts to maximize use of the outside temperature."

"That's rocket," said Eva, watching her sleeves tinge olive.

"Nice, huh?" Eight smiled. She resumed sorting through the supplies they had brought from the life capsule. Rovender knelt down and joined her.

A low animal call sounded out across the plain.

"Oeeah! Look!" Rovender pointed upward.

A pod of gigantic air-whales, each buoyed by large air sacs, drifted overhead. At once the whales sang out in a chorus that rang out across the afternoon sky.

"Whoa." Eight moved closer to Eva. "They won't eat us, will they?"

Rovender chuckled. "No, Eva Eight. They will not."

"They feed on knifejacks, don't they, Rovee?" Eva said.

"Yes," Rovender replied. "Among other things. I've seen them congregate around the spore farms near Solas."

"They are heading south," Nadeau whispered. "Where they will spawn."

Eva grabbed a tube of SpeedHeal ointment and approached the weakened Cærulean. He was lying in the cuplike leaves of the wandering tree, which held him like a cradle. Eva dabbed the ointment onto his lesions, then took a blanket from the supply pile and covered him. As she did so, he clutched her arm.

"See how they remain close, as a unit?" He

pointed to the pod. The air-whales soared high above, their multiple air-fins flapping in a slow rhythm.

Eva nodded.

"It is because they are happier when they are together. They are safe. They are strong."

"I understand." Eva patted Nadeau. "And we will get you to your village soon so that you may become strong once more."

"My time here is almost done, Eva. Soon I will become one with Orbona."

"We will find a way to heal you." Eva noticed dark blood vessels pulsing under his cheek. She realized they were not veins at all but thin wires.

"It is as it is," Nadeau replied, and coughed. "I have been freed by the very kind that would cause me harm. Even at the end of my journey, I still learn." A frail smile crept across his pasty face, and he closed his eyes.

"Let him rest," Rovender said. "He has obviously been through a lot."

"What can we do?" Eva asked.

Rovender led her around the tree and out of Nadeau's earshot. "By the look of him, I'd say he has but a couple of days before his spirit leaves his body."

Eva said nothing. She didn't know Nadeau very

well, but she didn't want to see him die. She didn't want to see anybody else die.

Rovender gazed out at the horizon. "I am guessing we are somewhere out in the Northern Wastelands."

"Yes," Eva said. "Hux . . . Huxley said we were." She tried to erase from her mind the memory of brave Huxley flying into those missiles, but the moment would not leave.

"If that's the case," Rovender said, hoisting himself up onto a branch of the wandering tree, "then we are on the outskirts of the Wandering Forest . . . and perhaps . . ." He continued climbing.

"What? What is it?" Eva climbed up after him. They both arrived at the topmost bough of the tree. From there Eva could see the vast wasteland spread out before her. It was different from the desert that surrounded the ancient ruins. The dust-covered plain was sprinkled with scattered boulders. Far in the distance large round monoliths rose from the flat horizon, creating a stony forest.

Rovender pointed toward the formations. "I recognize those standing stones. My clan's village, Faunas, is four or five days on the other side of them if we travel by foot. We should set off at once."

"But Nadeau can't make that. You said he won't . . . live that long." Eva felt the climatefiber tighten as a chill wind whipped past.

"Perhaps we can construct a stretcher of some sort so that he may rest. We can take turns carrying him, but we'll have to move day and night." Rovender began to climb down. Throughout the canopy the tree limbs creaked in the building breeze.

"There's got to be another way," Eva said as she followed him down. They joined Eva Eight, who had finished organizing their supplies.

"Well, our boy Hailey was right, Nine," Eight said. "We've got a handful of hydration tablets, two hydration kits, and a full canister of nutriment tablets. Though, everything looks old."

"Is there anything else we can give to Nadeau?" Eva asked.

"Nothing that will undo what Cadmus has done to him," Eight said, furrowing her brow. "I wish I could strap *Cadmus* down and shove wires into *his* brain."

"Rovender says their village is not far from here," said Eva. "We are going to take Nadeau home."

"A good plan, Nine, but I don't know if he's going to make it," Eight said.

Rovender looked over the sorted supplies. "Is there anything here that we can use to construct a stretcher for transporting him?"

"Maybe the crewman's coveralls that we were

wearing," Eight replied. "But we'll need something for supports."

"Hmmm, like a pair of big sticks," Rovender said, scanning the immediate area. Eva could see that there were no sticks anywhere. "This is not good," he said. "They confiscated all of my belongings back in the city. I don't even have my walking stick." Frustration rose in his voice.

"What if we cut some branches from one of these trees?" Eight asked. "They're thick, but maybe we can split them."

Eva looked up at the giant tree. Branches swayed and squeaked in the wind as if they were dancing slowly together. She remembered the first time she rode in a wandering tree and how it had carried her far from her Sanctuary.

"I have an idea," she said.

"On how to remove some branches?" Eight asked.

"No." Eva started throwing the supplies into the cup-shaped leaves of the tree.

"What are you doing?" Eight asked.

"Eva Nine?" Rovender approached her.

"Just help me get all the stuff picked up and climb on," she said.

Eva put her palms flat on the tree. She closed

her eyes and let her fingers slide into the grooved patterns in the bark. *We have someone with us who is dying—someone whose spirit is ready to leave this world,* she thought to the tree. *But he wants to be with his clan. With his forest. Will you take us?*

She opened her eyes and looked up. The topmost boughs played with the breeze, making high-pitched grating sounds. It reminded Eva of the air-whales' song.

"Well?" Rovender climbed up to his perch.

"What are you doing?" Eight remained on the ground, a look of bewilderment on her face.

The roots of the tree began to finger their way out from under its thick base. One by one they clutched the sand and rock, scooting the tree ahead ever so slightly.

"Get on!" Eva climbed up into the tree.

Eva Eight's eyes grew wide as the wandering tree lurched forward. With Rovender's help she pulled herself up onto a branch.

"Well done, Eva Nine. Well done!" Rovender said.

"How? How did you do that?" asked Eight.

Eva smiled. "I asked it. Nicely."

CHAPTER 24: FLOATERS

Dusk stained the landscape a deep violet as the wandering tree carried its riders toward the stony monoliths. The travel had been peaceful enough for Eva and her sister to rest in the cupped leaves while Rovender stood watch on the topmost bough. It was Rovender who woke Eva in a soft voice. "Eva Nine, wake up. We have stopped."

Eva sat up and rubbed her eyes. The setting of the sun had brought a drop in the temperature. She could feel the chilled fingers of the approaching night prick at her cheeks. "Where are we?" she asked.

"We have crossed the plain from where we landed and are about to enter the Valley of Standing Stones. But I fear the tree will go no farther."

Eva peered out into the dusky light. Hundreds of egg-shaped monoliths stood silently all around them. Their tops, higher than the wandering tree, were sheathed in thick moss. Eva reached out to the nearest stone and felt the damp hanging clumps of green before climbing down the tree to the gravel below.

"Activating lumen-wear," her tunic said. The cuffs and seams of her clothing began to glow brightly. Surprised and delighted at this newfound feature, Eva stopped to adjust the controls for the lights.

The tree's roots grasped at the ground near the closest monolith. Examining this curious action closer, Eva watched the wandering tree submerge its root tips into the pool of water at the base of the stone. *You need a break, huh?* She patted the trunk of the tree. *Thank you for taking us.*

"It's just taking a break and drinking," she called up to Rovender.

"Who is?" Eva Eight popped up from her leafy perch.

"The tree," Rovender said as he shimmied down the trunk past Eva's sister.

"Oh, right. The walking tree. Of course." Eight lay back down and pulled her blanket over her head.

"I'd like a drink of usquebaugh myself," Rovender mumbled. He hopped down to check on Nadeau resting on one of the lower boughs. "Will it continue onward?"

"I think so," Eva said, taking in her surroundings. "Though I don't know how thirsty it is. We may be here for a little while."

"And it looks like it may have trouble walking through all these rocks up ahead," Rovender said. Eva helped him tuck the blankets tightly around a sleeping Nadeau.

"We should climb up and see if there is a clear path," she said.

Together they climbed back up to the top bough, where Rovender had stood lookout. The lanky alien grabbed a small lantern from the supply bag and clipped it to his jacket.

"I wonder . . . ," he said, eyeing the stone they were closest to. "I wonder if there may be some food to be found up there."

"Let's have a look." Eva stepped to the edge of the leafy platform on the tree and grabbed a handful of the thick moss hanging from the rock. Hand over hand she pulled herself up to the round summit. Rovender quickly joined her. He pulled up a sprig of the moss and smelled it.

"There are turnfins that roost here frequently," he said. "We may be able to catch one."

"Any fruits or vegetables?" Eva scanned the overgrown surface of the stone. Long tubes ending in tufted tips sprang up in gathered clumps.

"None that we can eat." Rovender examined one of the tubes. "However, there seem to be other animals living up here."

Eva touched one of the tufts, and it quickly withdrew into its tube. A nearby tuft hooted and the entire cluster retreated into their pipe homes. "So you've been to this valley before?" she asked.

"Once, when I was young," Rovender said. "Others in my village have explored it more than I."

"What's it like?" Eva asked. "Your village?"

"It is a village of my people, just as your human city was," replied Rovender. He continued searching through the growth. "Tell me, Eva, was it everything you thought it would be?"

"I dunno." She wriggled her finger down one of the tube-creature's homes. "There were things I did like about it."

"Such as?"

"Well, the buildings were beautiful to look at, just like all the people. And there was this aviary full of living birds from long ago. You would have loved—" Eva quickly remembered why Rovender hadn't been there with her to experience it. She stifled a shudder. "But despite all of that, it didn't feel . . . right."

Rovender stopped foraging and looked over at her.

"Of course this was *before* I knew about Cadmus," she said quickly. "Everyone there was so happy, so content, but I felt . . . I felt . . ." It hurt Eva to admit that Rovender had been correct from the start. The words came tumbling out: "I felt like I didn't fit in. And it wasn't just the way I looked, Rovee, even after I got my new clothes. It was the way I thought. It was the way I thought about the whole world, not just what was going on in New Attica. . . . I don't know."

Rovender put his arm around the girl. "I *do* know, Eva. I do. Some things we must learn through experience. That is how one truly lives. It was important for you to visit the village of your people to gain understanding from them and within yourself. So it has been the same for me."

In the shadows of the tube-flowers there was a rustle.

"What is that?" By simply pointing, Eva directed the light from her cuff toward something small hovering just above the moss. The light beam fell upon it, revealing what appeared to be the upturned husk of a dried flower head, its wilted petals undulating below it. The top end of this husk opened, and a pair of clawed paws and a head poked out. The face was adorned with feathery feelers and two beady eyes shining brightly in the night. The diminutive creature chirped and drifted closer to Eva.

"That's just a floatazoan, or a floater," Rovender said. "You can't eat them. They taste of eukaberries, their primary food source."

"Aw, it's so cute!" Eva knelt down to the floatazoan. "Can't we keep it?"

"I don't think you want to, Eva. They—"

"Ow!" Eva rubbed her cheek. Sticky apricot-colored pulp adhered to her fingertips. "Something hit me in the face, and it smells *horrible*. Ew!"

"Eukaberry," Rovender said. "Floaters are very territorial, and have great aim." He rushed at the creature and waved his arms about madly. The floatazoan chirruped and retreated into the

shadows. "A loner like this will scare off easily. Let's hope there's not a colony."

Thunder growled across the horizon. Lightning pulsed through the sky, its bright electric veins muted by the clouds.

"A storm?" Eva watched the lights.

"It looks to be," Rovender replied. "Yet I smell no rain, nor feel the rushing breath of wind." He studied the sky for a moment. "Perhaps this is a storm of a different kind."

"Hey, you two," Eva Eight called from Rovender's lookout atop the tree. Her glowing sleeves left lighted tracers as she waved. "Find anything?"

"We are watching the storm." Eva pointed up.

Eight peered up at the clouds as the thunder continued. Far off in the distance, from the direction that they had come, a star dropped from the sky.

"Do you see it?" asked Eva.

"Yes, yes, yes. I see," Rovender said.

The star slowed, then disappeared on the horizon.

"What is that?" Eva Eight asked. "Could it be Hailey?"

"Would he come back for us?" Eva squinted. *Could he have survived that chase with the warships?*

"I don't believe it is Hailey Turner," Rovender grumbled. "I have a feeling it is from Cadmus. Douse your lights, quickly!"

Rovender and Eva hopped back onto the wandering tree, joining Eva Eight. They huddled under their climatefiber blankets and watched the horizon for more activity. Before long the tree had drunk its fill and shambled onward into the gloom.

The night still lurked about in a heavy fog as the first light crept over the Valley of Standing Stones. Somewhere in the distance a clatter of turnfins called out.

"This is as far as we can go," Rovender said as he hopped down from the low branches of the wandering tree. "We travel by foot from here onward. The forest edge should be less than a two-day hike from here. Once we are in, it is another day until we reach Faunas."

"Wait a nano," Eva whispered, approaching Rovender with the supply bag. "Yesterday you said Nadeau might have only a couple of days left."

"I know, Eva," Rovender replied in a hushed tone. "But what else can we do? It is up to his spirit now as to whether it shall remain here with us or leave him."

"Okay, then." Eva pulled a container of water from the supply bag. "Let's continue on."

"Yes, I think it is the best decision," Rovender said. He and Eva walked over to Nadeau, who was still resting in the tree.

Eva dribbled water into Nadeau's mouth from her open container. The Cærulean gave a faint smile and patted her hand. "Many gratitudes," he whispered.

"Hang in there," Eva said. "We'll have you home soon."

Nadeau gestured for Eva to come closer. "You must know something, Eva," he whispered. "My clan will not let Rovender into the village, despite my state."

"They won't?"

"No," he continued. "You must be encouraging, because it will not be easy for him or the others. Do you understand?"

Eva nodded, though she didn't really understand.

"How is he?" Eight asked with a yawn. She climbed down from the tree and shuffled over to Eva, still bundled in her blanket.

"Oeeah!" Rovender's head moved side to side as he stared at both of them. "It is uncanny how much you two look alike."

Eight smiled and squeezed Eva Nine. "It's because we are sisters—both of us born from the same home. A family reunited at last, right, Nine?"

Awkwardly Eva hugged her sister back, though her eyes remained on Rovender.

"And, Nadeau. How are you feeling?" Rovender took the ailing Cærulean's hand.

"He's okay, for now," replied Eva. She broke away from Eva Eight and joined Rovender.

Nadeau spoke in a frail voice, "I am waiting to see our clan, Rovender. Our family, before I say farewell."

"I am working on getting you there, my brother," Rovender said. He turned to Eva and her sister. "After I awoke this morning I discovered the remains of a fallen air-whale not far from here. I'm hoping I can find some bones to fashion a stretcher to carry Nadeau the rest of the way."

"That sounds good," replied Eva Eight. "I'll wait here with Nadeau, unless you think this tree thing is going to walk away?"

"No." Eva stroked the wandering tree's scaly bark. "I think it will stay put for a while."

"Good," Rovender said. "Eva, you can join me. I may need somc help carrying back whatever we find."

"Perhaps we'll catch some breakfast as well," said Eva in a cheery tone. "I'm starving."

"What? Didn't you grab some pills this morning?" Eight asked.

"I'd save those pellets as a last resort," said Rovender.

Eva smiled. "Yeah, you haven't had breakfast until you've had roasted turnfin."

"Roasted . . . turnfin? Really?" Eight blanched at this suggestion. For some reason this delighted Eva.

CHAPTER 25: LURE

Gravel and stone crunched under Eva's sneakboots as she hiked with Rovender across a flat plain in the misty morning sun.

"The remains are not far in this direction," he said. "It should take only a little time for us to reach it."

"That's fine. I'm sure Eva Eight will take good care of Nadeau back at camp while we are gone." Eva was happy to be alone with Rovender, though she wrestled with why she felt more at ease with an alien than with her own flesh and blood.

"Tell me," started Rovender as he continued walking, "you have reunited with a sibling you did not know of, a gift left from Muthr. Are you not excited by this?"

Eva shrugged her shoulders.

"That doesn't seem like much of an answer," Rovender observed. "You must feel something more than that?"

"It's weird . . . *She's* weird." Eva picked at her nail polish. "It's like we sort of know each other, but not really."

"Like all things, you must give it time, Eva," Rovender replied.

"Like we did with Hailey?"

Rovender let out a halfhearted laugh. "Yes. Just like the pilot, Hailey Turner—the one I trusted, who then tricked me. The one I wanted to kill, whom you saved. And the one who in turn saved all of us."

"What does that prove?" Eva kicked some green eukaberries lying on the ground. "Your method of understanding someone takes too long."

"But what does it reveal?"

Eva rolled her eyes. There was no way to sort out Hailey. "It reveals that people are confusing."

Rovender corrected her. "Not confusing. *Complex.*"

Eva sighed loudly.

"Despite all of that, remember to trust what you feel, Eva. What your heart tells you."

"Right now I don't know how I feel. Especially about my sister," Eva said.

"She has much disdain for Cadmus, which is understandable. However, I fear it muddies her spirit," said Rovender.

"Yeah," replied Eva. "And she knows nothing about life out here. I don't think she can even talk to the trees and stuff like I can."

A cacophony of birds fluttered up ahead of the duo. The sun-bleached bones of a long-dead air-whale jutted upward from the open plain. Its mammoth skull faced Eva, staring at her through hollowed sockets. The remains reminded her of the stripped airship deteriorating in Hailey's hangar.

From the ground, Rovender picked up a thin ivory bone, twice his body length. "This is a fin ray from one of the air-whale's fins. These are quite strong." He brushed off the dirt and other debris from it. "We need a couple more of these, and then we can focus on finding breakfast." He handed the fin ray to Eva. Despite its length the bone was light in her hands. Its tapered length gave it the appearance of a long white spear.

They approached the air-whale's gigantic skull. Its eye sockets were large enough for Eva to walk through. Hordes of turnfins took wing as Eva and Rovender searched for more fin rays.

"All that is left are bones," Eva said. She thought of the mounted specimens in the Royal Museum in Solas.

"It's been picked clean. Probably by these turnfins." Rovender overturned one of many porous plates from the air-whale's carapace. Underneath, a trio of largish rock-mimic insects scuttled for cover.

Eva stared up at the ribs. The wandering tree that had carried them could walk through the rib cage and not touch the top.

"Oeeah! What have we here?" Rovender picked up an odd-shaped bone from the remains and dusted it off.

Eva recognized it as a skull. "Is it a baby whale?"

"No." Rovender rubbed the barbels on his chin. "This appears to be the skull of a Mirthian individual. Like our friend Huxley."

A chill wormed its way into Eva. "Did the air-whale eat him?"

"No, no, no." Rovender set the skull down and continued picking through the bones.

"How did he die, then?" Eva's eyes darted out into the plain, half-expecting a Dorcean huntsman to jump out.

"Age, illness. Or perhaps he was attacked. Only his spirit knows for sure." Rovender pushed more bones aside with his foot. "This is what we need!" He found an entire fin worth of ray bones. He knelt down and began sorting through the fin rays.

"Does his spirit really know?" Eva picked up and studied the Mirthian skull. Even without skin and muscle it seemed to be smiling, just like Huxley.

"How do you mean?" Rovender asked. He bent one of the fin rays, testing its strength. The bone snapped in half. Rovender threw the pieces aside and grabbed another.

"I mean if his spirit *knows* how he died but is no longer here, then where is it?"

"Ah!" Rovender pointed to the enormous skull with the fin ray. "His spirit, like this air-whale's, has left the body, but still it continues on."

"On? On to where? Where will my spirit go when I am gone?" Eva took the fin ray from Rovender.

"You will know that answer one day, Eva." Rovender gathered several more ray bones and stood up, ready to leave. "But I believe that day is far off."

"But Nadeau . . . He will know soon?" Eva followed Rovender as they backtracked through the skeleton.

"Yes," Rovender replied. "His journey here is coming to a close. Even now he is preparing for the next."

Eva couldn't recall having much conversation about this topic as she was growing up with Muthr. Talking with Rovender about Nadeau's death put her at ease a bit regarding Muthr's passing. "So is death a journey? Is it to another place?" she asked. "Is it another planet?"

"Many have wondered this very question," replied Rovender. "But there is an old Cærulean saying: When your journey reaches its destination here, may you walk on through the memories of those still with us."

Eva followed her blue friend toward the skull of the air-whale. *Will Muthr be waiting for me on my next journey?* She remembered Rovender's words when Muthr was laid to rest. *She lives within you now.*

As they neared the skull, her thoughts were interrupted by a flurry of turnfins whooshing past.

"They are scared," she said, looking around for the danger.

Rovender nodded in agreement. "Something is wrong."

From behind the rib cage several floatazoans popped up, hurling eukaberries at the birds. The flock flew out over the open plain, dodging the projectiles before circling back toward the skeleton. More floatazoans emerged from behind rocks and bones and continued the volley of foul-smelling fruit.

The turnfins veered away from the floatazoans and fled back out into the plain. Several birds dropped to the ground, flapping helplessly, their wings coated in sticky pulp.

"Let's grab one!" Eva dashed out and seized a fallen turnfin by the feet. "We can wash this smelly stuff off."

"No, Eva. You—"Rovender did not finish his sentence. He was thrown back by a large sand-sniper surging up from below him.

The sniper scuttled over the open plain, toward the grounded birds—and toward Eva.

Please don't hurt me. Please don't hurt me. Please don't, Eva thought to it.

The sniper devoured each of the fruit-covered birds and then turned its attention to Eva, who was still holding one of the struggling turnfins. She dropped the bird and retreated step by step. The sniper clicked loudly, its antennae waving out toward Eva. In the dim overcast light Eva could see its many bioluminescent markings flashing in a myriad of colors.

I didn't mean to take your food, she thought. *I am very sorry.*

With lightning speed the sand-sniper snatched the turnfin and consumed it in front of Eva. She remained motionless in front of the monster, trying to hold back the nausea of witnessing a bird being eaten alive. In seconds the feast was complete and the sniper regurgitated a gooey ball of spittle into its pincered maw. It turned its giant head toward the carcass of the air-whale and spat the spittle ball onto the ground.

From unseen cracks and crevices hordes of floatazoans drifted out toward the gooey ball. They gorged on the spittle, leaving nothing behind but the bones of the turnfins.

That is disgusting. Eva crinkled her nose as the rancid stink of eukaberry wafted over her. The sand-sniper turned to face her once more and clacked loudly. The colony of floatazoans hovered near it.

Rovender pulled himself out from under a heap

of bones and stood. "Eva!" he called out. The floatazoans turned toward Rovender and began pelting him with eukaberries. Covering his face, Rovender scrambled toward the giant skull of the air-whale for shelter. The sand-sniper bolted after him.

"No!" Eva ran through the gathered floatazoans toward the skull. She scurried past the sand-sniper, which was trying to crack the thick cranium open with its mighty graspers. Eva dove into a gaping eye socket and scampered toward the back. Deep within she found Rovender. "Rovee! Are you all right?"

"Yes," he replied. "Just a bit shaken. What is going on?"

Eva tried to catch her breath as she spoke. "The floaters . . . direct the sniper . . . with the berries. I think it's attracted to the smell of them."

"Can't you talk to the floaters?" He scraped the pungent pulp off his hands and onto the ground. "Tell them we mean no harm."

Eva concentrated. Several floatazoans had now entered the eye socket, chirping and pointing at her.

Food.

The thought trickled into Eva's head like a distant birdsong on the wind.

Please, just let us leave. We won't take any of your food. I promise.

More floatazoans clustered together inside the socket.

Food. Food. Food.

I gave the sniper back his food, and I am sorry to have taken it.

The floatazoans began to crowd close to Eva. Their thoughts rose in a chorus.

Food. Food. Food. Food. Food. Food. Food.

From outside the socket the sand-sniper reached in with one of its graspers. The massive spiked pincers fell just short of Eva and Rovender.

Food. Food. Food. Food. Food. Food. Food. Food. Food. Food. Food. Food. Food. Food.

Please! Eva clutched her head as the floatazoans' thoughts filled her mind, now in a deafening roar.

A barrage of eukaberries beat down on Eva and Rovender. Eva kicked wildly at the throng of attackers, knocking them away. There were so many floatazoans crammed into the socket that new ones filled the places of their fallen comrades. Through the din of the attack, Eva heard a voice from outside.

It was a familiar voice—a cry—and it severed Eva's mental connection with the floatazoans.

It was Eva Eight.

Eva Nine pushed through the mass of floatazoans and dashed past the sniper. She emerged from the eye socket covered in eukaberry pulp.

Eva looked out across the plain, from the direction she had traveled. There, she saw her sister running toward her. Eva rushed out to intercept her. "No! There's a sand-sniper! Go back! It's too dangerous!" Then Eva saw something that stopped her in her tracks.

Behind Eva Eight rose the unmistakable shape of one of Cadmus's warbots. The machine's grinding movement paused, and it fired a spray of SHOCdarts at Eight. She moaned something incoherent and then stumbled, landing facedown in the gravel. Eva rushed to her and found her sister's back quilled with dozens of darts. Electric static crackled from dart to dart, sending Eva Eight into convulsions.

"It's going to be okay. I will get you out of here." Eva tried to remain focused as she plucked the darts from her sister's body with trembling hands.

I don't know where Rovee is, she thought, *or if I am going to be attacked by the floatazoans, or that sand-sniper.* A dark shadow fell over her. Eva looked up at the large skull-shaped body of the warbot now towering over her.

CHAPTER 26: WOUNDS

A thick glob of bright orange foam shot from one of the warbot's cannons and landed on Eva's forearm, gluing it to the ground. Eva tried to wriggle her arm free, but the foam instantly began to harden and became heavier.

The warbot spoke in a firm tone, "Short-range immobilization foam dispensed. Please remain stationary while your identification is confirmed." Its red laser scanned down over Eva.

She grabbed one of the large pointed SHOC-darts from her sister's back and tore at the tunic sleeve of her trapped arm. The climatefiber ripped, and Eva yanked her arm through the sleeve, free of the foam. She scrambled to her feet and bolted, leading the warbot away from Eva Eight.

As she fled, Eva could hear darts raining down onto the ground behind her. She sprinted back toward the air-whale skeleton. The mechanical motors of the warbot could be heard as it gave chase on swift stilt legs. *There is no way I can outrun this machine,* she thought, and looked over her shoulder.

Eva stumbled to the ground. Once again the shadow of the warbot loomed as it closed in. Eva realized that she had tripped over several floatazoans. Their many voices returned in her head as they flooded out from the skeleton, pelting Eva with more berries.

Food. Food. Food.

"Please remain stationary," the warbot instructed. "Eva Nine, defector of New Attica and spy for the alien races, you are to return with me to New Attica for immediate treatment and reprogramming."

Eva stood to face the machine. The barrel of the warbot's ElectroRifle followed her every move.

"You cannot escape apprehension. Either come with me of your own will or be immobilized like your sibling, Eva Eight," the warbot continued.

Eva unfastened her berry-drenched utilitunic.

"Make your decision now," the warbot said.

"Oh, I've made my decision." Eva hurled the heavy garment at the warbot. It splattered on the machine, covering it in thick globs of eukaberry pulp.

The warbot fired repeatedly as Eva made off

toward the skull of the air-whale. Dozens of floatazoans cried out as they were caught in the torrent of SHOCdarts. Eva felt the sting of darts enter her calves and thighs, followed by a jolt of electricity. She dropped facedown to the gravel, unable to move as her muscles spasmed.

From the ground she watched the unfortunate floatazoans who had also been shot become electrified. In moments the entire colony swarmed at the feet of the machine and covered it with eukaberries.

The sand-sniper flew past Eva, carried on its many legs. Though her limbs were immobile, Eva focused her teary eyes on the sniper. The monster faced the warbot chattering wildly, with every one of its graspers flexed.

"It's a threat response," Rovender whispered as he knelt next to Eva and began removing the darts.

The warbot addressed the sand-sniper. "Unidentified assailant, please back away immediately. I will be forced to immobilize you if you do not comply."

That invader wants your food, Eva thought out to the sniper. *It will take your food and kill all of your food-finders.*

Faster than her eyes could follow, the sand-sniper struck the leg of the warbot, instantly crippling it. Projectiles erupted out of the machine in every direction as it collapsed to the ground, but the volley of darts bounced off the sand-sniper's hard carapace. The sniper seized the body of the warbot with its pincers and crushed it.

While the sand-sniper and floatazoans focused on the warbot, Rovender slung Eva over his shoulder and hustled toward Eva Eight.

Even though the SHOCdarts were now removed, throbbing pain pulsed through the back of Eva's legs. "Ugh!" she said through clenched teeth. "It hurts!"

"I know you are in pain, Eva. But we have to hurry before that sniper loses interest in the dead machine." Rovender set Eva down on the ground along with the air-whale's fin rays that he'd been holding in his other hand. He began to pull the darts from Eva's unconscious sister. "Try to use the fin bones as a crutch to help you walk."

"They won't break?" Eva grabbed the ivory rods.

"Do not be deceived by their thin appearance. They are strong enough."

Eva pulled herself up to a standing position using the long bones. Her right leg was still spasming but her left had stopped, though it felt numb, as if it were asleep. Clumsily she hopped on her left leg, using the fin rays as support.

Rovender pulled off his pulp-covered jacket. He wadded it up and hurled it far in the opposite direction from their camp. The Cærulean picked up Eva Eight with both hands. "Come on," he said. "We haven't much time."

The wandering tree had gone, leaving Nadeau alone asleep under the shade of a standing stone. The feeling had returned to Eva's legs, though her wounds were still tender. She helped Rovender ease the now conscious Eva Eight onto a blanket next to Nadeau. Rovender threw the supply bag to Eva and flopped down, clearly winded. She handed him a bottle of water and rummaged through the first aid kit.

"SpeedHeal ointment, yes!" she said, pulling out the tube of cream. "Too bad I had to throw off that utilitunic. It would have taken care of me."

"You will be okay?" Rovender asked, still panting.

"Yeah," replied Eva. "My leg is a little sore, but I'll live."

"Well, you are better off than that Mirthian we saw," Rovender said, sipping his water. "Now we know what became of him."

"And what that ship was that we saw last night." Eva pulled off her sneakboots and her leggings, both plastered with dried pulp. The miasma of eukaberry was heavy in the air. "Do you think there are more warbots?" Eva asked.

"I do not know," replied Rovender.

"I can't believe he sent one after us," said Eva. She rubbed the ointment into the puncture wounds on her legs.

"I can." Rovender scooted over to a pool of water surrounding the stone and filled his bottle. "My guess is that his attack on Lacus and Solas is supposed to be a surprise—"

Eva finished his thought, "And he doesn't want us to warn them."

"Cadmus." Eva Eight sat up. "Damn him and his evil army," she sneered. "We need to warn your friends so they can do away with him," she said to Rovender.

"I agree, Eva Eight. But I don't know how that is possible," Rovender said. "We are many days away from Lacus and Solas. I do not think we will reach them in time, especially in our state."

"What of the shuttle?" Nadeau was awake.

Rovender grumbled into his bottle and sipped his water.

"Shuttle?" Eva handed her sister the SpeedHeal ointment. "What shuttle? What is he talking about?"

"There is a small ship at our village," Nadeau said. "Used primarily for diplomatic trips for our leader, Antiquus, to meet with Queen Ojo."

"Do you think he'd let us borrow it?" Eva looked at Rovender.

"No." Rovender stood and paced. "That isn't going to happen, Nadeau, and you know this to be true."

"But this is a matter of life and death for many of our sister clans, Rovender. Surely Antiquus will put aside past—"

"He will not!" Rovender shouted. He wiped spit from his mouth with the back of his hand. "He will not."

Eva's eyes were wide with surprise at Rovender's sudden anger. She looked over at her sister.

"I'm glad I'm not the only one who hates their leader," Eight said under her breath.

"The problem does not lie with the leader." Rovender grabbed the fin rays and the crewman's overalls. "Antiquus is a good leader, trusted by all. It is I whom they dislike."

"I know what you mean," Eight replied.

Eva approached Rovender as he laid out the bones on the ground. With his jacket gone, he was now adorned in a simple loincloth secured around his waist by a frayed fibrous cord. Without his big tattered jacket, Rovender seemed smaller. Lonely. Eva sat down next to her blue friend and helped assemble the stretcher.

CHAPTER 27: WILDLIFE

I don't know about you," Eva Eight said as she tramped between the stony monoliths, "but I think the wildlife here is just as dangerous as Cadmus's army."

"It can be scary," Eva said, "but it can also be beautiful."

They were hiking behind Rovender, who now pulled Nadeau in a stretcher of sorts—a travois—that dragged on the ground like a sled. The supporting rods of the travois gouged a pair of shallow ruts in the sand, which Eva followed. At one point Eva would have imagined that it was a magic path being rendered just for her, but now she found it harder to hold

on to such childhood daydreams. "Don't you think the wildlife here is beautiful, Rovee?" she asked.

Rovender was silent, as he had been for all of the afternoon, leading the way through the standing stones toward his village. Far ahead the skies darkened and distant thunder rumbled.

Don't you miss the comfort of our old Sanctuary, Nine? Wouldn't it be great to go back?" Eight said wistfully. "We could start our own community there. We would be able to come and go as we please and live safe from any outside dangers. That would be lovely, don't you think?"

"Uh . . . well . . . maybe." Eva played with one of her braids. She missed the comfort of her Sanctuary, but she enjoyed traveling around the landscape and learning about the different cultures of Orbona much more.

Rovender spoke over his shoulder. "Speak your truth, Eva Nine. Say what you mean."

"I am saying what *I mean*," Eva retorted. "And *I mean* there were things that I liked about living in the Sanctuary and things I didn't."

"Such as?" Eight's face held the slightest smile, as if she enjoyed Rovender's agitation toward Eva.

Eva replied, "I didn't like that we had to be a certain age before we were allowed to go up to the surface—"

"Be thankful you weren't old enough," Eight interjected.

"Muthr and I often argued about it," said Eva.

"Muthr." Eight scoffed. "Another one of Cadmus's robots serving his needs. A robot raising us? Some mother she turned out to be."

Eight's words pierced Eva as if she'd been struck by a sand-sniper.

"And if that place was really a 'Sanctuary' as we were told it was, we should have been allowed to feel safe within its walls for our entire life. Not be ejected by some mindless piece of machinery working for—"

"TAKE THAT BACK!" Eva Nine tackled her sister headlong. They both fell into a shallow pool at the foot of a monolith. "Muthr wasn't like that! She was just doing what she was told! She didn't know! You don't know!" Eva swatted wildly at her cowering sister.

"Eva! Eva!" Rovender's large hands seized Eva by the wrists. He pried her off Eva Eight and pulled her away.

"What is wrong with you?" Eight yelled.

"You don't know anything about Muthr!" Eva spat.

"Oh, I don't?" Eight fired back. "I think it is *you* who doesn't know anything, Nine. *You* don't know that all she was supposed to do was train us to live 'up here' on the surface. *You* don't know that on your sixteenth birthday you would be FORCED to leave the Sanctuary, alone, whether you had siblings or not. And that once you left, you couldn't return, ever—even if you traveled all the way to New Attica and back again. Even if all you wanted was to feel safe in the only place you knew. To feel loved. To have a family. A sister. A daughter."

"But Muthr didn't know," Eva cried. "She was under the control of the Sanctuary."

"Yeah, right!" Eight retorted. "Like it's the Sanctuary's fault, not Muthr's. She didn't care. I brought back supplies for her, food and clothing for you. . . . I even found an old fairy tale book to read you, *but she didn't care*. She could have overridden the Sanctuary computer at any time, but she didn't. She locked me out of my own home. *Our* home." Eight fell to her knees. "I could have taken care of you. I could have protected you. It's not right." She buried her head in her hands and sobbed.

"The WondLa?" Eva whispered. "You brought it?"

"I will never forgive her, Nine," Eight said, and sniffled. "I *hate* Cadmus for programming my only mother to push me away, and *I hate her* for allowing it to happen."

"But . . . Muthr didn't know." Eva looked over at

Rovender. "Rovee, you were there. Tell her. Muthr didn't know."

"Mother robot did seem to be under the influence of the machine that was your home," Rovender said. "But her heart was true."

"Oh, and you're going to listen to him?" Eight pointed at Rovender in an accusatory way. "He spends a few days with Muthr, and now he knows her better than I do?"

Large drops of rain fell from the tumultuous skies above.

Eva remembered how angry and frustrated she could be with Muthr. But there were also good memories from her upbringing in the Sanctuary—even from their search for answers. Eva Nine had never hated Muthr. *But what if she had locked me out?* It didn't matter now.

Eva walked over to her sister and hugged her. "It's going to be okay," she whispered to her in a soothing voice.

"You're right. I'm sorry. Seeing you just brings up these old feelings," Eight said, looking up at Eva. She pulled the damp tresses of Eva's hair from her face. "But don't you worry about what happened with me and Muthr. It was in the past." Eight wiped the tears from her face. "We are in this together now, right?"

Eva nodded. "Right."

Eight clung to Eva's thin shoulders, her fingers gripping her tightly. "I've felt like a stranger in a strange land during my years living in New Attica. No one truly understood what it is like to be Sanctuary-born. But you are here now, Nine, and you are all I've got," she said with desperation in her voice.

The rain began to come down harder. Thunder resounded overhead.

Raindrops pattered on the blanket stretched taught over a cluster of several stone monoliths. Underneath, Eva warmed her damp body near the campfire she had built. Her sister wrung out her soaked tunic while Nadeau slept in a bundle of blankets.

"You were right," Eva said. "The temperature has dropped now that the sun is down."

"Here, catch!" Eight threw the second pair of crewman's coveralls to Eva. "Like I said, I don't think they have climatefiber or a life-monitoring system, but—"

"It's better than running around in my undertunic." Eva pulled the coveralls on.

In the dark beyond the fire's light, the intermittent sounds of the wild called out.

"I hope there are no sand monsters out here that will eat us in our sleep." Eight pulled the lid from a food container and shook out a handful of nutriment pellets.

"We are too close to rocks for a sniper attack," said Eva, dropping a log onto the fire. "And I haven't seen any more floaters since our encounter this morning." Just as she had been during the escape from New Attica, Eva's sister seemed eerily calm after their blowup. In fact, Eva Eight seemed completely unfazed as she downed a handful of pellets. Eva thought to her the way she spoke to the sand-snipers. *Tell me you don't like it out here. Tell me you want to go back to New Attica or go live with the Toilers.*

"How is it that you know so much about the creatures here?" Eight asked. "There were no sand-snipes or floaterzoans in our natural history programs." She offered Eva some pellets.

"Tell me about it." Eva waved away the offer. "The Identicapture program on the Omnipod was useless."

"So how did you learn about all this stuff?" Eight grabbed another handful.

"Rovender," Eva said. "He knows a lot about a lot. I guess it's from all his travels exploring Orbona."

"Orbona?"

"Orbona is what the aliens call Earth." Eva pulled off her sneakboots and socks. She stretched her toes out toward the campfire. "I prefer to call it that too, since the Earth we learned about is really no longer here."

"I'll say," said Eight.

"You said you traveled from New Attica back to the Sanctuary?" Eva said, stoking the fire. "Didn't you see aliens and stuff then?"

"No." Eight focused on the awakened flames. "I hitched a ride back with the retriever who brought me to New Attica originally, Evan Seven. He had a baby son of his own and was a good guy. And he was cute."

"What happened?" Eva leaned into the conversation. Though she had watched many romantic programs in the Sanctuary, she and Muthr had hardly ever spoken of boys.

Eight let out a long sigh. "He stayed with me at the Sanctuary for a time, while I tried to convince Muthr to let us back in. When that didn't happen, I tried to persuade her to let me take you with me."

"You did?" It was weird to think that Eight had been in the Sanctuary while Eva was there.

"You were just a baby then, Nine. You wouldn't remember," Eight said.

Eva's mind flitted back to the memories from the Omnipod shown in Cadmus's medlab. There was that one recording that was out of order: *The older Eva arguing with Muthr in my bedroom wasn't me—it was Eight.* She imagined Eight and the pilot moving into the Sanctuary and raising Eva with Muthr, just like the image of the robot and the little girl and the adult on her tattered WondLa.

"Anyway, it didn't happen. Obviously." Eight's voice was flat. "So we left and returned to New Attica. I figured I'd wait for you there. My cute pilot took off with some radical group of explorers. I never saw him again. Men, right?"

Are all men like this pilot? Like Hailey? Eva wondered.

"But it doesn't matter now. We don't need any flaky pilots. Us gals can take care of ourselves out here in the wilderness."

Eva Eight's gaze remained fixed on the fire. In the dancing firelight Eva's sister looked different from when Eva had first met her. Under unkempt hair, dirt and smudged mascara now tarnished Eight's face. Eva could see the exhaustion in her sister's sea-green eyes. But there was something else in Eight's gaze too—resignation.

And yet the very thing Eva Eight had wanted—her WondLa—was no different from what Eva wanted. No different from what Muthr had wanted. As far as Eight was concerned, she now had the thing that had been missing in her life. She had told Eva how happy she was now that they were reunited, but there was great despair etched in those perfect porcelain features.

"Dinner!" Rovender said, emerging from the dark. In his hand he carried two halves of a skinned turnfin. He plopped down between the Evas and pulled a piece of fin ray from a bundle on the travois. He pushed the narrow bone into the ground at an angle over the fire and then skewered the meat on the top, creating a spit. "Stir those embers, Eva Nine, and let's get these started."

"Is that one of those weird three-winged birds?" Eight winced at the carcass sizzling on the spit.

"A turnfin, yes," Rovender replied.

"And you are going to eat it?" Eight scooted away from the fire.

"It's not so bad," Eva said. "I wasn't sure what to think about it either at first, but the meat is actually pretty tasty, and it's a good source of protein. Better than nutriment pellets."

"But it's . . . dead," said Eight.

"True, it has given its life," Rovender said. "But its energy, its spirit, will replenish yours. Respect that and enjoy the meal."

"You wanted to leave New Attica," Eva added. "This is it. We are now non-trackers living off of the land."

"Well, we don't have to live like animals." Eight scowled at the meat smoking on the spit.

With his eye on Eight, Rovender said, "Eva, while this is cooking, there is something I want to show you. Follow me."

"Sure," Eva said and put on her sneakboots.

In the drizzling rain Eva followed Rovender out into the night, leaving her sister to watch over Nadeau and their cooking meal. "You don't think anything is going to happen again, do you?" Eva asked. She looked back at the orange glow of the campfire. It was like a burning star under the muted moonlight.

"No, no, no," Rovender said. "We'll be gone only a moment. You have to take a look at this."

In the pale light Eva could see that he was leading her to a group of large standing stones overgrown with foliage. In fact, Eva realized that her sneakboots were no longer crunching over gravel and sand but were padding over soft patches of moss. "It's the Wandering Forest! Are we close to your village?" she asked.

"It is the Wandering Forest, Eva, but look closer." Rovender lit his small lantern and set it down near the base of a stone.

At first all Eva could see was movement, small and steady movement as if the moss on the stone's surface were vibrating. She leaned in for a closer examination and realized it wasn't vibrating.

"It's . . . it's growing," said Eva. Roots, like tiny pulsing veins, twined over the surface of the stone. Tendrils sprouted out in all directions and interlocked, weaving a pattern of rich olive green over everything. "Right before our eyes it is growing!"

"Yes, Eva," Rovender said. "I know where we are, and the edge of the Wandering Forest used to be another day's trek from here. But it has grown. Expanded. Soon all of Orbona will be green."

Eva watched as the growth overtook a giant monolith. "Earth plants don't grow like this," she said, astonished. "In our greenhouse they took weeks to germinate from seeds, even with fertilizer."

Rovender craned his head up as plumes of tufted plant-creatures sprung forth from the rock face. "This is what the Vitae Virus generator, that Huxley spoke of, has started. It restarts life where it once was absent, and spreads it. It is quite a gift."

Eva pondered this as she watched several odd insects flutter around Rovender's lantern. The insects whirred and flew into the lantern as if they were in a contest to see which one could get closest to the light source. "If the generator isn't in Solas," she said, deep in thought, "then it must be somewhere in the forest."

Rovender nodded. "If the generator is indeed there, Cadmus's forces will never find it." The rain had stopped, and the two made their way back to camp.

"But if the forest is expanding, Cadmus doesn't need the generator. Eventually the green will come to New Attica. His land will become fertile once again," Eva said.

"Fertile or not, Eva, the land is not his," replied Rovender.

"But New Attica. The land it is on is his, isn't it?" asked Eva. The Divination Machine's prediction of humans taking over what had been Solas drifted into Eva's mind.

"Land does not belong to anyone. We belong to the land. To Orbona. The planet must be free to breathe and grow as we breathe and grow."

"If only Cadmus knew about the forest expanding," Eva said with a sigh. *Would he call off the invasion?*

"If only, Eva Nine, but I doubt . . ." Rovender stopped and sniffed the night air. He doused his light. "I know that scent. It's munt-runner," he whispered.

"What?" Eva said. "Munt-runner?"

"Yes. I am sure of it. Come on!" Rovender took Eva by the hand and rushed back to camp.

CHAPTER 28: GHOST

As they approached their camp, Eva could hear braying and shuffling sounds around the site. From the shadows trotted a tall birdlike bipedal animal with a shadowy rider on its back. Leather reins hung from the pair of horns that grew from the mount's brow.

"Is that a munt-runner?" Eva whispered.

Rovender gestured for her to be quiet.

"Who's out there?" Eva Eight was standing at the fire swinging a broken fin ray like a sword. Behind her lay Nadeau, still bundled under his blankets. The rider entered the campsite, a young Cærulean seated in the munt-runner's saddle. His mount's wild scarlet eyes dilated as they neared the firelight.

"Come on." Rovender took Eva's hand and stepped into the flickering glow of the campfire at the center of the camp.

"Do my eyes betray me? Look what we have here, brother," the rider announced, gesturing toward Rovender. Another young rider emerged from behind a standing stone.

"The spirits of the dead are out this night," the second rider said.

"Indeed, for I see the drunken ghost of Rovender Kitt," added the first.

"Galell, it has been some time," Rovender addressed the first rider. "You were hardly older than a nymph when I saw you last."

"Do you hear that?" Galell said to the second rider. "The ghost speaks. It now mingles with dirt-burrowers . . . still lost without its clan." Both riders chuckled.

"Rovee's not—" Eva started, but with a gesture Rovender cut her off. Eight watched from the campfire, unmoving.

"Whether I am a ghost or not," Rovender said, "only your spirit within knows for sure. However, this ghost, along with these others, has traveled far to return one of our brethren back to Faunas."

Rovender pulled back the blankets to reveal Nadeau. The Cærulean looked paler than ever. His wan skin contrasted with the dark wires that pulsed beneath it.

"What in Orbona?" Galell hopped off his mount and rushed to the weakened Cærulean. He took Nadeau by the hand. "What has become of you? Who has done this?"

With shaky aim Nadeau pointed at Eva Nine. "It was their kind, but it was not—"

Galell did not allow Nadeau to finish. He wheeled around and pulled a sonic boomrod from his pack. The second rider hopped down holding a bolas. The munt-runners brayed and stomped, splashing puddles near their feet.

Rovender jumped between the barrel of the boomrod and Eva. His outstretched arms covered both her and her sister. "This is not what you think, brother," Rovender said, remaining calm. "They are helping Nadeau."

"I don't want to hear any more ravings from you, old ghost!" Galell kept his weapon aimed at Rovender. "We are taking Nadeau and these dirt-burrowers back to our village, where they shall pay for their cruelty. Their fate is now in Antiquus's hands."

Eva grabbed the spit with the charred turnfin

on it. She slung the meat off and pointed it as a weapon toward Galell.

"Try it!" Galell charged the boomrod and pressed closer. "You see this, ghost? They are all hostile. They'll kill us as soon as they have the chance!" The second rider whirled his bolas over his head in a rhythmic fashion.

"Enough!" Rovender said. "Eva, go with them. I don't want any more bloodshed."

"Come on, Nine. Let's do as he says." Eva Eight put a reassuring hand on Eva's shoulder.

Eva shrugged off the gesture. "No way, Rovee. We can—"

"Just. Do. It." He turned to her and Eva Eight. "I don't want either of you to get hurt. Let us try to solve this with words, not weapons. Understand?"

Eva dropped the spit down into the fire, sending up a flurry of incandescent ash.

"What?" she said, flabbergasted. "You—you're just gonna leave and let them take me?"

"It will be okay. This I promise." Rovender knelt down and hugged Eva. "I'll see you soon," he whispered into her ear.

"Let's go, dirt-burrower." Galell nudged Eva on with the barrel of his boomrod. He forced Eva up onto his mount. The second rider did the same with Eva Eight. From the saddle Eva watched Galell attach the travois to the back of his munt-runner. Nadeau, unconscious once more, said nothing.

"Galell, I must come with you," Rovender said. "I need to speak to Antiquus about this. There is more here than what you see."

"Wander off, ghost." Galell stepped into the stirrup of his saddle and climbed up onto his mount. "Your time in our village has long passed."

With a sharp kick from Galell, the munt-runner took off into the night. Eva looked back over her shoulder to check on Rovender. She expected a signal, a sign about what to do next, but the flames of the campfire had been extinguished and she could see nothing.

"Wake up!" Galell nudged Eva Nine hard with his elbow and nearly knocked her from his saddle. Eva blinked away the sleep and shook off the exhaustion that had overtaken her during their ride. The shadows of the night still hid among the bushes and trees as the early light of dawn flushed the sky gold.

The riders steered their mounts into a spacious clearing. Clustered in the center of this clearing were domed huts, each perched high on tapering stalks. Their mushroomy appearance brought to mind the large structures that made up Lacus. Somehow, in the construction of both villages, Eva could see that the builders had originated from the same planet, as Rovender had mentioned.

As the riders neared the cluster, Eva realized the domiciles were constructed entirely of woven materials. Dried leaves and coarse fiber had been meticulously intertwined to form the bizarre structures. Every façade was adorned with scrimshaw, as if each building told a story in pictures of those who dwelled within.

A lone Cærulean, standing on the roof of the tallest hut, let out a piercing cry, which ushered forth the entire village. In moments the villagers, whooping and calling out, surrounded the two riders. Everywhere Eva looked she saw Cæruleans who bore a striking resemblance to Rovender, but her friend was nowhere to be found. She glanced over at Eva Eight, who appeared dazed.

Galell pulled his weapon and addressed the gathering. "While hunting last night in the Valley of Standing Stones, I came across a ghost."

A whispery hush fell over the village.

"This ghost told me he was returning our long-lost brother Nadeau back to us from these dirt-burrowers." Galell pointed to Eva and her sister with his boomrod, then hopped off his mount. A murmur grew among the villagers. "See what these monsters, these callous creatures, have done!" He pulled the blankets away from Nadeau. Audible gasps and moans came from the crowd.

Eva turned on the saddle to see the poor Cærulean. He looked dead. His chalk-white skin, rigid form, and half-open eyes made him appear as if he'd been frozen alive. She leaned over to see if he was breathing, but several hands yanked her down from Galell's mount.

"I told you, Galell, I didn't do this!" Eva yelled, struggling against her captors. "We were trying to save him!" Eva felt fists box and strike at her. A scowling Cærulean began twirling a set of bolas. Eva craned her neck to locate her sister, but Eva Eight had been pulled from her ride as well and was obscured by the mob.

Rovender, where are you? she thought. *You need to hurry.*

"What is this?" a gravelly voice called out. "What has troubled you all on such a glorious morning?"

The crowd calmed and parted to form a pathway. From the back of the gathering came an aged Cærulean seated on a hoverdisc. He floated over to examine Nadeau, still strapped in the travois. The elder had long twisted whiskers and tattered ears that hung over his simple robes. Saying nothing, he placed a knobby large hand flat on Nadeau's chest. The entire village was silent. All Eva could hear was the elder's wheezing breath.

"Are you Antiquus?" Eva asked. Galell jabbed her hard in the ribs with the muzzle of the boom-rod, and she dropped to her knees.

The leader of the Cæruleans kept a hand on Nadeau and turned toward her. From the personal items on his hoverdisc, he plucked a hand-size metallic object shaped like a seashell. He placed the object in his ear and looked at her curiously.

"Are you Antiquus?" repeated Eva. She braced herself for another strike from Galell, but none came.

The leader raised his droopy brow to expose piercing ice-blue eyes, which studied Eva. "Antiquus I am, little one. What has become of our brother Nadeau?"

Eva tried to approach, but the Cæruleans held her tight. "I—I did not do this. My sister and I, along with Rovender Kitt, were trying to bring him back here before . . . before he died."

Antiquus's brow dropped back down, shadowing his eyes, and he resumed his examination of Nadeau. "Rovender Kitt. That name means nothing here."

"It means something to me," Eva replied. "Isn't this his village?"

"It is not."

Has Galell taken us to another village of Cæruleans? Rovender would never find them now.

"Poor Nadeau." Antiquus ran his fingers over the Cærulean's pale cheek. "His spirit yearns to leave, yet the electricity that now courses through him does not allow it."

"No," Eva said. "He held on because he wanted to come home before he let his spirit leave."

"I do not understand." There was sadness and confusion in Antiquus's voice. "How could you . . . Why would you do such a thing to another?"

"She didn't." Eva Eight spoke. "Cadmus Pryde did. The human leader."

"Hu-man? And what clan is the hu-man?" Antiquus asked.

"They are people," Eight replied. "Like Eva and me. But we had no part in this."

Antiquus grumbled, "So the sneaky raffid says when cornered by a pack of wild dargs."

"Why won't you believe us?" said Eight. "We could have just left him back in New Attica to die. Do you know what we've been through to get him here?"

Antiquus waved away Eva Eight's words, and she was pulled back into the crowd. Clearly he had heard enough. He removed his ear trumpet, uncoiled it, and placed it in Nadeau's mouth like a horn. From the folds of his robe the elder pulled a fine thin blade no longer than Eva's finger. Slowly he pushed the blade into Nadeau's throat. An audible exhalation could be heard escaping through the ear horn.

Eva winced and looked away.

"Safe journey, Brother Nadeau. You are free," Antiquus whispered, and closed Nadeau's eyes.

Cries of anguish burst from the crowd. The villagers freed Nadeau's body from the travois and lifted him high over their heads. Their wails began to harmonize into a chorus, creating a melancholy song of mourning.

Antiquus coiled his ear trumpet and put it back on. He turned to Galell. "Take these two to the isolation house. I must convene with the circle of elders so that we may determine what fate these hu-mans have earned for their actions."

"What a mess we're in," Eight said. "When is your friend Rovender going to come and sort this out?"

"I don't know," Eva replied. They were in a tiny hut set high above the village.

"Well, he better get here soon, or we are going to be joining Nadeau." Eight rummaged through the scant items in the room.

Eva scooted toward the doorway and peered down into the village. She could see Galell turning the large crank that wound the rope ladder that they had ascended. The nearest rooftop was at least fifteen meters below.

Galell finished retracting the ladder and stood guard as the other villagers constructed a large fire. A procession appeared from one of the huts carrying the shrouded body of Nadeau.

I am so sorry, Nadeau. We really tried, Eva thought. She scanned the surrounding forest, hoping a wandering tree could come to her assistance, but none responded to her mental pleas.

"Any ideas?" Eight sat against the back wall of the hut and pulled a blanket over herself.

"Rovee said that we needed to solve this with words, not weapons," Eva said. She watched as the villagers placed Nadeau's body onto the pyre. "Maybe we'll be able to talk it out with the elders."

"I don't think that's gonna happen, Nine," said Eight. "This old guy is just as bloodthirsty as Cadmus. Did you see what he did to Nadeau?"

Eva closed her eyes to force the image away, but it remained, just like the image of Besteel killing Otto's mate . . .

. . . and the image of the juvenile water bear

being frozen alive in the taxidermist's lab . . .

. . . and Muthr, broken and battered in the desert sand.

Just let me go, Muthr had said.

Maybe that's all Antiquus was doing . . . letting Nadeau go. She watched as a ribbon of smoke from the funeral pyre below drifted past the doorway of their hut. *Nadeau is on to his next journey,* she thought. *Hopefully it is one without any pain.*

A sense of comfort radiated from somewhere within Eva. Even though their situation appeared dire, somehow she knew it would work out. "It's all right. We are going to be fine. Rovee will come, and we'll figure this out," she said in a calm tone.

"How do you know that?" Eight replied.

"I—I just know." Eva smiled.

"I don't think you do, Nine," Eight replied. "Cadmus is going to kill or enslave every race on this planet, including humans, and you think it's all going to be 'fine'?"

Eva slid away from the door. "That's not what I mean. I mean *we'll* be fine. I don't know what will happen to everybody else."

"I thought I knew everything when I was a child your age. You've got a lot to learn," Eva Eight said and stared out the small window.

Eva ignored her sister's condescension. "Of course, I don't want there to be a war, she said. "I want everyone to be able to live together . . . to be happy."

"Your friends in Lacus aren't going to be too happy when a warship starts shooting everyone on sight."

"I know, I know. We have to meet with Cadmus," said Eva.

"Meet? Are you crazy?" Eight glared at Eva from across the hut.

"Rovee and I saw the Wandering Forest growing. It's bigger now than it was before. Eventually it will reach New Attica. Cadmus doesn't need the Vitae Virus generator. He doesn't need to invade at all."

"You are naïve, Nine." Eight shook her head as she spoke. There was exasperation in her voice. "Cadmus needs to be eliminated. Didn't you hear what those aliens said? *They hate humans.* They are going to kill *us* in retaliation for Cadmus's lab experiment."

Eva looked back out the doorway at the Cæruleans down below mourning Nadeau's passing. With the entire village gathered it reminded Eva of the peaceful Halcyonus back in Lacus. *How would Hostia treat me if there were a human invasion?* A flock of turnfins fluttered past. *I wish I could fly away like them.* She let out a long sigh and waited.

CHAPTER 29: TRUTH

The sun sank behind the treetops, turning the cloudless sky an angry vermilion. Eva looked down from her lofty cell and spied Galell climbing the long rope ladder up to her.

He entered the hut and threw a cloth sack onto the floor, causing the fruit within to tumble out. He pointed to Eva Eight. "You stay."

He turned to Eva Nine. "You—the elders want a word with you."

Eva Eight jumped up. "No! We are family! We stay together!"

Galell pulled out his boomrod and charged it.

"Stop!" Eva Nine pushed the muzzle of the weapon away. She rushed over to her sister. "I'll be all right," she whispered.

"You can't let them separate us, Nine." Eight clutched Eva. "I don't know about these aliens or their ways. We have to stay together."

Eva hugged her sister. There was genuine fear in Eight's eyes. "I'll be okay," Eva said. "Rovee will come."

"Rovender! What about me? What about us?"

"Stay calm." Eva patted Eight's hand. "Remember how you asked me to trust you?"

Eva Eight loosened her grip on Eva. She relaxed and nodded in agreement.

"Don't worry," Eva said. "All I can do is tell them the truth." She gave her sister another hug and then followed Galell down the ladder to the base of the isolation house.

On the ground an armed Cærulean began to crank the winch that pulled the ladder down from the hut. Eva glanced back up at Eight. She was watching from the doorway high above.

"Let's go!" Galell shoved Eva. "They are waiting." Eva scowled at him and followed.

Galell escorted Eva to a small, low-lying hut partially obscured by the stalked bases of the other homes. "In there, dirt-burrower." He pointed up at the closed curtain doorway.

Eva climbed up the short ladder to the doorway and looked over her shoulder to see that Galell remained on guard at the base of the ladder. He was not following her in.

"Do not keep them waiting! Go!" Galell said.

Eva pushed the heavy curtain aside and entered the hut. The scent of burning soap wafted over Eva, reminding her of Arius's dwelling. In the soft glowing lights she could see that the woven walls were decorated from floor to ceiling in ornate pictographs. Around the hut hung thick fibrous cords. Each cord looped out to the center of the floor from the wall into which it was woven. The loose end of every cord was tied around the waist of a council elder, all of whom were seated in a circle.

"Come in," said Antiquus. He sat cross-legged on the floor with an age-smoothed cane at his side. Behind him a tiny fork-tailed bird twittered from a wooden perch. Antiquus gestured to a floor mat at the center of the circle of elders, and said, "Please sit, hu-man. We have talked much about the events that we witnessed today. Now we have some questions for you."

Eva did as she was told and looked at the council of Cæruleans seated around her. She half-hoped to see Rovender among them, but he was not. Like their leader, each of the other elders was adorned in earth-toned garments offset by colorful jewelry made of beads, seedpods, and feathers.

Antiquus pointed to the ancient council member seated to his left. "Soth, you may begin," he said.

The Cærulean rose and ambled toward Eva. Her necklaces jangled with every step. As the elder woman searched through her knotted necklaces, Eva noticed a severed dried foot hanging around her neck. *Soth must be the shaman,* Eva thought. She remembered Rovender's story about her and the Great Migration.

Eva hid her feet, tucking them under her. "What are you going to do to me?"

"We just need to ask a few questions. And you must speak the truth," answered Soth.

"I always tell the truth," replied Eva. "You can ask me anything."

"We need to be certain." The shaman untangled a thin necklace. A small whistle dangled from its chain. When she blew it, three short trills reverberated through the hut, and the tiny bird perched behind Antiquus took wing.

As the bird hovered above its perch in midair, Eva thought of the holograms of brilliant hummingbirds that she had once seen. The shaman called out with a long whistle and walked behind Eva. The bird zoomed over, stopping just centimeters in front of Eva's nose. The shaman let out a final trill and received a *chirrup* in response.

Eva blinked involuntarily from the breeze generated by the bird's fast-beating wings. A fine glimmering dust drifted from the wing tips and blew onto Eva's face. She turned away from the dust, but Soth's hands gripped Eva's head and held her fast. "It will not hurt," the shaman said. "Just breathe it in, and the treowe, the truth-bird, will do the rest."

Eva did not feel the dust settle on her face. However, an overwhelming sense of calm took over her body, and her eyelids fluttered, as if she were fighting off sleep.

"Good," Soth whispered. "It is working. Let the bird in, hu-man."

The shaman's words sounded as if Eva were underwater, as if she were dreaming. Eva let out a large yawn, and the truth-bird flew into her mouth and landed on her tongue. She felt the tickle of its tail coil down her throat.

"She is ready," Soth said, and returned to her seat.

"Hu-man, tell us how it is that you came into our custody," said Antiquus.

Eva's mouth didn't move. Her mind reeled with shock when she heard her own voice answering the question, spoken by the truth-bird. "I escaped from New Attica, the human city, with the help of my sister, a retriever, a Royal Beamguide Scout, and Rovee. I stumbled across the experimentation on Nadeau in a lab deep in Attican Hall and could not allow it to continue. All of us agreed that

Nadeau could not be left behind. So Rovee led us here."

The elders looked at one another with confusion on their faces. "Who is Rovee?" Antiquus asked.

"Rovender Kitt," the truth-bird replied. "We crashed in the Northern Wastelands and lost Hailey and Huxley. From there we've traveled by foot to try to reach Faunas before Nadeau died."

"What do you care of a dying Cærulean's wishes?"

"Because everyone should be allowed the chance to say good-bye to those they love before they die."

Antiquus leaned back and said nothing.

"But Nadeau did not just want to die here with his clan," the truth-bird continued. "He wanted Rovender to return. He wanted you to hear the truth."

This sent murmurs among the council members.

"And what is the truth?" asked Soth.

"That the human leader is to invade Solas with a fleet of warships."

"An invasion?" a council member said, aghast. "Of Solas? Why?"

"To seize the Vitae Virus generator," replied the truth-bird from Eva's mouth.

"He will never find it," the shaman muttered.

"No one in Solas knows where that generator is hidden."

"And what if he does find it?" Antiquus asked Eva.

"Cadmus wants mankind to rule the world once more and control all of its resources."

Antiquus let out an audible gasp. "War?"

"Try as we might, we cannot escape war's cunning effect on society," Soth said. "It is as if—"

A commotion outside the hut interrupted her. The truth-bird fluttered out of Eva's mouth, breaking its spell over her. Eva remained seated, still numb from the effects of the trance.

Galell stumbled into the hut, winded. Blood trickled from the corner of his mouth.

"Galell?" said Antiquus. "What is this? Why are you—"

"He is running to tell you he has seen a ghost," Rovender said as he stepped into the hut.

Antiquus rose with the aid of his cane. "You will not desecrate this village, or this meeting, with your presence!" he said. "Please leave us, banished spirit."

"Not without Eva Nine." Rovender pointed to her.

"She is in our captivity now," Antiquus said. "Both she and the other one may come in handy if the hu-mans are to invade here with their machines of war craft."

"Bluh. That will do you no good." Rovender approached Eva. "You know nothing of humans."

"And you do?"

"I know what I know. But what difference does it make?" Rovender helped Eva to her feet. "I am dead to you. A ghost. A phantom."

Even in her stupor Eva saw that the frayed cord around Rovender's waist was identical to the cords wrapped around the other council members, the cords that bound each of them to the weave of the hut itself. She looked around the room.

"That was yours, wasn't it?" She pointed to a severed unraveled cord hanging from the wall. "You were part of this council."

Rovender's face was stoic. "Come, Eva. I have returned here only for you. Now we shall leave."

"Hold on." Antiquus raised his hand. "We need to know more about the hu-mans and what they did to Nadeau."

"You will learn of it soon enough," Rovender replied. "You think you may avoid the world by hiding up here, but eventually the world will come to you. And you may not like what you see, old one."

"Enough!" Antiquus pointed at Rovender with

his cane. “Seize this ghost and his fledgling.”

A gang of Cæruleans entered the hut, overwhelming Rovender and Eva. Both were bound and tied.

“Bring him here!” Antiquus pointed to the center of the room. He looked over at the shaman. “Soth, call the bird.”

Rovender opened his mouth before the truth-bird flew in. Eva watched as it settled on his tongue. A pointed head peeked out from between Rovender’s lips.

“You will tell us all that we need to know,” Antiquus said, and took his seat as the head of the council.

“You know the truth already,” the truth-bird said in Rovender’s voice.

“Watch your tongue, ghost, or I shall have it removed,” said Antiquus. “Tell us why the hu-mans did what they did to Nadeau.”

“I do not know,” replied the truth-bird. “Perhaps it is an attempt to understand us so that they may control us.”

“Could they achieve this?” Antiquus looked over at Eva.

“They have many machines and an arsenal that is unmatched on all of Orbona,” the truth-bird replied from Rovender’s mouth. “They will stop at nothing to achieve their goal.”

These words sent the council whispering to one another. *This is no different from what I said,* Eva thought. *It's as if they don't believe the truth even when it's being told directly to them.*

"His answer is based only on what *he perceives* as the truth," one of the elders said. "This drunk has spent his exile wandering from our village to the hu-man village."

"Has he?" Soth asked. She turned to Rovender. "How do you know that the hu-mans hold such power?"

The truth-bird replied in Rovender's voice, "Because I have traveled far from here—into the ancient ruins of the Eastern Wastelands, down to the southern tip of the Bliek Mountains, and west to the shores of the Barren Sea. The humans have more primitive machinery than Ojo, to be sure, but there is much of it and it will fulfill their commands."

Eva thought of the alien pedestrian she'd met when she'd been escaping from Solas in the Goldfish. Even that battered hovercar had impressed him. The aliens did not have a lot of Tech like Cadmus.

"If he is right," one of the elders said, "it's going to be like the Second Solar War all over again."

"You have journeyed far, Rovender," Soth continued. "Why have you returned here from your leave?"

"You mean," Antiquus said, "why did he leave in the first place and turn his back on all his kin?"

"You know this answer," the truth-bird said. "When my partner and nymph passed into the next world, I could no longer stay. Grief greeted me at every corner in this village. I was reminded of them everywhere I looked. I saw their faces in my brothers and sisters. I saw their spirits in my dreams. It was a longing pain that could never be soothed."

Eva tried to wriggle free from her binds. She could see Rovender's body begin to tremble. She wanted to hold her friend tight and tell him she was here for him.

"Yet you abandoned us all, even as we tried to help you," Antiquus said.

"Our traditional rituals did little to ease my pain. I needed to—," the bird started.

"So you turned your back on them? Our spirit-healing rituals have worked for generations, unchanged from our home planet. So it has always been. Who are you to disavow them?" Antiquus's voice rose in anger.

"I am not from our home planet. I am from Orbona," the truth-bird replied.

"And here, on Orbona, in our village, you left us all without any warning?" Antiquus leaned on his cane and pulled himself up, clearly agitated by Rovender's words. "When the sickness claimed more of our clan, you were not here. When our munt-runners fled from Dorcean poachers, you were not here. When our scouts started vanishing mysteriously—"

"I left because none of you could heal me. I left because I didn't know why I was still alive. I left because I didn't understand why I survived and my loved ones perished."

Soth looked over at Antiquus, but he said nothing.

The truth-bird continued, "I *was* a ghost, an apparition, destined to wander aimlessly forever. I cared about no one and nothing, not even myself . . . until I met the human girl, Eva Nine."

"This hu-man?" Antiquus pointed to Eva.

"Eva gave me purpose. She filled my heart with hope once again. My spirit told me she was special. My spirit told me to teach her as if she were mine—teach her about us . . . about Orbona . . . about everything. Little did I know that she was teaching me."

Tears rolled down Eva's cheek as she listened to Rovender speak. Her friend had been beaten and bruised by Besteel, authoritons, and sand-snipers, and yet these words that he spoke, the truth, seemed to hurt him most.

"What has she taught you?" Soth asked.

"A heart of compassion is just as hard to hold within you as one of indifference," the truth-bird replied.

Antiquus was silent. The council looked at him for a reaction.

"Say something," Soth said to Antiquus. "For you now know his truth."

Antiquus cleared his throat. "I knew that you ached for the loss of your loved ones. So, too, did the village. We all mourned their passing."

"But you did not show it," the truth-bird replied.

"A leader must be steadfast no matter what horrors he faces. He cannot show pain, Rovender. It can be interpreted as a sign of weakness." Antiquus's voice was hushed. A whisper.

"I did not want a leader," said the truth-bird. "I wanted my father."

Antiquus's voice was shaking now. "And I wanted my son back, my little carefree son who was always by my side. Always playing. Always laughing. Not burdened by tragedy. Not broken by destiny's fickle decisions."

"A child needs his parent at all times, Father. Not just when life is smiling down upon him."

Antiquus ambled over and gently removed the truth-bird from Rovender's mouth. He held Rovender's head in his trembling hands and spoke. "You are right, my son. You are right."

The council of elders cheered and clapped.

Eva wriggled free from her binds. She rushed to Rovender, but stopped short as she watched him embrace his father. Arius's chanting drifted into her mind like a long-forgotten lullaby. *Soon there will be a reunion, but it will end falsely in death and then truly in rebirth.* Eva dried the tears from her cheeks and smiled.

CHAPTER 30: FAMILY

"If this conflict is inevitable," Antiquus said, "we must do what we can to help our sister clans."

"We need to get to Lacus," Eva said. She was sitting with the council members next to Rovender. Most of the village was now crammed into the hut, including Eva Eight. "We must warn the Halcyonus, and I need to speak to Arius."

"Arius?" Soth said. "The Arsian? How do you know her?"

"I've met her," Eva said. "She told me my future and gave me this." Eva rolled up her sleeve.

"An Arsian glyph!" Soth's eyes were wide. "Little nymph, you have been marked."

Eva rolled her sleeve back down. She didn't have to look to know that all eyes were on her. "Is that a good thing?" she asked, a bit hesitant.

"A mark can come to represent good, evil, or otherwise," said the shaman. "It depends on what actions are associated with it."

"And since you've risked much to return our dying brother, against the wishes of your own leader, I'd say that this mark will be a mark of good," Antiquus said.

"You know, the Ars—including Arius—are very reclusive beings. They are highly selective in who they communicate with," Soth said. "Can you recall any of Arius's predictions?"

Eva concentrated on conjuring more of what Arius had said. "There was something about a gift that none could have or take. . . . I don't know. . . . I can't remember. It's in my head, but it never comes when I want it."

"A gift?" Antiquus said.

"The greatest gift of all is life," Soth replied.

"Maybe she was talking about the Vitae Virus generator?" Eva added.

Antiquus nodded. "That certainly is a gift given that none may take."

"Cadmus is going to try," Eva Eight spoke up.

"As I said, he'll never find it," replied Soth. "It is buried deep in the Heart of the Wandering Forest, protected by a powerful entity."

"A being that can see right into your very spirit," added Antiquus. "It will know if someone impure of heart were to cross its threshold."

"The signposts," Eva said. "I remember when we saw those, Rovee."

"Warnings to all who trespass," Rovender said. "Whatever dwells inside there is beyond our understanding. Only a few who dared enter have returned."

"And they are always changed," Soth added. "Different from before they ventured into the Heart." The gathering murmured in agreement.

"Father, may we take the shuttle so that we may travel to Lacus to help our sister clan, the Halcyonus?" Rovender asked.

"I am still confused as to why the hu-mans would lay siege to Lacus instead of directly attacking Solas." Antiquus rubbed his dewlap in thought.

"I saw what looked like an Ars working with Cadmus, but he was different," Eva said. "For some reason they want Arius before they attack Solas."

"That is not good," Antiquus moaned. "Not good at all."

"Why?" asked Eva.

Soth reached up to a shelf and took down an oblong piece of carved wood. The shellacked wood was decorated with the design of a round smiling creature. Soth twisted the top of the carving, and it split in half, revealing a smaller wood carving inside, like the nesting dolls Eva had seen in her dream. The shaman pulled the second doll out from within the first and opened it up.

"When we arrived in Orbona, there were four Arsians who traveled with us." Soth now had all four dolls placed in a row. "Two sisters and two brothers."

"Yes," Eva said. "I also met Zin at the Royal Museum, and he told me this. He has two sisters: Arius and Darius."

"That is correct," Soth said, arranging the dolls in pairs. "Arius seeks the premonitions of the future. Darius seeks the wisdom of the past."

Eva recognized the dolls now. They were fanciful depictions of Arius and her siblings. "What does Zin seek?" she asked, pointing to the doll representing him.

"Knowledge. Which is why King Ojo asked them to

accompany us on our journey," replied the shaman.

Eva remembered how intrigued Zin had been by every artifact he'd collected, and all the questions he had asked her.

"But what of the other?" Rovender asked.

"Loroc, the other brother. He sought strength."

"I don't know," Eva said, examining the doll depicting Loroc. "This guy didn't look that strong. Big and scary? Yes. But he didn't seem very strong."

"Strength is not just in muscle and bone," Rovender said.

"That is right," Soth added. "Emotional strength is more powerful."

"I don't know." Eva returned the Loroc doll to the others. "This being had two pairs of eyes and more arms than Zin or Arius."

"Hmmm," Soth said. "That description is different from what I know Loroc to look like." She tucked the dolls back within one another and put them away.

Eva remembered her conversation with Zin. Despite his chirpy voice there had been sadness in him. Hopelessness. "Zin said his sister Darius had died. He was looking for Arius and didn't know where she was," said Eva.

This unsettled the gathering. Many murmured among themselves.

"Darius did visit us many years ago to seek our counsel," Antiquus said. "She was not well."

"We tried to heal her, but it was hopeless," Soth added. "So we sent word to King Ojo."

"Loroc arrived some days later," continued Antiquus, "and Darius and Loroc left together. We never saw either of them again."

"We did not know that she had passed," Soth said. She held a palm up to the air. "Hopefully, her spirit has found serenity."

The council did the same. "Spirit find serenity," they said in unison.

"You must leave at once to warn Arius and help the Halcyonus," Antiquus said. He gestured to Galell. "Please find Hækel and have him ready the shuttle for Rovender and Eva Nine, and her sister."

Galell left, and the assembly began to break up. Eva and Rovender helped Antiquus onto his hover-disc, and they followed him out of the hut and into the center of Faunas. The nighttime village was aglow under hundreds of hanging lanterns.

"Eva Nine," Antiquus said, and took her hand. "I am truly sorry for many things that we learned today, but mostly I am sorry in how you were received by our clan. Will you forgive us?"

"Of course." Eva smiled. "I am just glad to see Rovee return home."

"You did good, Eva." Rovender knelt down and placed his hands on her shoulders. "There was much healing done to my spirit tonight. I am glad you were here to see it."

Eva hugged Rovender tightly. From the entrance of the elders' hut, she could see the silhouette of Eva Eight watching them. Eva smiled at her but could not tell if her sister was smiling back.

A low vibration came from above. Over the treetops a squarish ship with a bulbous windshield hovered. Its dual engines were incredibly quiet compared to the noisy *Bijou*. The gathering of villagers cleared the way, and the shuttle set down in the center of the village. A scruffy, smiling Cærulean pilot stepped out.

"Hækel, whom you have known since nymph-hood, will take you all to Lacus," Antiquus said to Rovender.

"The shuttle is fueled and ready. We shall leave at your word, Rovender," Hækel said.

"I don't know what you did in there, Nine, but it worked. I thought we were done for," Eight said as she stepped up alongside Eva. They watched Rovender and Hækel talking excitedly in front of the shuttle. "Looks like your friend Rovender got the good fortune of returning home. He is a lucky one."

"So are we," Eva added. She reached out and grabbed Eight's hand.

Eva Eight looked down at Eva's hand in hers. "You two are pretty close," she said.

"Yeah," Eva replied. "We've been through a lot. After Muthr died, he promised he'd always be there for me. "

Eva Eight was quiet as she watched Rovender bid farewell to his fellow villagers.

There was a tap on Eva's shoulder. She and her sister turned to see Galell holding his boomrod and charger. "For you, Eva Nine," Galell handed the weapon to her. "May it protect you all."

"Thank you, Galell." Eva handed the heavy weapon to her sister. "I hope we never have to use it."

"I am sorry for my actions. Please have it in your heart to forgive me."

"Of course," Eva said.

Soth walked up to Eva and took her hand. "Many gratitudes to you both for returning our departed Nadeau. My life is richer for crossing paths with you, Eva Nine. I hope your journey ends well." She placed a braided necklace around Eva's neck. From it hung a glass vial half-filled with dirt. "This is the soil from our home world. To remind you on your travels that you are always home."

"Thank you, Soth," said Eva, tucking the necklace into her coveralls. "I'll keep it close."

Eva and her sister boarded the shuttle. Rovender stopped at the bottom of the ramp.

"My son," Antiquus said as he reached out to Rovender, "you have taught this old creature much today."

Rovender embraced his father.

"I am so sorry," Antiquus whispered. "Despite the darkness that looms over our world, I am lightened to hold you once again."

"Me too, Father. Me too," Rovender said.

"I know your mother's spirit is happy now as she watches over us."

"I feel it too," Rovender said, and smiled.

"Perhaps some of the Halcyonus would want to come here?" Antiquus said. "We are inland, but we are also out of the fray . . . for now."

"I will offer," Rovender replied and walked to the top of the ramp. "And we shall be back. I promise."

"Safe journeys." Antiquus held up his palm.

The ramp closed and the shuttle lifted off and soared into the night.

From the closed cockpit Eva watched the treetops rush by as the shuttle sped over the forest.

"How long do you think it will take?" Rovender asked.

"We should arrive before sunrise," Hækel replied. "I am going to travel east, to Lake Concors, and follow the shoreline south to Lacus. Once we are at the lake, I will attempt contact with Solas."

"Keep us over the forest in case we should need to land in a hurry," Rovender replied. "We do not want to face off with any of Cadmus's warships."

"You can say that again," Eva Eight said with a snort.

"This is good to know," said Hækel. He turned from the flight controls momentarily and unlatched the cockpit door that led into the cabin. "You all must be quite weary from your travels. Why not retire for the remainder of our journey? I shall wake you when we are near Lacus, or if anything else should arise."

"We could use the rest," Rovender said, exiting the cockpit.

"Thank you, Hækel." Eva patted his shoulder.

"Many gratitudes to you, Eva Nine. It is good to see our brother Rovender in our village again."

Eva closed the door to the cockpit and joined her sister and Rovender in the small cabin of the shuttle. Eight was examining Galell's boomrod.

Eva shuddered. "You don't want to be on the

other end of the barrel when that thing goes off. Trust me."

"I hope we do not have to use it, but it is comforting to know we have some sort of weapon," Rovender said. He opened a storage compartment and pulled out three Cærulean-made flight jackets. He threw one over to Eva, then one to her sister. "Let us rest if we can. There will be much to do once we arrive at Lacus."

"Do you think Cadmus is there already?" Eva asked as she curled up in her seat and pulled the heavy jacket on.

"Hard to say." Rovender fastened his coat. "Like us, the Halcyonus prefer a quiet existence. There is no way to communicate with them directly."

"I hope we're not too late," Eva said. "I'd hate to see anything bad happen to Hostia or her family."

"As would I, Eva Nine." Rovender reclined in his seat and closed his eyes. "Let us all hope for the best."

Eva awoke to the sound of arguing. She looked over at Rovender, who was snoring softly in his seat. Through the closed cockpit door she could hear Eva Eight's voice.

What's going on? Eva approached the cockpit.

"I don't care what he said. Just make this stop

first, and then we'll continue, okay?" Eva Eight said. There was the sharp edge of anger in her voice.

"Stop where?" Eva asked as she opened the door. "What are you talking about?"

Hækel said, "Eva Nine, your sister wants me to set down in the Wandering Forest. She—"

"I was thinking, Nine. We can stop all of this by getting to the generator first," said Eight.

"What?" said Eva, noticing Galell's boomrod in Eight's hands. "No. We don't have time for that."

"But if we have the generator, then we can bargain—"

"The device lies in the Heart of the forest, Eva Eight." Rovender joined Eva in the doorway. "We can't go in there."

"It's just trees." Eva Eight gestured with the muzzle of the weapon to the landscape beyond the cockpit window. "Listen. We *have* to take the generator before Cadmus finds it."

"Cadmus isn't going to find the generator!" Eva yelled, losing her patience. "He's going to invade Lacus, if he hasn't already!"

"We must help our friends." Rovender spoke in a calm tone. Slowly he reached for the boomrod in Eva Eight's grasp. "Please just hand me the—"

"NO!" Eva Eight pulled the weapon away from

Rovender and backed up. "We are taking that generator!" She charged the boomrod.

"What are you doing!" said Eva.

"It would be best to put that down, Eva Eight," Rovender continued in his calm manner. "You do not want this weapon going off in here. It would be bad for all of us."

Tears welled in Eva Eight's eyes. "Cadmus has taken everything from me! He has taken my family, my home, and my freedom. He is not taking this, Nine. I am taking it from him. For once there will be something he can't have!" Eight aimed the boomrod at Hækel. "Now you land this thing in the Heart of the forest, or I'll force us to land!"

Through the cockpit window Eva could see poking up through the canopy the tall spires that circled the Heart. Without a word she looked over at Rovender. Eva Eight spied the exchange.

"What?" she said. "What is it?"

"The Heart—we just passed over it," Hækel said.

"We can come back and look for the generator after we help the Halcyonus," Eva said.

"Yes," Rovender added. "I will personally take you to the Heart myself, Eva Eight. Just put down the—"

"Too late." Eva Eight fired the boomrod at the shuttle's control panel.

CHAPTER 31: HEART

Eva Nine gripped the back of a cabin chair and pulled herself up. Smoke, heavy with ozone, curled into her lungs. She coughed, sending jolts of pain stabbing through her chest. Holding her sides, Eva found her only relief was to inhale in short, shallow breaths.

Somewhere a hatch on the ship opened, and the smoke began to clear. Eva realized the shuttle was on its side. In the cockpit Hækel was still strapped to his pilot's seat, though unmoving. Behind Eva, lying crumpled near the open ramp at the back of the shuttle, was Rovender. "Rovee? Rovee?" She crawled over to him. "Are you okay?"

He did not respond, but Eva could see his chest rise and fall. Rovender was alive but unconscious. She grabbed his heavy jacket and dragged him toward the open ramp. Both of them tumbled off the ramp onto the mossy ground below.

The cool night air was silent around the smoldering wreck. Eva stood slowly, holding her throbbing ribs. Dizzy, she nearly fell back down, but an icy hand seized hers.

"Come on, Nine," Eight said, her voice shrill. She was holding the boomrod in her other hand. "I need you to show me where the Heart of the forest is."

Pain blurred Eva's vision. "No! We . . . we can't leave them," she said, pointing to the shuttle. "And something's wrong with me. It hurts when I breathe." She went to activate the life monitor patch on her utilitunic, then remembered she had thrown the eukaberry-drenched garment at the warbot.

"I still have my tunic and it can heal you, Nine." Eight opened her flight jacket to reveal her dark blue utilitunic beneath.

Eva reached out for the tunic. "Take it off. I need it!"

"I will," Eight replied, closing her jacket, "but first you have to take me to the Heart. I am getting that generator."

Eva slumped back down, defeated. "Okay," she whispered. "I'll—I'll take you."

"Good! Get up and let's go! We are doing this

together!" Eight yanked Eva by the hand, and they disappeared into the depths of the Wandering Forest.

"I'm not going past here," Eva said. They were standing in an open field feathered with twisted bracken. A gentle breeze rippled over the ferns, causing them to whisper in the moonlight. Eva knew they were whispering to the noduled spires that stood here and watched the forest. She remembered Rovender explaining that these spires were signposts warning those who would trespass into this forbidden area.

"You are coming, Nine." Eight looked up at the pointed spire. "I don't know how big this generator is, so we may need your talents to call up one of your tree friends to carry it out for us."

"Call one yourself!" Eva eased down to the ground, sitting next to a spire. The hike through the forest had been exhausting. With every breath she took, Eva's sides felt as if they'd been seared by shards of hot glass. "I—I need to go back and check on Rovee and Hækel."

"You don't get it!" Eight's voice pierced the night, sending up a covey of startled turnfins. "Your alien friends will all become enslaved if we don't find this thing. We have a chance to get to it first. We have a chance to have the upper hand. For once Cadmus will have to listen to us. He'll have to give us what we want."

"I thought all you wanted was for us to be together. To be a family," Eva said. "What more do you want?"

Eight's sea-green eyes were turbulent and stormy. "I want to see the look on Cadmus's face when I tell him I know where the generator is hidden and he can't have it. I want him to beg me for it, and I want to deny him—the way he denied me the life that I wanted."

Eva gripped the spire to support herself as she rose. Her sides throbbed. "You wouldn't even be here—*I wouldn't be here*—if it weren't for Cadmus and what he created."

"I don't want to be here!" Eva Eight yelled. "I didn't want this. I wanted Earth, the Earth we learned about in our programs. The Earth with cities, people, and culture, not this . . . this alien wilderness."

"Well, you don't get that old Earth. I don't get it either. And none of the aliens here, who left their home planets to start their lives all over again, get that. We all have to live here, on Orbona." Eva coughed hard. The agony was so intense that her vision went white from pain. Scarlet drops of blood spotted her hand.

Eight gazed up at the moon. It was hiding behind Orbona's rings. The light shining down made the tears on her cheeks glisten. "If I don't get it, then neither does he." She aimed the boomrod at Eva. "You're coming with me or we are both dying right here."

Eva reluctantly followed Eight as she waded through the bracken, past the spires and into a dense curtain of foliage. Tree limbs creaked and snapped, unseen birds squawked, and insects chirruped in a nocturnal choir. Even the noisy movement of the Evas' traipsing through the undergrowth did little to deter the calling of the forest's denizens. *The forest must know we are here,* Eva thought. *What did Rovender say about the Heart? There is something you have to have . . . or be, in order to enter.* Eva hugged her sides, dizzy from the nausea caused by her pain.

At once the sounds stopped and Eva found herself at the edge of the forest, looking down from a ridge into a wide glade.

"What on earth!" Eight said as she joined Eva at the tree line.

Strange plants, similar to the microscopic fungi Eva had seen in holograms, reached out toward the moonlight. Brilliant bioluminescence pulsed inside each plant, bathing the entire glade in a whitish glow. Though the plants wavered in concert as if they were underwater, Eva could feel no breeze. In the center of the glade was what appeared to be an impact crater.

"This is it!" Eight said, grabbing Eva by the hand. "The generator is in there. I know it!"

"I—I can't go on." Eva coughed, and almost passed out from the surge of pain that racked her body.

"We are so close, Nine!" Eight's voice rose to near hysteria. Her eyes were wild with madness. "I'll give you the tunic once we are at the generator, and you'll be fine. Come with me! Come on!"

They stepped down into the glade, and the waist-high plants leaned toward them, like tentacles reaching for a meal. Eight swatted at the plants with the boomrod, causing them to recoil and flash their lights. All manner of small creatures danced through the foliage. "I bet it's right in the center of this impact crater."

"We shouldn't be here," Eva whispered. Fear caused her breathing to quicken, which in turn caused more pain. It felt as if her lungs could not hold any air. Once more she coughed. Once more blood stained her palm.

They climbed up the earthy outer wall of the crater. "We are almost there, Nine!" Eight cackled as she clawed up toward the summit of the crater wall. "We've got this! Cadmus will—" Eva Eight looked down into the crater, frozen in her steps.

"What is it?" Eva asked in a whispery voice. With shaky hands she pulled herself up to the edge of the crater's rim. Eva peered into the depression and realized it was not a crater after all.

It was the exposed ruins of an underground HRP Sanctuary.

"This can't be." Eva Eight jumped down onto the roof of the Sanctuary. "Where is the generator?"

Eva slid over the rim, joining her sister. She could see that the Sanctuary's roof was partially collapsed, revealing several rooms within. *This is the Heart of the forest?* Eva scooted toward the opening in the roof. *Perhaps there is still a utilitunic or MediKit in the supply room.*

"The generator came from the aliens, not humans, right?" Eight said, standing at the edge of the collapsed roof. "Could it be somewhere else in the forest?"

As if in response to the question, a chorus of animal calls erupted from deep within the ruins. Both girls backed away as bizarre creatures, the likes of which Eva had never encountered before, burst forth from the Sanctuary. The creatures crawled, slithered, galloped, and flew out into the forest night.

"Do not run. Do not be afraid, my children," a melodious voice intoned. "We have guests, pilgrims from our old Earth who have come to be purified, to find their true selves. Their essence. Their composition, makeup, and matter."

Eva watched as a large diaphanous entity rose from the remains of the Sanctuary. Its form stretched, coiled, and twisted with multiple pseudopods, as if it were a gigantic amoeba. An electric glow rippled through its flowing membrane. The light within the entity seemed to pump through a fine network of veins, bringing to mind the wiring diagram of the *Bijou* that Eva had seen.

"What? Who are you?" Eight shielded her eyes from the light emanating from the entity. Its vibrant presence clearly dumbfounded Eight, dousing her mania.

"The Heart, the spirit, of the forest," Eva whispered, hugging the pain in her chest. She scooted away from the opening in the roof.

"I am the Keeper of Balance," the entity replied. It moved through the night air as if it were swimming through water. "I am the Spark of Life. I am the Mother of All Nature."

Muthr. Eva thought. *Its voice sounds like Muthr's.* The entity whirled toward Eva and examined her in its glowing light. Its voice entered Eva's mind.

I am Muthr. I am your mother. I am the Mother.

"We mean you no harm here, Mother," Eva Eight said. "We are just looking for a machine, an alien generator. If you could show us where it is, we'd—"

"Generator?" The Mother whisked back toward Eva Eight. "The generation here is done by no machine. It is accomplished through metamorphosis. Is that what you seek?"

"No," Eight said. "I must find the generator. I need to get to it before anyone else does."

"Why?" The Mother drew closer to Eva Eight.

"Be-because I don't want the human leader to take it," Eight replied with a hitch in her voice. She creeped toward Eva.

"So you would take this 'generator' so that no other might have it? You would seize it? Steal it away? Safekeep it?" The entity stretched one of its pseudopods to block Eight's path to Eva.

"Be careful what you say, Eight," Eva wheezed, "and what you think."

"Seize the generator and safekeep it?" Eight repeated. She looked over at Eva, then back at the Mother. "I suppose, yes," she answered, though Eva could hear a waver in her words. "Can you show me where it is?"

"There is hesitation in you," the Mother said. "You are concealing your truth. Let me see into you. Let me see your spirit, your truth, before I show you where the generation occurs."

Eva's sister let out a short shriek as one of the Mother's pseudopods wrapped around and constricted her.

Eva stretched out a hand to her sister. Their fingertips brushed before Eight was lifted up. "What are you doing, Mother?" Eva asked. Eight tried to wriggle free from the Mother's grasp but was absorbed into her ectoplasm.

A blinding burst of light exploded from the entity. Eva closed her eyes tightly, but an afterimage remained. In it Eight remained motionless while her garments and belongings evaporated in the flash. Eva slowly opened her eyes and discovered her sister suspended inside the Mother. Like the entity, Eight's body had become transparent. Eva could see Eight's skeleton and veins through translucent skin and muscle.

"I don't want to be here. I didn't want this." The Mother repeated Eva Eight's words in Eva Eight's voice.

"Let her go," Eva said. "Please, Mother, let her go."

"Her unfulfilled desires have hurt her deeply," the Mother said. "See, here, how her hatred has poisoned her." Eva watched an inky darkness pump from Eight's heart and circulate throughout her body. "I have no tolerance for hate."

"She has been hurt, yes." Eva closed her eyes and tried to push out the agonizing pain of her injury. "I am hurt, Mother . . . Muthr."

"Indeed, this one has been hurt. However, she in turn would hurt others. She has hurt you." The Mother continued examining Eight. "I see no need for this to carry on."

Eva opened her bleary eyes. She could see her sister's pumping heart. Slower and slower the heartbeats became. "No!" Eva called out. "Don't kill her!" She coughed hard and slumped down onto the roof of the Sanctuary. "She just wanted to have a family," Eva whispered. "That's all anybody wants."

"A family? Yes," the Mother said. "To look over and care for her own as I do for my little ones." The entity stretched one of its pseudopods back down into the Sanctuary. "However, to raise them in the world, she must be at one with the world. So it shall be."

Eva watched as a brightly patterned flower, like an orchid, traveled up the pseudopod inside the Mother's body.

"I shall soothe her troubled spirit," the Mother said. The flower drifted toward Eva Eight, still suspended in the entity's body.

"What are you doing?" Eva asked. Her voice was barely a whisper.

"I am regenerating her," the Mother answered. The flower went into Eva Eight's open mouth and through her translucent body. Eight began to jerk and twist, struggling within the entity. Eva watched as her sister's legs fused together and her toes stretched out into winding tendrils.

". . . changing her for the better," the Mother mused.

Eight's hair grew in great length in every direction, twisting and knotting as it spiraled outward.

". . . curing all that ails her . . ."

Her skin wrinkled and cracked as it hardened and browned.

". . . reinventing her . . ."

Arms stretched into branches. Fingers became leaves.

"I have evolved her. She will venture back into

the world anew. She is now free from my bosom."

The Mother released the transformed Eva Eight—who was another being now, composed of both a tree and a human. Her body creaked as she twisted to face Eva.

"I am sorry," the Eva-tree whispered. Tiny flower buds popped from woody vines that had once been Eva Eight's hair.

I'm dreaming, Eva thought. *I must be delirious from the pain.* She closed her eyes and curled up into a ball. *I am going to die here, in the Heart of the forest.*

A glowing pseudopod stretched out to Eva. With cold, weak, trembling hands she took the pseudopod and hugged it close to her chest. It was warm to the touch.

Eva Nine's breathing slowed.

Where will my spirit go when I am gone? Eva had asked.

You will know that answer one day, Eva, Rovender had said, *but I believe that day is far off.*

"Rovee, you were wrong." Eva whispered. "I hope you remember me."

I'll see you soon, Muthr, she thought. *Let's go on the next journey together.* As she exhaled a dying breath, Eva could feel the Mother's pseudopod winding its way around her battered body.

CHAPTER 32: EVOLUTION

Eva Nine felt as if she were soaking in a warm bathtub. She tried to move, but her exhausted limbs wouldn't allow it. Though her eyes remained closed, in her mind she saw a blurry vision of a woman holding her close. She wondered, *Am I dead?*

"No," the woman answered. Eva tried to focus on the details of the woman and saw a slight smile on her face. It looked like Muthr's silicon smile. The woman combed her long fingers through Eva's hair, untangling it and rendering it more colorless with each stroke. "You are not dead. You, who would plead for another's life with your dying breath, are now within me. I am healing you."

Healing me? How?

"Open your eyes and you will see," the woman replied.

Eva opened her eyes and found herself inside the glowing entity, Mother. As had happened to her sister, Eva's skin had now become translucent, revealing broken ribs and a punctured lung. The glowing ectoplasm of the Mother flowed around and through Eva's body, healing her as it did so.

You have . . . wires inside of you, Eva observed. *Mixed with arteries and veins.*

"That is correct," the Mother replied. "I am a chimera. A being composed of both machinery and living tissue."

"Chimera." I know that word, Eva thought. *Are you a Muthr?*

"Once upon a time I was that simple machine, programmed to create life, care for it, and send it off into the world. But I have changed. I have grown, evolved beyond what I once was."

Evolved. Eva looked out through the entity's translucent skin. Outside, in the night, the lone tree figure of Eva Eight stood watching. Unmoving.

Will you evolve me as well? What shall I become?

"Evolution is adaptation. Mutation. To survive by accepting the changes in your reality." The Mother carried Eva down into the Sanctuary ruins. From within the entity, Eva could see the overgrown remains of rooms that she knew all too well. "You are interesting, little one. You have already evolved. You are different from your sisterkind and those that I created here long ago."

I am? Eva looked out into the Sanctuary at the generator room, where the human embryos had been cultivated. The room was now little more than rubble with more bizarre plants growing from it. Several floatazoans hovered in the room's entryway.

"You are closer to your ancestors in that you are more attuned with your fellow flora and fauna."

You're talking about how I can communicate with Otto and the trees.

"It is your compassion that I sense within you. It is an energy beyond any I can create." A white light pumped from Eva's heart and circulated through her body. "You feel empathy toward others, no matter what their makeup—be it plant, animal, extraterrestrial, or robot."

Muthr.

"Yes, and like your Muthr, I still reside here," the

Mother continued. "I still create life and send it off into the world. So it has been for me. So it shall always be."

You still create new life? Eva glanced back at the demolished generator room. *How?*

"I allow the beings here to do what I have done—drink from the Water of Life," the Mother answered. "The primordial ooze from which all living beings flow forth." The Mother brought Eva to the other side of the Sanctuary, below the collapsed roof. Where the gymnasium and greenhouse would normally be, there was now a small pond. Its green surface shimmered with fluorescent life-forms swimming about within it, while large otherworldly plants lined the shore. The Mother released Eva from her ectoplasmic body and placed her at the edge of the pond.

Eva stretched and yawned, feeling no pain. In fact, she felt as if she had awakened from a deep, restful sleep. Though her skin had returned to its usual rosy tone, her clothing and her hair were devoid of any color. Eva ran her fingers over her ribs and inhaled deeply. Her wounds had been healed.

"Thank you," she said.

"Your compassion must be encouraged. It must be fostered," the Mother replied. "Taste the water and teach others how to adapt as you have. Teach them how to thrive in our reimagined world."

Eva looked out at the water. Floating on the surface were the orchid flowers that the Mother had fed to Eva Eight. Farther out, half-submerged in the center of the pond, was a metallic device shaped like an enormous seed. Under the layers of algae that coated the device, Eva could make out the distinct image of an eye with a horizontal iris—the heraldic symbol of the Ojo family.

"The Vitae Virus generator," Eva whispered. "It fell here and filled the pool water with the virus."

A lone floatazoan drifted into the room. Eva watched as it dipped one of its petal-like feelers into the pond water. It placed the feeler into its mouth and licked it dry. The animal twisted and contorted as Eva Eight had done. It doubled in size, and its arms grew in length. It turned and regarded Eva with watchful eyes. Intelligent eyes.

You, it thought to her. *Me.*

All at once Eva understood how the Vitae Virus worked, the virus that was thriving in the water.

The water that the Sanctuary's resident Muthr had somehow ingested . . .

. . . the water that all the greenhouse plants had been exposed to . . .

. . . the water that all of Earth's surviving microorganisms were exposed to—the algae. The tardigrades. The insects . . .

. . . the water that grew the orchid Eva Eight had ingested.

They are always changed, Soth had said of those who entered the Heart of the forest. *Different from before.*

"Drink from the pool and awaken what is already within you," said the Mother.

"I am not like the others," Eva whispered. She thought of Gen, Hailey, and her sister.

"You are not," the Mother agreed. "Embrace that notion. Open yourself to accepting who you truly are. Only then will your spirit soar."

Arius's chant echoed from the back of Eva's mind. *For the waters of life will quench your thirst, heal all wounds, and allow your spirit to soar.*

Eva knelt down and dipped her hands into the cool green water of the pond. Cupping them, she scooped up the water and brought it to her lips.

She closed her eyes and drank.

Eva awoke to a chorus of soft hooting. She jolted upright, startled. "Where am I?"

Several turnfins called out from the opening in

the roof above her. Eva stood as the night's events replayed in her mind. Peering out into the darkness of the Sanctuary, she searched through the abundance of life growing around the pond for the Mother, but the entity was nowhere to be found.

Eva looked down at her reflection in the surface of the pond. Aside from the white hair and clothing, the face that looked back at Eva was unchanged. She climbed up to the rim that surrounded the Sanctuary and looked back as a predawn light snuck across the sky. Rooted to the shadowy roof of the Sanctuary, the Eva-tree danced with fluttering turnfins in a cool morning zephyr.

"I must go," Eva whispered to her sister. "Will you be okay?"

"I shall. It is as if a weight has been lifted from me," the Eva-tree answered. "I am home."

"I am happy for you." Eva ran her fingers over the Eva-tree's bark skin. It was warm to the touch.

"You were right, Nine. About telling Cadmus of the expanding forest."

"I just don't want anybody else to die." Eva's eyes were downcast, her mind heavy with the memories of Hailey, Huxley, Nadeau, and Muthr.

"Then show him." Leafy fingers on willow-branch arms reached for Soth's necklace, still

hanging around Eva's neck. The Eva-tree plucked an orchid from its many blooms and placed it in the vial with the soil from the Cærulean planet. "Show Cadmus his thinking must evolve in order for his people to thrive."

"Thank you, Eva Eight, my sister. I will." Eva set off through the glade.

She passed the ring of spires that marked the Heart of the forest and came to a rest in a field of bracken. Closing her eyes and inhaling deeply, she could sense every tree, animal, and insect in the forest. Her perception of her surroundings was awakened, focused, and sharp. She let her mind stretch out deep into the wood—then it stopped, recognizing a familiar spirit.

I am near. Come to me, she thought.

Eva stood in the bracken and stared up into the gilded dawn sky. A whooshing sound came from the distance, and a great beast landed a meter in front of her.

You. Me. Happy.

"I am happy to see you too, Otto." Eva reached out her thin arms and embraced the giant armored water bear. A warm dry tongue licked her head.

"We have to hurry. There is much I have to do. Can you help?"

Yes. Always. Help.

Eva climbed up onto Otto's back and straddled one of his rust-colored scutes. "We need to check on Rovee and Hækel first," Eva said. "I need you to take me *here*." She visualized the area in the forest where the shuttle had crashed.

Hold. On.

Otto cocked his fan-shaped tail under his belly. He snapped it down onto the ground with tremendous force, which sent them hurling up over treetops. Before long they landed at the crash site next to the wrecked shuttle.

Eva slid off Otto onto the moss-covered ground and discovered that Rovender was no longer where she had left him. "Rovee! Rovee!" Eva called out as she ran toward the shuttle. "Rovee, where are you?"

"He is not here," Hækel called out from inside the entranceway. "Eva Nine? Is that you?"

"Yes," Eva crawled into the ship. "Where is Rovee? Is he okay?"

"He is fine," Hækel replied, staring at Eva. "He went looking for you. With both you and your sister gone, we feared the worst."

"Oh, I'm okay." Eva played with a strand of her white hair. "Are you all right?"

"I'm a little bruised, but I shall survive," replied

Hækel. "Actually, I think I may be able to get the shuttle operating once more. The boomrod damaged only the steering controls. Fortunately, I keep quite a few spare parts. But it is going to take some time before we are airborne again, especially with the ship lying on its side like this."

Otto, can you push the shuttle back upright? Eva thought.

Yes.

Outside, Eva could hear the ship creaking as Otto nudged up against it.

"Hold on to something," Eva said to Hækel. The Cærulean did so, a look of confusion on his whiskered face.

Slowly the ship rolled back into the upright position. Eva and Hækel exited down the ramp.

"Good job!" Eva scratched Otto behind the ears.

"A giant water bear." The Cærulean pilot put his hands on his hips, marveling at the behemoth. "I've never seen one of these this close before."

"Don't be afraid. He's an old friend," Eva said. She took Hækel's hand and placed it on Otto's forehead. "Otto," Eva continued, "I need you to go find Rovee. Can you do that for me?"

Yes. Bring. Back.

"Thank you." Eva played with Otto's barbels. "Bring him back safely."

"Eva Nine!" Rovender hopped down from Otto's back and ran to the girl. He held her tight while the water bear hooted and sang. "Are you all right? I feared the worst."

"I am okay, Rovee," Eva said, clutching Rovender. "I'm just glad to be back from the Heart."

Rovender's eyes went wide. "That is why your hair and your clothing is colorless. You have been cleansed by the spirit of the forest. Is this what has happened?"

Eva nodded in agreement. "You were right about trusting what I feel inside. Even though Eight and I were from the same place, and the same blood, we were just different inside, you know?"

"I do know," Rovender replied.

"I knew deep down that Eight wasn't thinking clearly," Eva said with a sniffle. "I guess I thought it would go away after we left the city, but it didn't."

"Her pain was deep." Rovender wiped a long tear from Eva's cheek. "It was a scar you could not heal, Eva. No one could."

"I actually think she is healed now." Eva smiled. "I'll tell you everything on our way to Lacus."

"You are right, Eva. Time is short." Rovender grabbed supplies from the ship and loaded them into a backpack. "Let us go. Hækel, we shall return."

"I will be here," the pilot replied. "Safe journeys."

"Safe journeys," Eva said, climbing up onto Otto.

Thunder threatened from above. Everyone looked up to see a large warship rumble overhead. Its immensity blotted out the morning sun, shadowing the forest in darkness. Several other warships followed in formation.

"They are heading toward Lacus," Rovender said.

"We are too late," added Hækel, with a sigh of defeat.

"Not yet," Eva said, patting the water bear. "Otto, get us there as fast as you can. Okay?"

Hurry. Help. Go.

"Hold on tight," Eva said as she crouched low and gripped the edge of the water bear's plated scutes.

"I have almost forgotten how much I do not enjoy this," Rovender said, joining her.

With a snap of his mighty tail, Otto shot up into the sky, carrying his riders toward Lacus.

CHAPTER 33: LACUS

From the shade of the forest, Otto stepped out onto a vast salt flat. The water bear hooted and sheared off a large patch of moss from a nearby tree. "Otto needs to take a break," Eva said. "All this jumping has worn him out."

"Fine with me," Rovender replied, and stood up on Otto's back. He pulled a spyglass from his supply pack and stood to scan the horizon. "Do you recognize our location?"

"Yes. We are at the flats, on the eastern side of the forest," she said.

"That is correct. We are just south of Lake Concurs and Lacus."

The mineral scent of the lake's waters drifted past on the midday breeze. The scent took Eva back to the first time she'd journeyed out here with Rovender, Otto, and Muthr. Then they'd been searching for any sign of humans living on the planet. It seemed like such a long time ago.

Eva squinted in the direction Rovender was scanning with the spyglass. Clouds gathered over the lake, merging with the haze coming from the horizon. "Can you see Lacus? Are they okay?" she asked.

"No. We are still too far away," Rovender replied. "Hmmmm."

"What is it?"

"I see dust up ahead caused by movement. There is something heading toward the forest." Rovender pointed.

"Cadmus?"

"It is difficult to say." Rovender rubbed his whiskers in thought.

"There is only one way to find out," Eva said.

Otto shuffled toward the movement, traveling in the shade of the tree line. By afternoon they'd arrived at the southern tip of the lake. And there they discovered the source of the dust clouds.

"Hostia! Fiscian!" Rovender jumped down and

rushed toward the Halcyonus family. Like the Cærulean, the colorful residents of Lacus walked on backward-bending legs. But they were shorter in stature and adorned in decorative garb.

From high atop Otto's back Eva gazed out at the shoreline of the lake. Hundreds of Halcyonus were streaming away from their fishing village. Each carried but a few items bundled in baskets and sacks strapped to their backs. Flocks of turnfins cried out from above as if lamenting the exodus. Behind them rose the towering knobby structures that made up the village. Hovering over the towers was a fleet of Cadmus's polished warships, each reflecting the late day sun. Eva's heart pounded, as if it were trying to escape her chest.

She slid down to the ground to help Hostia's family and spied Zoozi, the youngest, clutching his wooden puppet. Zoozi ran and hid behind his mother. Hostia, Fiscian, and their older daughter, Mægden, stiffened as Eva approached them.

"This is so terrible," Eva said. "Are you all okay?"

"We . . . are fines." Hostia pulled Zoozi back, away from Eva. "What has happens to you?"

"I've been to the Heart of the forest. I—"

"There she is!" a Halcyonus screeched from both mouths. Eva turned to see an elderly crone jabbing a finger at her. The crone continued, "There is the harbinger of alls this!"

"Me?" Eva gasped. "I—I had nothing to do with the invasion."

"You and your machines." The crone's eyes were fiery orange. "You broughts this on us. On all of us!"

"That is not true," Rovender said.

"It is!" the crone countered. "And you delivered her to us, Rovenders!"

The exiled villagers now began to crowd around the crone. Eva backed up against Otto.

You. Me. Leave.

Not yet, Eva thought to her companion. *We have to help them. They are scared.*

A herd. Still.

Yes, they still have one another, despite their situation, she thought.

Tell. Them.

Eva climbed back onto Otto's back. Halcyonus villagers were gathering in a noisy throng, surrounding Rovender.

"Listen!" Eva cried out. "Listen to me!"

The din of the crowd lowered. All orange eyes were now on Eva.

"I know you are scared, and I am sorry that this has happened. But believe me when I tell you that it was to happen whether I arrived at your village or not."

"Who does this to us and why?" Hostia asked aloud. The gathering grumbled.

Eva swallowed. She knew the truth would upset them. Hostia and her family had been so kind to her. Rovender looked up at Eva and nodded.

"It is hard to say this, but the warships are from humans, like me," Eva said. "They are planning to invade Solas."

Eva waited for the retaliation—for an attack on her—but all the villagers remained silent. The looks on their exhausted, frightened faces said everything.

"I am here with Rovender to help you. He will lead you all to shelter in the forest, where we can shuttle you to anywhere you want to go."

"Go? Where we wants to go?" Hostia said, exasperated. "Eva, our home is Lacus."

"Your home is where your family is," Eva replied. "Where someone waits for you and thinks about you." She looked over at Rovender. "You all still have that."

"And you?" Fiscian asked. "Have you found your family? Is this them that causes our fear and forces us from our homes?"

"They are like me, but I am not like them," Eva replied.

The Halcyonus rumbled at this answer.

"I will go to Cadmus, the human leader, to try to end this." Eva slid down to the ground and walked into the crowd. "You have no reason to trust me or my words, but listen in here"—Eva put her hand to her chest—"when I tell you I am going to do everything I can to get your village back."

The crowd parted, and Eva walked along the shoreline toward the village. Rovender came up next to Eva and grabbed her wrist. "Are you sure about this? You have seen what those machines can do," he said.

"I have to stop this," said Eva. "Cadmus doesn't know about the generator and the growing forest. And I still need to speak to Arius."

Rovender knelt down on one knee and placed his hands on Eva shoulders. "What if they have gotten to Arius already? What if Cadmus does not wish to hear your words?"

"I have to, Rovee. I feel that this is what I have to do." Eva forced an uncertain smile.

"Then Otto and I will accompany you," Rovender replied.

"No. You and Otto should take the Halcyonus

back to the shuttle. I know exactly how they feel right now—frightened, without shelter, and unsure of what's to come. If anyone can guide and protect them, it is you. Otto will stay behind to help you. He'll do whatever you ask, trust me," said Eva. Somehow she felt better, as if speaking her plan aloud made her more committed.

Rovender held Eva in his arms for a long moment before speaking. "Please be careful. I do not know what I would do if I lost you."

Eva hugged him close. "I'll be okay."

"Before you go, I want to give you something." Rovender pulled off the frayed cord from around his waist.

"Your cord from the council?"

"As Antiquus's son, I was next in line to be the leader of my village," Rovender said as he tied the cord around Eva's waist. "But leadership is not inherited. It is earned through action. You are a leader, Eva Nine. A hero. And you are my WondLa."

Eva embraced Rovender. "I love you, Rovee."

"I love you too. Please return to me safe."

"I will. I promise," Eva said, and then she continued alone, along the shore, toward uncertainty.

CHAPTER 34: CONSUMED

The waves of Lake Concors lapped at Eva's shoes while the wind twirled her long white hair. She was standing at the footbridge that led over the lake's surface toward the first tower of Lacus. The enormous tower housed an entire community in stacked globular huts held high above the deep green waters. The tower was also connected to four others by a network of rope bridges and skywalks. In the evening sun hovered a fleet of warships casting a dark silhouette over Lacus. From the shoreline Eva could see that the ships were unloading cargo into the village.

A brightly colored blanket, abandoned by its owners, fluttered across the pebbly beach. Eva grabbed the blanket and wrapped herself in it, concealing her face. She stepped onto the footbridge and set off toward the first tower.

As she passed under the arched entryway, Eva was nearly knocked into the water by a rush of fleeing Halcyonus carrying an unconscious fisherman. The fisherman's head lolled to one side, revealing the recognizable puncture wound of a SHOCdart in his neck.

Stopping for a moment, Eva closed her eyes, allowing her senses to run along into the homes in the first tower. She could feel the presence of Halcyonus everywhere—their panic and confusion. Just ahead of her she sensed another creature's fear.

Still tethered to the boards of a swaying footbridge, a fisherman's turnfin let out a lonely cry. Eva untied the leash from the bird's neck. "It's okay. You can join your flock now," she whispered, and dropped the leash to the planked walk.

"Before you leave," Eva said, stroking the turnfin's sleek head, "can you fly up and tell me which bridge would be safest to take?"

The turnfin squawked and flew out over the tower.

Eva continued on her way, rounding the gigantic piling of the first tower. Within the tower she could hear people shouting and machines grinding. Quickly the sounds were interrupted by the staccato of weapons firing.

Fly closest to the water. The turnfin's message drifted into Eva's mind.

"Thank you, friend," she whispered to the lone bird circling high above. Eva stepped onto a swaying rope bridge that sagged into the water before connecting to the second tower. She trod along the thin planks of the bridge and watched a group of villagers retreat in the skywalks above. *I hope I can get to Arius in time,* she thought. She could sense that the soothsayer was still in the village.

Eva was halfway across the bridge when she heard the explosion from the first tower. She spun around to see a warbot standing in a gaping hole where, just moments before, huts and shanties had stood. With great grasping claws the warbot systematically began cutting the cables that held the rope bridges.

One by one the collapsing bridges splashed into the lake, spilling villagers along the way. On long slender rafts fishermen frantically navigated between the fallen bridges to rescue survivors.

Eva heard a loud *TWANG*, and the woven rail on her rope bridge went slack. Without hesitation she bolted toward the second tower. *TWING!* The second rail was gone. Eva looked behind her. The warbot was cutting the remaining supports for the rope bridge. She wouldn't make it to the tower in time. She crouched down and clutched the wooden planks as the bridge collapsed. It fell into the lake, joining the tangle of severed skywalks floating on the surface. The other end of the rope bridge was still attached to the second tower, making it more a ladder now than a walk. Hand over hand Eva climbed up the remains of the bridge into the tower's base.

The spiral staircase that led through the tower was littered with deserted belongings. Eva crept up the steps, past broken lanterns, a trampled wide-brimmed hat, and toppled fishing baskets. She came out into the central courtyard, surrounded by the familiar tiers of rounded huts and shanties. Everything was in the shadow of the giant warship looming overhead in the low sun. Eva hid behind an upturned cart and watched, waiting for warbots to descend from the belly of the ship—but none came.

They are not invading? That's weird, Eva thought. *Maybe they are searching for Arius still.*

"Human child, Eva the Ninth," a voice whispered as if carried on the lake's cool breeze. It was a sing-song voice she recognized, though it was noticeably more melancholy. "Nine Evas, the child human."

"Arius?" Eva whispered aloud.

"The human returns," the voice sang. "The return of humans."

Eva set off, through the abandoned walkways, toward Arius's abode. "Arius, I need to speak with you. I fear you are in danger."

"See me you must, Eva the Nine. You must see me."

"There is another—like you—working with Cadmus, the human leader." Eva ran now. Higher and higher she traversed, up to the topmost tier. "It may be your brother."

"Another like me. Me and the other."

"Arius, you have to leave!" Eva said. She bolted past rows of houses, stopping at a large round hut with a narrow stairway alongside it.

"Before you, I shall leave. I shall leave you behind."

Eva took the stairs two at a time and crossed a narrow swaying footbridge that led to a small woven shanty—Arius's home.

"In come," a voice said. "Come in."

Eva burst through the door, knocking over the stacks of offerings that covered the entry room floor. "Arius! Arius!"

A voice hissed into Eva's thoughts from above her. *Save yourself from consumption. Save my master.*

Eva looked up and saw Arius's enormous pet gadworm coiled up among the rafters of the hut. *I have to talk with your master,* she thought to it. Eva pushed aside the heavy tassled curtains and entered the back room.

The Prime Adviser floated next to the window in the dusky light. His unhinged mouth was open unnaturally wide, like a snake devouring a bird's egg. In his mouth was the adviser's prey—Arius.

"No!" Eva screamed.

The Prime Adviser closed his mouth over the soothsayer, consuming her. His body rippled and grew. Nine new stumpy arms sprouted from his torso, and an extra set of eyes opened, giving him three pairs in all.

Eva recoiled from the adviser, tripping and falling to the floor. She scuttled back through piles of gifts into the shadow of the curtains and toppled a stand with a tray full of Arius's favorite food—fresh gadworm eggs.

Master is not master, the gadworm thought to Eva. It slithered along the rafters, into the room,

and released another egg, which splattered onto the floor next to Eva.

The adviser spoke. His words resounded as if three voices were speaking at once. "Eva the Ninth, your past has led me to my sister. My sister is now the past." He tossed Eva's Omnipod at her. It landed and slid across the floor.

"Loroc," Eva grumbled.

"I am Loroc. I am strength. I am power. My sister Arius has now joined my sister Darius. I can now see the past. I can now see the future." He floated closer to Eva.

She scrambled to her feet and bolted from the room, but Loroc seized Eva by the hair and pulled her back toward him.

"Today is my reunion with Arius. Tomorrow it will be Zin. Then I will be complete at last."

"What then?" Eva struggled against her captor, but it was no use.

"King Ojo's many wishes will come to pass. And many will pass on from this new king's wishes."

"You'll be the king?" Eva thought of the sandsniper holding her at the ancient ruins. She relaxed, fighting all urges to wriggle free of Loroc. She thought out to the gadworm even as she was speaking to Loroc. "But what about Cadmus?"

"Cadmus is winning a battle today so that he may lose tomorrow," replied Loroc. "I will do to him as I am to do to you."

Help me, Eva thought out. *Help free me . . . for Arius. For your master.*

"I am going to kill you," Loroc said. He took hold of Eva's head as if to snap her neck, but then let go and fell backward as something large dropped from the ceiling.

Momentarily freed from Loroc's grip, Eva scrambled to her feet and glanced back at Arius's giant gadworm dragging Loroc into the entry room. It wrapped its segments tightly around him, constricting all movement. With no other means of escape Eva jumped up onto the window-sill and clawed her way to the roof. She stood amidst a large flock of turnfins and looked out from the topmost point in Lacus. Far below she could hear the angry waves of the lake crashing against the tower.

The wind whipped at Eva, causing her to stumble. On hands and knees she crawled through nests of roosting birds.

The center of the roof exploded, sending debris and frightened turnfins flying in every direction. "Your scampering will do you no good, little creature." Loroc floated up through the hole, larger than before.

Eva retreated to the rounded edge of the roof.

"You cannot escape your fate," Loroc spat.

"You cannot escape yours, either," said Eva, standing to face Loroc. She recited Arius's words,

> *"A nymph, born of the earth, forged by*
> *machine,*
> *will lead a way through hate, through fear,*
> *through war."*

"I have seen my future, nymph." Loroc spoke in a haughty tone. "You may be 'that' child, but you cannot stop what has begun."

"Neither can you," retorted Eva.

"Perhaps. But know this: I do not fall by your hand. You, however, shall fall by mine." Loroc lunged at Eva.

Dodging his attack, Eva slipped and fell from the top of Arius's home. She landed hard on the roof of a neighboring shanty one story down. Though shaken by the fall, Eva rose among the nesting turnfins and faced Loroc once more.

She thought out to the birds, *Attack the intruder. He'll destroy your nests.* The flock of turnfins descended upon Loroc in a flurry of snapping beaks and beating wings.

Eva stretched her arms out from both sides.

I wish I could fly.

Several large female turnfins left their roosts and fluttered around Eva, their tiny claws pricking her arms and shoulders as they landed on her. In unison they flapped and rose.

Eva's feet slowly lifted from the roof of the shanty. Her white hair danced around her face as she watched Loroc retreating from the attacking birds. The turnfins carried Eva away as the red sun sank into the horizon, soaking the world in darkness.

EPILOGUE

Eva Nine

Eva Nine sat on the bough of a wandering tree as night cooled the land. The tree was traveling south on the border where the salt flats met the Wandering Forest. Eva had instructed the tree, like the turnfins, to carry her far from Rovender, Otto, and the Halcyonus, for fear that Loroc would give chase. She waited for a warship or a warbot to come blasting out of the forest in ambush, but none came.

What do I do now? Eva had hoped Arius would have answers. She had hoped Arius would still be alive. "Arius, can you hear me?" she called out.

There was no response.

I need to help Rovender, but the Halcyonus all hate me. I could go warn Zin and Queen Ojo, but I'm sure they are aware of Cadmus's attack by now. I can't go back to New Attica. . . . Where do I go?

As she looked out and watched the fog roll in from Lake Concors, Eva sensed something. It was a feeling. A signal coming from far out in the salt flats.

Danger.

She stood up and scanned the horizon. In the murk she saw nothing, though the feeling was stronger now. Several voices, feral and different from any she had ever heard, were on the prowl and closing in on their prey.

"Will you please follow them?" she asked the tree. The wandering tree obliged and ambled out onto the flats.

Before long Eva noticed largish creatures running through the fog past the trunk of the tree. She peered over the edge of the bough but saw little detail. Their movement reminded her of sand-snipers, but these creatures were smaller.

Eva hopped down to one of the tree's lower branches for a clearer view.

Who are you? She thought out to the creatures.

We hunt. We eat. We share, many voices replied.

One of the creatures ran by. It looked somewhat like a small pale-patterned sand-sniper.

Out in the fog Eva could hear their clicking calls. She also made out the distinct sound of scratching—like claws scuttling on metal.

What are you eating? she asked.

We open. The egg. We eat, the creatures replied.

The wandering tree approached the creature's prey.

It was the *Bijou.*

The ship had crash-landed on the flats and was now crawling with a dozen ghostly white sand-snipers. The creatures were snapping at the hull with their powerful graspers and yanking off pieces of the ship in an attempt to enter it.

"No!" Eva jumped down from the tree. *There is no food here for you. Only danger. Disperse!*

The ghost-snipers scurried off the ship and disappeared into the fog. Eva could hear them chittering and circling just beyond her vision. She listened to their voices. They were planning another invasion on the ship once more snipers arrived.

Eva was not sure if she would be able to hold them all off.

"Wait here," she said, and patted the trunk of the tree. Then she ran off toward the *Bijou*.

The smoldering ship was on its side with its landing gear extended. The hull was riddled with bullet holes and covered in thick gunky foam. Through the cracked windshield Eva could see sparking wires in the cockpit. She ran over to the entry ramp. The ramp was cracked open and crates were spilling out, blocking any entry. "Hailey! Hailey! Are you in there?" Eva called. She put her arms inside the open ramp and tried to push the crates aside.

A hand from within grabbed hers, and a muffled voice called out, "Eva?"

One of the crates tumbled away, revealing a bruised and battered teenage pilot.

"Hailey Turner." Eva helped him out of the wreckage. "Am I glad to see you."

"Me too." Hailey limped out from the ship. "Remind me to tell Vanpa he was right about Cadmus."

Eva laughed despite the situation. She sensed more ghost-snipers gathering in the fog. "Come with me," she said, helping Hailey over to the tree.

"You look different, Eva. Did you change again?" Hailey studied her in the moonlight.

"Yeah, I did change." Eva pushed her white bangs from her eyes. She thought about all that she had been through since she'd first met the pilot. "But this is me. The real me."

Hailey smiled and stroked her hair. "I like it. It suits you."

Eva climbed up onto the nearest branch and reached out with her hand. Taking it, Hailey hoisted himself up next to her. The wandering tree meandered away from the wrecked *Bijou* and into the fog of the night.

End of

BOOK II

The Northern Wastelands
Faunas
The Valley of Standing Stones
TO
New Attica
The *Bijou*'s Life Capsule Landed Here
Regional Map of
Orbona
Not to Scale

N
Lake Concors
Solas
The Heart of the Forest
The Wandering Forest
Lacus
Sanctuary 573
The Wastelands
The Ancient Ruins

THE ORBONIAN ALPHABET

A common alphabet is used by the inhabitants of Orbona. The chart that follows is the key to unlocking their written language. The main alphabet consists of thirty-two characters (as opposed to the English alphabet, which comprises twenty-six), and many of these are derived from symbols of familiar objects, actions, or ideas. They are shown in alphabetical order with the compound letters at the end, although this is not the order Orbonians would use. Orbonians would align similar symbols alongside one another so that their youth could identify different characteristics more easily.

Orbonians write in a vertical manner and from left to right. Compound words are often broken up, with their individual parts written alongside one another as seen here in "the Wastelands":

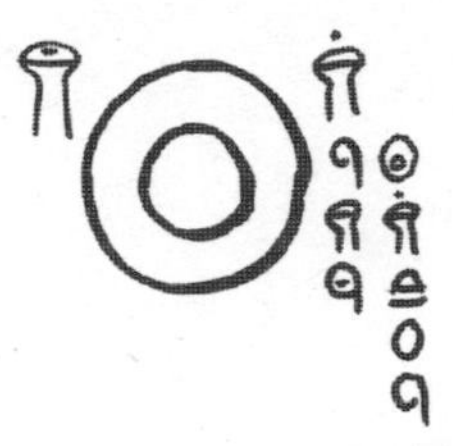

Capital letters are larger versions of the lowercase letters. Proper nouns use a large version of the letter with the remainder of the word written to the right of it, as can be seen here in the word "Lacus":

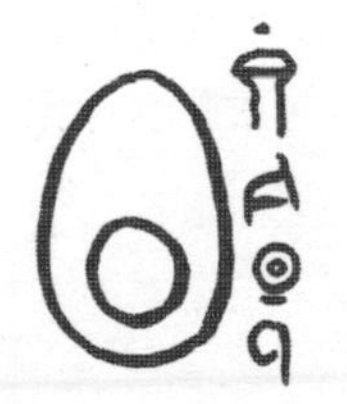

There are many shortcut symbols for small words like "of" and "the," both of which are included on the chart. However, the focus here is on the main alphabet so that readers may be able to decipher Orbonian writing in this and future books.

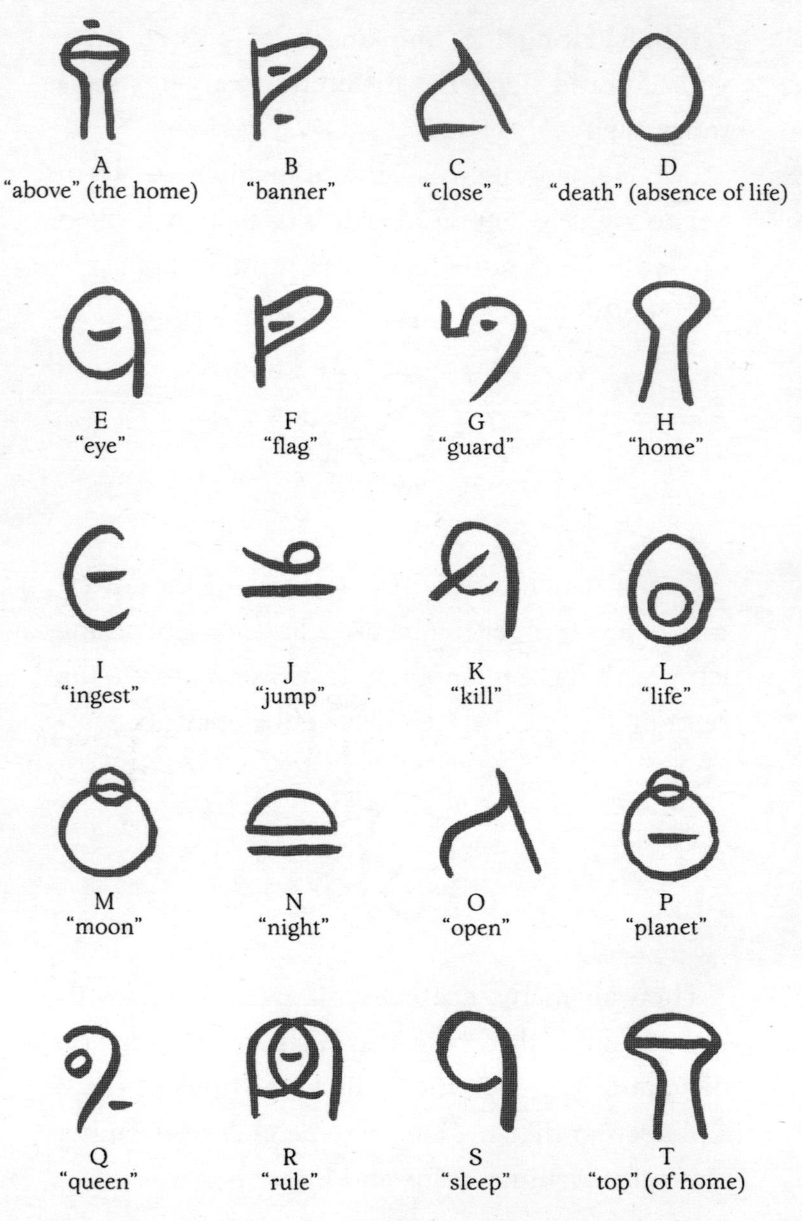
A
"above" (the home)
B
"banner"
C
"close"
D
"death" (absence of life)
E
"eye"
F
"flag"
G
"guard"
H
"home"
I
"ingest"
J
"jump"
K
"kill"
L
"life"
M
"moon"
N
"night"
O
"open"
P
"planet"
Q
"queen"
R
"rule"
S
"sleep"
T
"top" (of home)

U
"universe"

V
"voxfruit"

W
"world"

X
"examine"

Y
"yell"

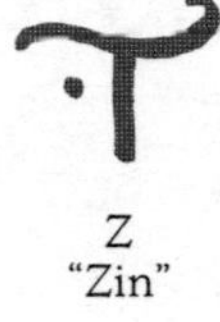

Z
"Zin"

Æ

er

eez

id

tch

th

the

of

ACKNOWLEDGMENTS

Just as Eva Nine has transformed and matured as a character, I feel that I too have grown as her storyteller. And, like Eva, I needed help from my friends to do it.

As always, I thank my ever-faithful managers, Ellen Goldsmith-Vein and Julie Kane-Ritsch, as well as publicist Maggie Begley, who have continued their unending support for this story, for me, and for all that I do.

I can't express my gratitude to the team at Simon & Schuster Books for Young Readers quite enough. Jon Anderson, Justin Chanda, and Anne Zafian continue to inspire me with their incredible enthusiasm and passion for quality bookmaking. Of course my editor, the always-vigilant David Gale, helped guide me through the harrowing plot of this second book in the trilogy.

I am indebted to my two story gurus, Steve Berman and Heidi Stemple, who aided me with those adventurous turns and momentous twists that needed the extra attention. Trusted friends Holly Gibson-Fischer; Rob Carlo; (the illuminating) Paige Kelley; and my assistant, Ashley Valentine, offered feedback and cheered me on.

I enjoyed enlightening conversations with old friends like Jeff Miracola, Jim Gaynor, and Colin McComb, who provided ideas for aspects of Eva Nine and New Attica. Additionally, I had inspiring story discussions with Ari Berk and Chase Palmer. I am grateful to you all for taking the time to talk.

While the words and plot slowly came into focus for Eva and company, my sketchbook began to fill with visions of futuristic cities and alien landscapes. Scott Fischer was with me every step of the way, critiquing and offering creative solutions. The digital aspect of the illustrations was completed with the help of the diligent David White. All of this was done under the guidance of my effervescent art director, Lizzy Bromley. I am proud to share the art in this book and for that I thank you all.

Lastly, I must thank my two heroes—my wife, Angela, and my daughter, Sophia. Your love and support kept me going day in and day out. I could not have created this without you. You are my WondLa.

Never abandon imagination.

Tony DiTerlizzi

is the visionary mind that conceived of the Spiderwick Chronicles. He has been creating books with Simon & Schuster for more than a decade. From fanciful picture books like *The Spider and the Fly* (a Caldecott Honor) to young chapter books like *Kenny and the Dragon*, Tony has always imbued his stories with a rich imagination. His series the Spiderwick Chronicles (with Holly Black) has sold millions of copies worldwide and was adapted into a feature film.

Inspired by stories by the likes of the Brothers Grimm, James M. Barrie, and L. Frank Baum, The Search for WondLa series is a new fairy tale for the twenty-first century.

Books by TONY DITERLIZZI

THE SEARCH FOR WONDLA

JIMMY ZANGWOW'S OUT-OF-THIS-WORLD MOON-PIE ADVENTURE

TED

THE SPIDER AND THE FLY
Written by Mary Howitt

G IS FOR ONE GZONK!

KENNY AND THE DRAGON

ADVENTURE OF MENO

by Tony DiTerlizzi and Angela DiTerlizzi

BIG FUN!

WET FRIEND!

YUMMY TRIP!

UH-OH SICK!

THE SPIDERWICK CHRONICLES

by Tony DiTerlizzi and Holly Black

THE SPIDERWICK CHRONICLES

The Field Guide

The Seeing Stone

Lucinda's Secret

The Ironwood Tree

The Wrath of Mulgarath

Arthur Spiderwick's Field Guide to the Fantastical World Around You

Care and Feeding of Sprites

BEYOND THE SPIDERWICK CHRONICLES

The Nixie's Song

A Giant Problem

The Wyrm King